Of the Emperor's Kindness

Of the Emperor's Kindness

A Comedy of Imperial Manners

Book 1 of the Imperial Vices series

Chaz Brenchley

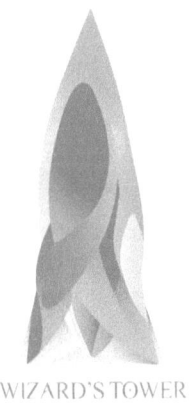

WIZARD'S TOWER

Wizard's Tower Press
Rhydaman, Cymru

Of the Emperor's Kindness

A Comedy of Imperial Manners
Book 1 of the Imperial Vices series

Text © 2025 by Chaz Brenchley
Cover art & design by Ben Baldwin
Book design by Cheryl Morgan

First published in Great Britain
by Wizard's Tower Press, October 2025

Paperback ISBN: 978-1-917950-13-8

http://wizardstowerpress.com/
http://www.chazbrenchley.co.uk/

Contents

Advance Praise

"Highly readable, immersive, clever and unsettling. What an absolutely fascinating book." — KJ Charles

"Beautifully written, with a fascinating world, a deceptively simple plot, and complex and compelling characters, Of the Emperor's Kindness left me breathless. An utterly gorgeous book!" — Melissa Scott

"I will read anything Chaz Brenchley writes. His prose is melted butter with tarragon, and his characters and world-building equally delicious. Open this book to any page, and you will find something to delight you." — Ellen Kushner

This one is for Jeannie
and all the crew of the
Writers Drinking Coffee podcast,
with love, and thanks for listening

V

ONE

What did she mourn so, alone and far away?

It was the difference between grief and mourning: the one pain, and the other a measurement of loss. The one sent her out into the streets of the beloved city, frantic for company, for noise and colour and movement, hurry and hunger and life; the other kept her stilled at home, as quiet and internal as a memory.

Her moods swung unpredictably, unfathomably between the two. Even now, even after a year and more. She had cast off the formal white of mourning, but that was a lie to the eye, for the comfort of others. Of course she was still in mourning for her people, for her culture, for her land. Here was no paltry quotidian loss, the mediocrity of individual death; she would mourn Verantha for ever, for all the life that lay ahead of her.

Aye, and grieve for it too, with every drink and every dance and every dalliance, for as long as her body would indulge her. Home was home, was belonging, an absolute sense of settlement; she had lost a home and found a home, and would be torn hereafter.

Home was this overlarge house in the park, all her own and everything within it. Home was this rampant, exuberant city, which she had learned like learning the body of a lover, reaching under the skin. Probably, properly that meant that home was also the vast sprawl of the empire entire, although she was an alien here and not in any wise a citizen or subject to any authority, even to the emperor himself. She'd rarely left the city, though, in all her years here, and then only for the occasional weekend's skiing with friends in the mountains, still in sight of Feremendas, the reach and ambition of it, from the imperial palace to the teeming docks, from the slums to the arenas, from the covered marketplaces to the gorgeous parks. The city was like all the empire distilled into a single drop, or so they told her, so she was willing to believe. She didn't need to travel. She could linger here, and rejoice in the surge and wonder of it, and feel that the world had come to her. The truth of course was quite opposite, but a girl could surely lie to herself in the privacy of her own head, especially when she in her own person embodied a far greater lie. In principle, in the eyes of law and power and politics, she did not and could not exist.

Tonight she was mourning and no longer grieving, apparently. She had abandoned a riotous party on a houseboat on the lake, and crept home with her boys, alone. Everyone was willing to pretend that she took two graceful beauties with her for protection; in truth, all her friends adored them, the boys themselves loved the attention and the pretty clothes, and as often as not they had much more fun than she did, by dint of being much more fun than she was. Really, on nights like this she should just send them to the parties without her. As her ambassadors—

But no, that wasn't funny. On nights like this, it really wasn't funny.

Safe back, she sent the boys down to change into house tunics and gossip with the cook over a pot of tea and something hot to eat. Herself, she climbed the first flight of stairs to the suite of rooms she had claimed for herself— really, this house was ridiculously big and always had been, even when there were more here than just herself; rank has its obligations and appearances matter, and even so—where she knew Estar would be waiting for her. Still breathing hard, probably, after pelting up from the kitchens the moment someone reported footsteps on the path.

She ought probably to have a real maid, rather than an overworked kitchen girl given yet more to do. But then she ought to have more staff all through the house, a proper brigade, a household; but she didn't need a household just to serve her, and besides, she didn't want to be a burden on the empire, more than she was already. The emperor insisted that all her expenses be met by the palace; it was a kindness in him to parallel his many other kindnesses, and appallingly generous, and so she skimped whenever she could and spent the bare minimum of his money.

Well, mostly. The boys were an indulgence. For her friends' pleasure, though, as much as for her own. That ought to count for something.

Estar had been a different manner of indulgence, a street-child who didn't know her own age or parentage. Malance had found her begging, and brought her home to save her from a worse life later, as she grew. She was still growing now, all legs and elbows; and still a little wide-eyed at her promotion from skivvy to lady's maid, even if she did still have to do all the skivvying as well. Malance had worried a little about the child's rough hands on her finest silks and velvets, but regular applications of goose-grease had helped with that, alongside Estar's own passionate attachment to her mistress's wardrobe. She'd likely throw herself into the lake in misery, stones in her pockets, the first time she so much as laddered a stocking.

Tonight she helped Malance out of her gaudy party dress and into a simple robe, then scuttled off to make tea that they both knew would never be drunk.

Malance curled up in a window-seat, gazing out across the shadows of the park, intercut with paths of light where coloured lanterns dangled from the trees. Greater lights at greater distances spoke of other houses much like hers but busy, important, occupied. Manned with a full complement of servants, to attend a full and functional household. Not one rescued urchin, two ridiculously decorative boys and a decrepit cook she only kept because he had been here for ever and had nowhere else to go. As a staff, they were a joke, ridiculous. But then so was their work, so was she: one lonely grieving girl, forever cut off from home and family, spending money that wasn't hers to maintain a position that wasn't hers either except that the emperor had made it so, because he was a kind man and wanted to keep her safe, no reason else.

Estar was back with the wholly superfluous tea, asking if she should light lamps in the bedroom yet.

Malance sighed, and said yes. And then, "Oh, Estar? Go back down and bring me up one of the boys, would you? Either one, it doesn't—oh, damn it, no. Bring them both."

Those boys hadn't been cheap, as pretty as they were. She'd bought them anyway; she might as well make use of them. Mourning demanded focus, but grief craved distraction, and she could pivot so quickly, one to the other.

She went to sleep—eventually—between two warm and welcome bodies; she woke to just the one. Amil had slipped away already, to work with Estar down below. She could hear the clatter of the scullery pump, even up here.

Almost of its own accord, her hand slid down over warm and sticky skin, sleek muscle. Felid opened his eyes, smiled, reached for her.

Malance laughed a little regretfully, kissed his cheek and pushed him away.

"Go down and help your brother," she said. "Send Estar to me."

"Yes, lady."

He slithered out from under the covers and padded away, quite naked, quite unabashed. In fact, she thought he was preening, strutting a little under her eye. Vain creature, and rightly so.

He and Amil were brothers only by adoption, hers. The one had been raided from a fishing village, so far away she still had no clear idea where it lay, and in honesty neither did he; the other from right here in the city, snatched as an urchin in the street, an unluckily lovely child. They'd been sold and trained and sold again, finally brought together and sent to market as a matched pair, which justified—or was supposed to justify—the ludicrous price she'd paid. At the last she'd found herself bidding against a palace official and the factor of a wealthy merchant family, and stupidly determined to save the boys from either one of them.

She still didn't, couldn't regret it. They were a joy to her, in a life that offered few. She cherished and adored them, and thought—well, hoped, at least—that they loved her in their turn, in their way. She was their lady, their own; they were her boys. Hers.

Estar brought washing-water and a towel, lit a small fire, helped her to dress. For once, she did actually need the help. This was Friday, and the emperor would hold court. As ever, he would expect to see her there. She was in his debt, more ways than she could count; also, she simply liked the man. This Friday, as every Friday, she would be there. Dressed soberly but richly, as was her habit at the palace: the sobriety to speak to her situation, the richness in compliment to him.

She left Estar tidying her suite, and went down to the kitchen to tease her boys and sit with ancient Mechet, drink his execrable coffee, dip day-old bread in a dish of melted butter and call it breakfast, try not to drip on her dress. Envy her friends their undoubted and well-deserved hangovers, their long late lingering in bed. Any other day she might have done the same, even perhaps with one of them. Not on a Friday.

Come the time, she sent Felid running down to the park gate and the road beyond, to fetch her back a carriage. She did have stables of her own, a yard, a carriage-house. She ought to keep horses and a smart turnout, drive herself perhaps to save the cost and inconvenience of a man. Or at least a mount or two, ride in the park, ride all around the city. She did not. Not, again, on the emperor's coin. Her boys were very used to running to the road with a coin or two and riding back behind a cabriolet. It was a makeshift way of getting around, but it suited her sense of propriety. Anywhere closer to hand, anywhere between the park and the lake, she preferred to walk. The imperial palace was distanced by design, though, the emperor holding aloof from his subjects, even the grand ones. A call at the palace was always a ride.

Today's driver was a familiar face, one of her regulars. Malance was tolerably sure they had taken to waiting on that particular stretch of road, anticipating her needs or desires. And not only on Fridays; any time she needed a carriage, in daylight or dark, her boys could always seem to find one. Her suspicious soul wondered if someone from the palace had quietly made an arrangement, if these particular men had no need to seek other clients elsewhere, if all their needs were met so long as one of them was always ready when she called. Really it would have been easier to make her a gift of horses, carriage, stable lads and grooms; but the emperor was a quiet man, and preferred to see things arranged without fuss or notice.

Of course that meant she couldn't even thank him. Which would also be his preference, she knew.

She didn't take her boys to formal court. They would spend this Friday as every Friday, in their workaday tunics, scrubbing floors and running errands, scolded by Estar if they slacked or dallied. They might be exceedingly pretty, but Malance did feel she ought to justify their price somehow. In her head, she did. The emperor would laugh at her, if he knew; her friends did laugh at her, and flaunt their own devoted beauties, who had never lifted a hand to a day's work in all their pampered lives of service.

Through the endless and endlessly fascinating streets of Feremendas, from the raucous bazaars to the wide and quiet avenues, from winding shambles to great straight military roads; all her drivers knew to take her by slow and different ways, that she might look and listen to everything, to make her journey one more stitch in her understanding of the city. She always started early, just for this.

The emperor was a quiet man, but his palace spoke volumes on his behalf. Still properly known as the New Palace, despite being five hundred years old and more, it was a city within a city: a walled complex where thousands lived and studied, lived and laboured, lived and died without ever actually needing to step outside its gates, though they mostly did. It sat on an artificial hill raised wilfully above low-lying Feremendas, a little distanced and overlooking everything, even as the city had slowly spilled all around it. Overseeing the world, or an unfair portion thereof; the fates of millions were decided—quietly—within these walls.

Without needing to ask, her driver brought her to the Strangers' Gate, as he always did and always would. Felid had already paid him for the trip, but she gave him money anyway, just in case the emperor actually was subsidising him behind her back. Petty revenges were one of the currencies of court.

A liveried servant stepped forward to hand her down from the carriage, though she hardly needed it. There were no armed guards outside the palace wall; the emperor loved his people, and chose to believe that they loved him in return, and so kept his soldiery out of sight.

This gate, however, was not for his people. This was the Strangers' Gate, and it was kept closed by long tradition, meeting those strangers always with denial first, to remind them that they were admitted on sufferance, on recognition, that this was the Eye of the World.

The gatekeeper had a sharp eye for his favourites, though. Malance rarely had to linger long. Today she'd barely set foot to flagstone before one leaf in the vast stone-clad edifice was swinging wide in welcome and there he was to greet her in person, dressed in all his pomp and modest authority, delighted with himself and his little kingdom here. And delighted by her, by her coming, by her weekly holding true.

"Madam Ambassador."

As ever, Malance flinched inwardly at that. She still hadn't decided whether she loathed the honorific more, or the deceit. She was twenty-three years old, and no one should be calling her "Madam". And the rank was a courtesy, a fiction, the best protection the emperor could offer her in her sudden calamity: ambassador from a country that no longer existed, appointed to a court that most likely had no idea why the empire had ever offered an exchange of ambassadors in the first place.

It was a kindness, of course; and an embarrassment, of course; and an awkwardness she had no idea how to manage or to overcome. There was no value in tantrums, though sometimes she did just want to scream. There was no consequence to plotting—though she did dream and dream of all her many revenges yet to come—even if she'd had anyone to plot with. She was, so far as she knew, the last Veranthan in Feremendas, which meant the last in the world. Certainly she had been able to find none remaining in the city; and elsewhere they were all Clathian now, their own land swallowed up entire by the world's opposing power. The very name of Verantha had been forbidden, expunged, as with all the other little countries the kingdoms of Clath had swept across, swept up. Only the emperor was powerful enough to ignore that directive; only he of all the lords of life had little fear of Clath, and could afford to maintain a Veranthan embassy in his capital, both to spite his opposition and to offer a home to one abandoned, desperate, stateless girl.

Her house was officially that embassy, the last surviving little piece of Verantha in all the world, and she its sole citizen.

She had wept over this, of course, and raged against it. She had wanted to run away, to go back to her own land, to fight the Clath occupation. Surely, some of her people must be fighting yet. But the emperor had refused to let her go. Her predecessor in the post had vanished overnight, along with all his household. Malance chose to suppose that he and all of them had gone in search of that resistance, though none had left a note to say so. She'd been out all that night, seeking succour among friends, and returned in the morning to an empty house.

She'd have followed soon enough, if she'd only been allowed. But a page had come, a summons to the palace, from the emperor himself. There must be a Veranthan ambassador here at Feremendas, he had said, or where would any of her scattered frightened people know to turn? Her house was Veranthan land; she herself *was* Verantha now, a symbol and a beacon. Verantha would come to her, he said, if she only stayed visible, if she only stayed here.

Besides, he didn't say although she heard him clearly, *no country large or small has successfully risen up against Clath, once overrun; why, how could she suppose that tiny Verantha might? Or why, how, that she might help?*

He said none of that, but he was right. Of course he was right. She stayed, though she despised herself for doing so; she accepted his protection and his money both, though she despised herself for both of those as well. Her self-impoverishment—with, obviously, a pair of rather lovely exceptions—was a slap in the face to his generosity, and she found it desirable or necessary to despise herself for that also, she just wasn't quite sure which. Meanwhile she waited for other lost Veranthans to trickle into the city and find her, but none yet ever had.

Alone, she greeted the gatekeeper and asked after his wife and children, trying to chat with an acquaintance rather than condescend to a person of lower status. He beamed in gratitude at her condescension, as he did every week. Nowhere does status matter more, than at a gate.

With her own favoured status assured for another week, she walked on into the palace grounds. This whole complex might be a city in itself; if so, it was a city in a park. She had seen nothing more of the empire, but all of Feremendas-city was a haven of greenery, at least this side of the slums and rookeries. Somehow she had that image lodged in her head against all logic and all report, that groves and ponds and winding pathways were the very image of the empire at large. Perhaps it was a fantasy of consolation, that she needed something to pit against the green hills and valleys in her memory, lost to her now and for ever.

Sometimes when she was drunk she would sing songs of Verantha. Sometimes when she was sober she'd persuade her friends to learn them, so that they could all sing together when they were drunk.

Sometimes when she was alone—as now, as always, the last Veranthan—she mocked herself for that morbid obsession with what was gone. She had come to Feremendas at sixteen, ostensibly for a season, no more, to put a finishing gloss on her understanding of the language and to learn something of the world beyond Verantha. She'd always shown herself to be a somewhat unusual Veranthan, restless and inquisitive, eager to be gone. She had loved this city from the first, and begged to stay; and so in honesty had only ever known her homeland as a child. Here was her home of choice, here were the people who loved her for who she was,

18

not who she used to be. She knew the city and the city knew her, in ways—so many ways!—that her place of birth did not. What in honesty had she lost then, after all? What did she mourn so, alone and far away? Perhaps it was all for show, for the emperor's offered comforts. Or for the emperor's comfort: perhaps he needed to see her sorrow, so that he could be kind.

This Friday as every Friday, she faced the long walk through the parkland and the fountained courtyards to the reception hall, with scores of other buildings rising to either side, the only district of Feremendas that was a stranger to her, as she to it. And this week as every week, she heard the Strangers' Gate opening again and again at her back, for every ambassador would attend the court, hoping to catch the emperor's ear, to raise issues or grievances or possibilities of trade. Every ambassador had work to do, but her. She would merely … attend.

This Friday as every Friday, she heard hooves and rattling wheels at her back, she was overtaken by carriage after carriage. Her meagre cabriolet might not pass the gate, but ambassadors with their own equipage could ride all the way to the hall door.

This Friday as every Friday, she heard the jingling of a belled harness, two sets of horses' hooves slowing to a sedate walk beside her, a voice calling down. "Lady, shall we ride together?"

She'd been counting on that. This Friday, every Friday.

She swung herself up into the slow-rolling open carriage, and settled herself gladly beside its occupant. Brion Mercady, Ambassador for the Outlands, a spontaneous cluster of independent polities far beyond the empire's borders, in no danger of being subsumed. He was a fat, contented man, as devoted to politics as he was to food. What little she knew of diplomacy at this high level was largely thanks to him, and in no small measure to these brief carriage-rides through the emperor's gardens. What news there was, whether internal to the palace or external to the empire, he was safe to know it, and willing to share; and willing to coach her through the intricacies of court intrigue. Oh, and willing to gossip, that too. Perhaps they were all the same thing.

He said, "Malance, you look pale. And thin."

"You always say that."

"Because it's always true. That old man you keep in the basement is no good for you. Let me send you one of my lads. I know just the one, he's craving a kitchen of his own."

"I can't do that, Brion. Mechet would die of shame."

"And thus we are all better off: Mechet is freed from care, a respite frankly long overdue; I have rid my own kitchens of a restive soul and performed an act of charity for which you will certainly be grateful, and as you know—as I have taught you—gratitude is a currency among people of our kind; and you will grow plump as you ought to be. It's perfect. I am brilliant today, I find." He folded his hands comfortably across his own rather more than plumpness, and went on, "Also, I know you children love the night, but let the sun see your skin sometimes. Daylight is good for you. So also is sleep. Allow your body an early night, once in a while."

"Yes, Brion," she said dutifully. "Thank you for your guidance."

"Which you will of course ignore. You know it, I know it; why do I bother? Tell me that."

"Because you worry about me, just as you worry about your restive cook and everyone else of your household and a great many people else. You hold us all in the palm of your concern."

"Ah, is that what I do? Perhaps. Perhaps you're right. I am a worrier, I know. In service to which, let me tell you about this latest approach from the Palatinate. It's sure to come up in conversation, at least, even if the emperor doesn't raise it himself, which he is quite like to do..."

S ome minutes later—none the wiser, perhaps, but at least far better informed—she stepped down from the carriage and waited politely while Brion hauled himself out, taking advantage of the moment to thank his driver by name, as she always did. This Friday, every Friday. The day was a sequence of rituals, and they began well before the court had gathered.

The great doors of the reception hall stood wide, and just as well; each one needed a dozen hands to shift it, and they closed with a dreadful clangour. She had experienced that once, just the once, from inside the hall, and she'd thought her ears were bleeding merely from the noise. It had been actively painful, and in general the emperor was kind enough to leave them standing ajar while he held court.

Stepping through that vast doorway—and finding it as always somewhat forbidding, the least welcoming of door-ways, so that she was glad as always to be swept along in Brion's confident wake—she still remembered to smile at the men standing guard here, to greet the servants and pages lined up in formal welcome. It was another of her little quiet revenges, to demean herself in these grandees' eyes before they could find their own reasons to demean her. She had been meant as an interpreter, no more: here to ease the flow of trade—such as it had been—between Verantha and the empire, working dutifully out of the embassy by day and free to frolic citywide by night. Of course she did still frolic, but it was a frenetic, desperate kind of fun she sought these after days, bitter and hunting and never to be satisfied. Fifteen months now, and she could still be overwhelmed.

The emperor's reception hall was overwhelming in itself, an everlasting wonder, the work of a hundred years: so high it could almost have had weather, extravagantly broad and impossibly long, and yet all so immaculate in proportion and in craftsmanship that no aspect could ever be called grandiose or overdone. Some magic of design made it that when the emperor spoke from his seat on the dais—not in the centre of the hall, no, but towards the farther end, and somehow exactly where it ought to be—everyone could hear him, no matter the crowd.

Of course Brion was too nonchalant and too urgent both to stop and gawp, so Malance had to gawp as she trotted after. This Friday, every Friday. She swore never to grow accustomed to this magnificence, never to be blasé as all the court otherwise affected to be.

Brion, she was convinced, was blasé in truth, not in the least awed by his surroundings. He was a man of purpose, of many purposes, and he would seek to fulfil them all; and first of all was the side-hall that he headed for—this Friday, every Friday—that was itself large enough and imposing enough, it could have served the Council as their audience chamber back home.

Here was where all the court foregathered, before the noon bell summoned them. Here was where cronies met and mingled, here plots were hatched and despatched, proposals honed to the razor sharpness they'd need to penetrate the iron hide of the imperial bureaucracy—and so, of course, here were the tables of food and drink, pages in crimson livery passing hither and yon with wines and delicacies laid out on silver salvers. Brion liked to pretend that this was what he came for, and all that he came for; Malance was prepared to allow the first, though no one could believe the second.

He summoned a page with a flick of his finger. Half these children were scions of the noble families, fostered to the palace as a first step into their inevitable future among the upper echelons of the imperium, here to make friends and build alliances, watch the great at work and at play, learn the processes of power. The other half were city orphans, street-children, some abandoned babes, raised under the emperor's kindly eye and destined for a life of service. No matter their origins, they all bunked together in long dormitories, shared the same food, the same work, the same strict care and watchful guard. It was the emperor's fancy not only to dress them all alike, but to have their hair cut just the same, short and cute; with the younger ones, it wasn't always immediately clear if they were boy or girl, never mind if they were high-born or low.

This one was a girl, but only just, still little more than a slender sapling with a smile; she might have been twelve years old, or not. As was her practice, Malance smiled back. Brion hadn't noticeably looked at the girl at all. His attention was wholly on her tray.

"Crab roes on toasted crackers, smear of mustard, excellent, yes. I taught him that, the emperor, you know. Had to send one of my lads to show his kitchen staff. Smoked fish in pastry, yes, but what's the fish?" There was only one way to be sure. She watched in amusement, as he chewed and swallowed. "Ah, the carmine trout. Perfect. And—goose sausage, is this? Or duck? No, it's not the season for duck, unless it's smoked. No, goose, certainly. In my country this would be a gooseneck pudding, but they do things differently here. Be a good child"—no, he had definitely not troubled even to determine the page's sex—"and fetch us each a glass of flintered wine, will you? No need to take your tray, such heavy things, I'll hold that for you while you scamper. Off you go, now."

And of course by the time the girl was back her tray was empty, and he had scanned the tables from afar and told her just how to replenish it, and how swiftly she ought to return.

Malance sipped her wine—he knew that she liked it, which was why he had asked for it, which was typical of him; she still had no idea after all these weeks whether he actually liked it himself, so she had just tucked that particular anxiety away under "Oh, Brion likes everything," which did still seem to be holding true—and watched with delight as he nibbled and picked, nibbled and picked again, talking all the time, relishing the mere fact of food in a way she could never approach.

"You will like this, and this, and this," he said, pushing treats across the tray towards her. "Not that, and don't even think about that. Fire-pepper slices on baked shrimp paste: you would expire on the spot." Even he was sweating a little, after eating three of them. He took a hefty swig of the chilled wine, and would undoubtedly have scolded her into eating the bites he'd selected for her, if they hadn't been interrupted just as he drew breath.

"Outlands! The very man I was looking for! Ah, and your shadow, of course. Good day to you, young lady. I do beg your pardon, I should say 'Verantha', of course. Now, Outlands, about this Palatinate nonsense..."

She tried to be amused, she did try, at the various ways these diplomats sought to offend neither the emperor whose guests and clients they were, nor the powerful Clath kingdoms who could ruin a country's trade in a season or else simply swallow it down entire, the way they had swallowed her own. They had decreed Verantha not to exist; he had appointed her its ambassador. Fast footwork was required, to tread on no one's toes unduly hard.

This particular man—another big one, though he was all chest and shoulders, all hair and volume and height—had decided from the first to treat her as the emperor's pet, and her proper title as some pet name bestowed upon her by her master. She could hear the quotation marks, every time he said "Verantha". Which was infuriating, but he was that kind of man; he would have infuriated her anyway. She didn't trouble to greet him even with a nod; she only watched quietly as he peeled Brion away from her, tray and treats and all. That was fair enough. Brion had already done more than she could reasonably ask of him, keeping her abreast of the news and bringing her in under the shelter of his own imposing presence. His shadow, yes: that charge too was entirely fair. She should turn away now and make contacts of her own, even pick her own choices from the laden trays and tables, perhaps, because he was right, of course she ought to eat...

24

So she turned, and was abruptly face to face with the other reason she came this Friday and every Friday.

She came for the emperor, of course, because she owed him that and more, much more; she came for Brion, for the pleasures of his company and the knowledge, the insights that he shared; she came for herself, to build her own networks of contact and trust, to do her job in so far as it existed, in so far as it could conceivably help.

And she came for this: to look this creature in the eye and let her be reminded that so long as Malance was here, under the emperor's aegis and formally recognised within the open circle of his court, the woman had not—quite—achieved her lifetime's goal.

"Clath," Malance said, the proper greeting from one ambassador to another, though she spoke the word as cold as ice, as hard as stone, as sharp as the dagger at her belt.

For a moment, she thought Ambassador Attanborn would say nothing at all. It had happened before, that she only turned her back in a public refutation, all the more destructive when it came from a supposed diplomat. To Malance she would always be *General* Attanborn, as she was when she led the gathered Clath armies to destroy Malance's homeland so utterly, and thereby earn herself this privileged posting.

This Friday, though, after a pause for thought, the woman did deign to speak with her.

She said, "That precious piece of land you try to claim has been divided—you may have heard?—between two provinces of the Clath realms. Its borders have been ploughed under, its population redistributed, its archives burned, its governing class abolished. Why can you not acknowledge that it is gone?"

Of course she'd heard. Brion had told her, even before the emperor did. She liked to think he'd even known before the emperor, unlikely as that seemed. It was the ultimate cruelty, it seemed to her, not even to see the value of Verantha as an entity in herself, merely to seize hold of her geography and destroy all else.

But that was Clath, and she was long inured to cruelty, she who had come here to game and sport and make waves, make a new life far from home. She smiled as she had practised smiling, with not a shadow of warmth or care, and said, "Verantha is not gone, so long as I am her ambassador."

That was the weight she carried, the hope-without-hope, the compass of her mourning and the expression of her grief. Occasionally, she got to use it as a weapon.

The great bell in the tower overhead began to strike, leisurely, imperious, compulsive. It was followed almost on the instant by more bells, further bells, all through the palace complex and all across the city. Noon spread through Feremendas like ripples on a lake, all from a single drop of water; the emperor kept the time, while his people waited for him to pass it on.

Glasses were set down, or handed to waiting pages. Greasy fingers were wiped on linen napkins, hanging ready over the shoulders of those same pages. Plotting was postponed, conversation broken off, one last high voice hushed. Not hurrying, of course, but moving swiftly none the less, the city's elite filed out into the main hall again, and Malance with them.

The emperor was never late. Sometimes she suspected that the first telling stroke of noon might be delayed till he was ready. At all events, the bell had not yet finished counting off the hour before he was there, passing swiftly and easily through the throng, unattended save for a couple of his pages. Not a tall man, not particularly handsome or particularly old, he wore the same dull imperial crimson as the children at his heels, his clothes barely more ostentatious than their own. Nothing about him spoke to power, except that everything did. He held all the focus of that great hall;

the silverstone walls caught his reflection as a blur of shadow, more potent than any of the glitter and gorgeous array of his court in full pomp.

His own people bowed or knelt or curtsied low as he passed, as he recognised them with a glance or perhaps a word, though he paused to speak with none of them. Not yet. The strangers in the hall—and strangers yet, for all that some had represented their governments here for decades—offered their own respect in the manner of their own countries, but not so deeply. Pride and independence knelt to no one.

Malance waited for her moment, and bowed as one of her people would to a father figure, bespeaking gratitude and acknowledging fealty. As she straightened, his eyes smiled at her and he murmured "Verantha," exactly loud enough to be sure that Clath would hear it.

She knew full well—of course she did, she wasn't stupid—that she was being used here, that she was one more weapon in the constant struggle between Clath and Feremendas. It was a struggle of a hundred years already, and not any kind of war; their forces had never met on the battlefield. Not yet. Rather it was a struggle for influence in trade and politics worldwide, a slow kind of wrestling match, shifts of weight and pressure, the aggressive upstart trying to heave aside the veteran power. Of course Malance couldn't be a significant weapon in such a contest, only a pinprick, an irritant casually picked up and casually wielded. She knew it, and was grateful anyway, willing to serve this man in any way he asked for. Willing to be wielded, willing to prick as often as he wanted. And more, on her own account. Occasionally she wondered if this was a more dangerous game than she knew, if Clath might one day weary of being pricked and simply have her killed—she couldn't think "assassinated", not of herself; how could she matter that much, to anyone?—but she played it anyway. For him, and for Verantha.

Six steps climbed to the dais; he took them two at a time, more spring than stretch, while his pages scampered to keep up. On the dais stood what was often described as the most uncomfortable chair in the world, for all its padding and cushions. Its arms and back were gilded, its upholstery once more in the imperial colour, but it was still very much a chair and not a throne. He wouldn't have sat a throne, this man, any more than he'd have worn a crown, even if either one had traditionally come with the role. He might head the most powerful nation in the world—there was some debate about it, mostly from Clath, who held that Feremendas' star was in decline, while theirs was rampant—but his predecessors had established a low-key imperial style, and he'd embraced it wholeheartedly.

He took the chair, while his pages arrayed themselves behind. There were no seats else; comfort made courtiers tedious, it was said. A standing audience was a brief audience. Briefer, at any rate.

His court pressed closer, that inevitable impulse towards the heart, the lure of what's strong. He smiled down in greeting and said, "Well. The Palatinate, then. Who's first? Darien?"

His chancellor bowed in acknowledgement, and moved to stand on the second stair up, where he could be clearly seen without in any way impeding the emperor's view.

"Ambassador Jenn"—another bow, towards the man he named—"brought me this proposal in good earnest, I know, but..."

She didn't know if it was common practice elsewhere to debate government policy in open court, before the world's ambassadors. It was very much the custom here. Perhaps that was another expression of confidence in power, to let Clath and others hear what Feremendas thought, and what intended. She'd seen some few of the reports that Brion sent home after these audiences, and she diligently, defiantly wrote her own once she'd learned the way of it, for all that she had nowhere now to send them.

That was almost the worst of being Verantha, all that remained of Verantha: that she had no task here except to *be* here, to hold that name alive. There was nothing for an orphaned ambassador to *do*.

She listened carefully anyway, and worked out her own responses to the issues, because those were Verantha's responses now; she spoke for her country—except that she didn't actually speak, she never had spoken at court except at her formal reception, when the emperor gravely accepted the credentials he'd had written out for her—and it was important that she held actual arguable positions on the matters at hand, for all the world as though she were really an ambassador and Verantha still a real country. There had never been many of her people here to represent, for they weren't generally a travelling folk; and those few had packed and gone almost as soon as the news came through, trying to find their way home to family or friends, wanting to do something, anything to help the survivors recover. Malance had only stayed herself because of this, because she was the last one in the embassy and that mattered, and because—of the emperor's kindness—she held title and position now, she *was* Verantha so long as she was here, so of course she couldn't leave.

She would have died for her country, had her country asked that of her, had she had the opportunity. Now she felt obliged to live for the selfsame reasons, and to stay in the embassy that was technically the last surviving little piece of her homeland, and to be the emperor's plaything in whatever games the man might have in mind.

And obliged every Friday to come here to this hall, and to make notes for her impotent reports, and to linger afterwards when people gathered once again into little groups and murmurings. Sometimes the emperor would stay awhile himself, move from one group to another, talk to those who remained. That might be why they lingered; probably it was. Sometimes, as today, he would call an end to the audience with a few quick words and melt away with one or two counsellors, or none.

Generally she'd linger close to Brion—very like a shadow, yes—and leave more or less when he left, though they wouldn't go together and she wouldn't ask a ride. Today he had been swallowed by a larger group, to argue out the Palatinate issue in depth; she had nothing to contribute and no one to represent, and was feeling more of a fraud even than usual, so she lingered alone with her back to a pillar, trying to look deep in thought rather than merely abandoned.

She didn't have to keep up the pretence for long. A page appeared at her elbow, a boy this time, older, taller, starting to fill out a little. She was set to wave him off—no, there was nothing he could bring her, thank you—but he spoke first, which was unusual.

Not even from his voice could she tell if he were noble or base-born. Children are natural mimics, picking up accents from the air around, and they had diligent tutors besides; it was almost eerie, how all the pages sounded so alike.

He said, "Lady, his grace would be grateful for a word with you."

Then she recognised him as one of the emperor's favourites of the day, following his master in and out; then she gaped at him, almost had him repeat himself, because his message was so improbable.

His grace was the emperor, always. *A simple title for a simple man*, his people said, and loved him for it. Her own feeling was that in truth it was a very misleading title for a very complex man, but never mind that. Not even the most senior ambassadors at court expected to be summoned to private meetings with the man himself, not on a Friday. They might meet one-to-one with the chancellor, or any other high officials today; they might see the emperor alone or in company, any other day of the week; but Fridays were sacrosanct and all about the empire. Strangers were let listen and take note—or take notes, yes indeed—but they were rarely called on to speak and certainly never summoned to the emperor afterwards.

Perhaps he'd decided to end this charade, take back the keys to her house, send her away from the city? Perhaps there had been a shift in his relationship with Clath and he was obliged to give ground, and she was the easiest, most obvious, least costly way to do that. Perhaps that had been what she was here for all along, to be a handy sacrifice at need. Perhaps he'd chosen to tell her himself because he was a kind man, and he knew how this would devastate her, and—

Perhaps she should bite down on her reckless imagination, and wait to learn. Learn to wait. Concentrate on following the page, step by step, because her feet felt strangely unfamiliar and she wasn't at all confident that her legs would hold her up.

Out of that dreadful doorway, out of the portico's shadow, and a turn away from the road that would have taken her back to the Strangers' Gate. Along a path that meandered beside a brook, through a flowered meadow; it all looked so utterly natural, it must have been entirely artificial. Besides, this very hill had been built exactly to hold the palace, and all that it contained; everything up here was artificial. She should remember that.

She heard a soft, enquiring whistle from a grove of trees on her flank. There was a figure there, standing not quite in the light; she gestured a hasty stay. The boy she followed didn't seem to turn his head, didn't seem to react at all to the exchange, shouldn't have been able to see either the figure nor Malance's response. She was morally certain that he had observed every detail, and would report it all. To whom? To his master, perhaps; all these pages were the emperor's own, sporting his colour, obedient to his will. His eyes and ears throughout the palace and beyond, throughout the city. They might be organised into a hierarchy, though, each rank reporting to their seniors; or to someone not in that line at all, a palace steward or a secretary, who would filter and distil and lay only the briefest of documents on the emperor's desk when they were done.

She had been in the city seven years now, and had drunk deeply of it every day, and still she didn't know enough.

It was said, of course, that the emperor knew everything. Some said by supernatural means, or else by a network of spies and agents, for whom the pages were only a pretty cover in all too visible livery.

She didn't know. She didn't even know how Brion dredged up his information, given how rarely he left his house, unless it were to track down some exotic foodstuff fresh come from far away. She didn't know how he'd learn that either, but he would.

The brook tumbled over a lip of stone into a pool with lily pads, with fish; and here was a pavilion, as simple as it was lovely. Of course the emperor would be here. There could be no finer setting for the man. She almost expected him to open the door himself.

That didn't happen, naturally not. The page opened it instead—*good servants don't knock*, though it had taken a good servant to teach her that, and she had been obliged to teach her own—and bowed her through.

And yes, here was the emperor, waiting for her on a sofa, quite alone.

He smiled at his page and said, "Thank you, Ash." The boy nodded, respectful but abbreviated, a sketch of a bow; that must be the regimental custom, as it were, permissible to all who wore the livery. Certainly it would save time and fuss, and he was said to abominate fuss. The boy—*Ash*, very well, one more thing learned today—went to join his sister in service, where she stood quietly attentive against the far wall. The emperor turned his smile on Malance now, and said her name. Her true name, that name, not the other that she carried, the title he had given her when it didn't even lie within his gift.

He didn't stand—*the emperor stands for no one*—but patted the seat beside him. "Come, sit. Thank you for joining me," as if she or anyone would have had a choice. In his own palace, and very much his guest. "Flintered wine is your choice, I believe? Do try a glass of this."

He poured it with his own hands, somewhat outraging both his pages, but they were probably used to that.

She realised that in all her bewilderment and worry she had forgotten to offer him her own respect, that perfected bow. It seemed too late now, so she simply went, and sat, and took the glass he passed her.

From his hand into hers: the very notion was dizzying, never mind the accidental, inevitable touch of their fingers as she took it.

She raised the glass to him in salute, the very belated very least that she could offer, and took a sip to cover her confusion.

The wine was extraordinary. Not too chill to taste, just the cool of a pond in autumn; and that taste was like nothing that had passed her lips before. She struggled briefly for any way to frame it. There was the acid wash of the flintering process, of course, bright and sharp, a blade's edge against the palate; there was a depth that was new to her, layers of flavour and revelation, as though time itself were unfolding in her mouth. And a long, slow, comfortable touch of sweetness to follow, to round it at last into a coherent whole, a tale told. A taste. One sip could last her for an hour, she thought, just to think about it.

Perhaps that one sip had lasted an hour. He was watching her, amused, infinitely patient.

"You like it," he said. "I'm pleased. I'll have a case delivered to your house."

"Your—your grace," she stammered, and then seemed to lose wherever that sentence might have gone, and fell abruptly silent.

"Excellency?"

Now *that* was absurd, from him to her. And it gave her the chance to recover, as perhaps—probably—it had been intended to. Oh, he was subtle, this man. And enjoying himself far too much, and all at her expense.

"In any sensible arrangement," she told him firmly—oh lord, was the wine coming to her head already? Could it be that potent, as well as everything else that it was?—"the greater title would go to the greater position. With all respect to your predecessors, and to you, your empire is occasionally rather silly in its choices."

Definitely, it must be the wine. He was probably watching for it. He was certainly laughing.

Suddenly achingly vulnerable out of nowhere, she stumbled on. "...Please, will you call me Malance again? Almost nobody does now, I always have to be 'excellency' or 'lady' even in my own home," except when her particular friends were visiting. And, "Oh, except when Clath is in hearing, of course. Then I always have to be Verantha."

"I will do exactly that, Malance. You have my word," and a touch of his glass against hers to seal it, which was certainly a signal that she had to sip again.

Ah, well. If the emperor chose to make her drunk and tease her, that was surely his prerogative, though she could think of few reasons why he might want to. Or why she was here at all, if he wasn't going to dismiss her from his court and his city. *I'll have a case delivered to your house*—that honestly didn't sound much like dismissal.

"Your grace," being bold now, for nothing else would help her here, "how may I serve you?"

"You serve me already, by serving the memory of your country," he said slowly, "and I wanted to be sure you understood that. There may be ... moments, at court and elsewhere"—*moments with Clath* was what she heard—"and news from home that will go hard with you, hereafter. I don't keep you at hand just to sting her, nor to be stung yourself."

"Use me as you will, your grace."

"Oh, I shall. But I did want to apologise in advance, and to assure you that you have lost nothing of my regard. In token of which," and he wafted his glass vaguely in the direction of his pages, "these two are coming to the end of their time with me, and I intend to pass them on to you. That will confirm to the world your status in my eyes, since I never do that. Also it might help to bring a little, ah, order to your household. They are a vile insinuating pair of reprobates, but they do know what they're about."

Startled, she stared from him to the pages. He truly never did that. These two must surely be sixteen, perhaps nudging seventeen, which did truly mean that they must shed his livery soon enough; but the lordlings generally went home to their families at the end of their service, at least for a while, and the low-born stayed to live their lives out here in the palace as trusted servitors, in whatever role best suited them or him.

The youngsters of course said nothing, but they'd been all too obviously indignant earlier, when he usurped their privilege to serve her wine himself. Now they were calm, expressionless, the perfect attendants once again. *They knew*, she thought. *He told them earlier. But did they agree, or were they simply told? Are they servants gifted to me, or noble children loaned on promise of eventual return? Or one of each? Oh, help...*

She had no help from them, their schooled faces telling her nothing, while his was all mischief, and so no help at all.

"Your grace is too kind," she said hesitantly, "has been too kind already. I don't need more." Specifically, she didn't need more servants. Nor imperial eyes imposed upon her privacy, which must be the meaning behind this. Another meaning, rather, atop those that he had already confessed. How were things to grow harder for her, when they were so hard already? He hadn't said, so would not say, that was certain. But he wanted his people in her household, that was also certain; and not to hide the fact of it, to make it abundantly clear to all who followed his doings, which meant all the court and all the ambassadors and especially Clath and more.

"Malance, it is my desire," he said. "Trust me, they will be good for you. And for your house," a little sternly, as though he deprecated the ramshackle nature of her life as his protégée. "You don't even have a housekeeper, I know, and you ... were not made to keep house."

She tried to bite back a smile, failed, confessed it with a giggle. "Your grace, I was not made for ... any of this," a gesture that contained her house far off and all her people with it, and also her courtly dress which he had paid for, and her presence here at court and most particularly here in his private pavilion. She should have been a young and carefree functionary, let loose in his city for her own delight. Nothing that she had now was her worth or her choice or her desire.

"I know it, but even I can mend only one thing at a time. Take my imps, and let them ease at least some part of your burden. Beat them if they're troublesome," he added. "I do. It changes their behaviour not at all, but it is very good for my temper."

They stood easy, reacting not at all, unless the girl perhaps made a gesture to rub her bottom, as though it were still sore; it was hard to tell, when they stood with their hands neatly disciplined behind their backs. Clearly, the emperor was talking nonsense. Their tutors might perhaps have beaten them, when they were smaller; certainly not him, and certainly not recently.

Certainly not her either. She said, "Of course, your grace," to reassure them, and wondered what in the world she was to do with two new servants in the house. Especially when either or both of them might be lordlings in disguise. Could she even ask? How could she ask? Traditionally the rule was that no one ever asked, but if they were no longer in the emperor's service, at least on the face of it...?

Oh, she had no idea. Things would sort themselves out. Or more likely not, but she was weary of worrying about everything, all the time.

He rose abruptly, so she scrambled to do the same, understanding that this most unlikely of interviews was over.

"Good," he said. "Don't trouble to take them now; I know you have someone waiting. I'll send them down to your house later, with that case I promised." She'd barely touched her glass—but then, neither had he. Perhaps this was symbolic of an emperor's life, that he left a lifetime's-worth of glasses behind him, barely touched. It was ... very much not symbolic of her own, where she veered unpredictably from reckless indulgence to reckless abstinence, and back again. And again. And no, there was no more order in her life than in her household, and these children couldn't hope to touch that. Report back, no doubt they would; no doubt that was what he wanted. Though he seemed to know so much already, to know it all, and...

Wait. How, how in the world...?

She lifted her eyes to his one more time, and he smiled as though he knew everything that was in her head, as well as in her house or in her life.

"Tell my disrespectful niece not to whistle so raucously in my gardens," he said gently, "it disturbs the birds. She has lovely manners when she chooses; let her show them, at least within my hearing. Oh, and tell her also that all tonight is hers, to do as she likes with it. I shall not expect her back until the morning. Indeed, I forbid her to return. I do not want her; that is her punishment for kicking up such a racket. The gates shall be locked against her. Yes, tell her that. I shall see her at breakfast, perhaps, and not before."

Let her riot through the city and then fling herself on your mercy, he was saying, *she'll enjoy that, and so will you. If she doesn't make it home for breakfast, never mind.*

And he was right, of course, and Malance was enjoying the prospect of it already, but—oh, *damn* the man, how in the world had he *known*...?

V

TWO

A momentary flower in Marmon's throat

Both pages saw her out onto the pavilion's veranda. Both saw that they need see her no farther; both gave her that same odd deep nod—or was it a shallow, a very shallow bow?—that they employed with their current master; both turned and left her without a word, without a sign. Were they cautious, curious, conspiratorial? Contemptuous? Or just resigned to their new duties, following the emperor's will in this as in all things else?

She could read them not at all; they offered her nothing. Well, nothing but immaculate service, no doubt. And perhaps a route, a back way to the palace—but she had that already.

She stepped down from the veranda and crossed a lawn to the pond's edge, where Vivi sat on the low wall teasing the fish with a length of grass.

"He knows," Malance said, by way of greeting.

"Of course he knows. He always knows."

"Did you tell him?"

"I have never actually needed to tell him anything, in all my life." Vivi stood abruptly, tossing the grass-stem into the water. "Nor, of course, has he ever told me anything that mattered. He is the most infuriating man. As soon as I saw where you were going, though, and who was taking you, I knew that he would know."

"Oh, you know them—of course you know them. Do you know the girl's name, at all?" The boy's was Ash, but the girl's hadn't been mentioned.

"Yes, that's Alder. Why, do you want to become better acquainted?" Vivi had a particularly irritating smile, sly and sidelong, that she employed with purpose and on just the wrong occasions. As now. "She's a little young, but..."

"Oh, be quiet." An ambassador to the imperial court did not slap at a scion of the imperial family, nor shake her by the shoulders, so Malance only smiled back, a little ruefully. Vivi could score points in any conversation; wordplay was her life's blood, her native language and her most particular, most intimate skill. "I don't actually need a ruse to become better acquainted, that's going to happen anyway. The emperor has given both of them to me. It just seemed politic to know her name, before I find her in my house."

Just for once, she was pleased to see, she'd managed to startle even Vivi.

"He ... *gave* you two of his pages? He never does that!"

"No. He pointed that out himself. He did say it was sure to cause comment." And she had asked all that she intended to ask, about the two of them. Anything else they wanted her to know, they could tell her themselves.

"Comment? It'll cause cataclysms. Outrage. And envy, naturally. Everyone will want them, if you've got a pair. Oh, how much trouble has he stirred up now? And more to the matter, *why* would he do such a thing? I mean, he's been kind to you, I know—all the city knows—but this is *spectacularly* generous. You really don't know what you're getting, do you?"

Malance shrugged. "A pair of pages? And I have nothing for them to do, I don't need them. I think he meant them as some kind of prior compensation, for something dreadful that's going to happen soon. Maybe they can help with that, whatever it is? I don't know, Vivi. I really don't *want* them, but he wouldn't let me refuse."

"Of course not. A gift from the emperor? That, you do not refuse. And don't worry, they'll find plenty to do. Your house will never be the same again."

"Oh—that's the other thing. He says you're to stay with me tonight. I'm sorry my house is so awful..."

"Does he, indeed? Well, don't you be so despondent about it, that's rude to me and not a flattering look on you. Maybe I'll borrow one of your boys for the night, though he'd need to clean a room out first."

"Oh, you can take my bed. The sheets are clean, at least. I'll sleep on the sofa."

"Excellent plan. Look, it's cheered you right up. Now come on, everyone is waiting. Well, actually no, everyone will have started without us, but they're probably still moored down at the jetty. They'd better be."

So saying, little Vivi tucked her arm comfortably through Malance's and tugged her into movement. Another path, more trees; she really didn't know quite where they were or which way they were going. Her head was spinning entirely, and not at all from the wine. Well, maybe a little, although she'd barely drunk it. Vivi's perfume was intoxicating on its own account, as though she'd bathed in a smoky herbal tea, hints of bitterness and promise. And the silk shirt and trousers she'd opted to wear tonight were dark, unrevealing, alluring; and the simple string of pearls at her throat was nothing like her usual array of exotic, aggressive jewellery; and Malance said, "You were intending to come back with me tonight anyway, weren't you?"

"Absolutely. I don't need my honoured uncle's consent. Nor his instruction." Her eyes were bright as any jewels, catching the lowering sun. She might even have planned that, practised it; Vivi lived a very *intentional* life. "I don't know what the rest are going to think, mind."

"Don't you? I do. They're going to think the very worst of both of us—and they'll be delighted. And want all the details tomorrow. I shall be ... diplomatic." For once.

"Oh, you always are."

They had started arm in arm; now they were hand in hand, as the path brought them to an unexpected set of stairs. Unexpected by Malance, at least. She'd had no idea this was here, overhung as it was with trees. There was a cacophony overhead, among the branches; birds of some kind. She really should learn the city's birds, one of these days. Years, no doubt it would take years. A long lifetime, perhaps. She might have one of those, eked out in imperial charity. Perhaps she'd become a cherished antique, Madam Ambassador for a long-forgotten land, still lingering at court and going through the motions when even her own memory of Verantha had faded into dust.

Perhaps not, though. Probably not. The emperor had been warning her of something, even if he wouldn't tell her what.

Maybe this night with Vivi was another gift from him, or meant to be. *Prior compensation*, yes. Maybe there wouldn't or couldn't be more, after whatever-it-was came to pass.

At the foot of the stairs, where she'd almost been expecting a gate out into the city beyond, there was a path instead, circling the hill, running just inside the encompassing wall.

Vivi tugged her to the right, towards the river. This was all new to her; opportunities to explore the palace complex— even with an undisputed insider—came few and far between. And Vivi preferred to racket about the city with their friends, whatever chance she could. The palace wall must always have been a constriction to her, rather than a lure. Malance understood that entirely, and found an echo of it in her own divided feelings when she was younger, how she had loved her homeland and wanted to leave it as soon as ever she could. Even so, she did regret not having more opportunities to wander in this city-miniature, with this girl to act as guide and answerer of many questions.

Where the river touched the palace grounds, there stood the imperial dock: jetties like dark fingers reaching out into the water, the emperor's little fleet of pleasure-boats moored alongside or in one of the sheds to north and south. Too big for any shed, his favourite *Jade Princess* dominated the rest, but she was staid and silent today. All the noise was coming from a smaller craft at the far end of the dock, where a dozen bright revellers were waving and calling their names.

"I believe that's what my grandmother calls 'an excess of high spirits,'" Vivi said drily, still towing Malance along. "She says that, and then she laughs, and then she looks wicked."

"Well, you were right. They absolutely did start without us."

"Of course they did. Never mind that I passed them in, that I provided the boat and the crew. And the spirits."

She wasn't really grumbling; it was just duty, a rite observed. A social obligation, to be astonished by youthful discourtesy, as though she'd never demonstrated it on her own account.

Their friends were spilling down the gangway, running to meet them now.

"Where have you *been*?"

"We had to start without you!"

"There's this amazing shrimp concoction, I don't even know…"

Too many voices, too many faces, too many *hands*. This was what made Malance run away from fun, more nights than not: that same unbridled delight in themselves, in their company, in this moment and their plans for the night ahead and their lives beyond. They knew her sorrows, and they had all known sorrows of their own, and none the less. They were young and privileged and secure, ambitious and confident, clever and eager and ready for anything. They lived in the greatest city of the world, and they meant to taste and touch and experience all of it.

And she loved them and envied them and some nights she needed them and some nights she did not; and she never could predict which way that particular blade would fall. Her days at court always left her wanting them, wanting this; it's why Vivi had been waiting, to scoop her up and carry her away. Her meeting with the emperor would have sent her home, to sit and think and be solitary within the walls of her own house. Her meeting with Vivi after that—

Well. She was here, and she hoped to stay awhile, and to enjoy herself and her company, and then to leave together, she and Vivi. Someone pressed a glass into her hand, her free hand, the one that didn't apparently belong to Vivi now. She kissed those faces that presented themselves for kissing; hugged bodies awkwardly with one elbow, as both her hands were taken; spilled wine, inevitably, on someone's gorgeous shirt. Obviously, no one cared.

They were architects and artists, musicians and milliners, the idle and the very, very busy. They were ridiculous and irresistible. They were individually desirable, and collectively seductive. Between them they had an unfair measure of significance, influence and prestige already, young though they were.

Vivi was the only royal, because they had actually been Malance's friends first, unlikely though that seemed. Hard though that was to remember, sometimes. As today, for example, which was indeed all Vivi's doing. Whether she had adopted them or coopted them, Malance remained unclear. Certainly, though, she had taken possession. Like the empire over a thousand years of growth, annexing whatever it liked or valued. Not like Clath, though, seizing and burning and swallowing up. She wanted to be very clear on that.

Malance took a defiant gulp of her drink—oh, not wine: or not just wine, it had been perfumed somehow with a hint of anise, spiced with something else, something that teased the edges of her tongue with fire—and coughed with surprise, and was duly laughed at and thumped none too helpfully on the back while she wheezed and cursed them all. Careful sipping would be the order of the day hereafter, though she was totally going to track down the genius who'd come up with this and extract their method, by torture if need be. Old cooks could still be taught new tricks, and this was brilliant, when it wasn't setting her mouth aflame.

Up the gangway, single file only—Vivi finally had to relinquish her hand, though she did wait at the top to reclaim it—and here was the rest of the party, standing by to be kissed and hugged in their turn. Veranthans were much less physical in their affections, less demonstrative, *quieter* all around. She did love how tactile these people were, and how demanding. Sometimes, she did love it.

Tonight, she was determined to love every second of it. She drank again, and waved her cup wildly for a refill; and was abruptly if briefly sobered, when a girl in that very familiar livery came pattering over with a jug.

"You borrowed the emperor's pages? On a *Friday*?"

"Why not? Court is over; he doesn't need them now. He doesn't need them *all*. He has dozens, and dozens more to spare."

He did: and he somehow kept all of them always busy, at least as far as she had ever seen. Always dashing, when they weren't standing in quiet, poised attendance.

Well, he had two fewer now. She still didn't know what to think about that, so decided not to think about it at all.

Instead, she took a firmer grip of Vivi's hand and did the towing for a change, pulling her right up into the bow, where someone had foolishly relinquished the best seats on the boat.

"I won't hog you all night, I promise"—*I'm going to have you all night, after all*—"but I'm not ready to mingle yet. Are you *sure* your uncle won't miss this many of his pages?" She'd just spotted another tiny one on the jetty, standing by to unmoor.

Apparently this vessel was entirely crewed by competent children. She had no doubt of their competence—so long as they could see over the wheel, at least—but she was distinctly dubious about the legitimacy of this adventure.

"He isn't really my uncle, you know," which was transparently not an answer to her question, but as a diversionary tactic it was a masterstroke.

"He's not?"

"Uh-uh. He's a *relative*—some sort of complicated cousinly thing on all sides, going back centuries, we're shockingly inbred—but not that close. I came to the palace, I came to *him* to be fostered and trained."

She stopped there, which seemed a little abrupt—until finally Malance understood her. "Vivi, you didn't! You weren't!"

Vivi nodded emphatically. "I did and I was. Eight years his page—and then I didn't want to go, and he didn't want to let me, so of course I stayed. There are a fair few of us in the complex, fosters that he allowed to stay or else he chose to keep. We all call him Uncle, just to keep things simple, and he calls us whatever he likes. And goes on making use of us whenever he likes, as if we were all still in livery. Which we all are, probably, inside. Once a page, always a page. I think. At least, it hasn't worn off yet."

"All right, I want to hear *all* about this. Start with day one, when you arrived at the palace, and go on from there."

"Oh, it started long before that. We used to visit for the summer, and I believe he took a fancy to me then. But I don't want to talk about it here. It was important to tell you, to help you understand a lot of things about me, and about the palace—but I don't want the others to know, or at least not yet. It's a very private kind of service, or it feels that way to us, even though we're out in public all the time, in full view. We're all known by page-names while we're in livery, not our real ones. People only notice the livery, I think, not our individual faces; I've hardly ever been recognised, out in the city, even by the people I used to run errands to. Palace folk know, of course—they saw me shift from page to family, which is *not* the easiest transition, let me tell you; I may have made something of a fool of myself in the process—but not many outside the wall, and I'd like to keep it that way."

"Of course. I won't say a word," but oh, Vivi was going to be saying a great many words as soon as they were private; and Malance was going to be listening with a very, very focused mind.

Well, it was actually possible that Malance would be listening with a very, very giddy drunken mind, if things went on this way. Perhaps she should slow down, probably.

The chances of her being sensible, though? With this crowd? Vanishingly small. And she was struggling with so much, in her head and in the palace and in the city too; maybe for one night she could just drown it all…?

At any rate, for now she wasn't moving. She glanced over the side again, to where that worryingly small child was waiting by the bow rope; and thought that of course Vivi could attract a crew of pages if she'd been one herself, if it wasn't strictly against their rules. Would she have insisted on experienced sailors, though, or did she simply promise them a treat?

Malance drew breath to ask, and was interrupted by a reassuringly mature voice, calling out a string of orders. "Stand by! Hands aloft! Cast off fore and aft! Let fall the topsail!"

Vivi had seduced or commanded at least one of the emperor's boatmen, by the sound of it. Even so: those were all pages swarming up the rigging now. One professional, then, and a crew of willing amateurs. Perhaps this was a common task, when the imperial family chose to go cruising on the river. Perhaps Vivi too had scuttled up to loose those sails and come down to haul on ropes, and no doubt swab the decks and do a hundred tasks else and blister her hands and get tar all over her livery the way these youngsters were. While loving every moment of it, no doubt, if Malance was any judge.

But here was the girl again with that moisture-beaded jug, and it was rude to say no; and suddenly that little lad below was scrambling over the ship's side right there beside her, where he must have cast off his rope and then simply climbed up it as the boat drifted out into the current. He grinned at her amiably, exchanged a more complicated look with Vivi—yes, this was conspiracy, definitely—and turned back to coil the cable neatly, with an air of having done all this many and many a time before.

Malance revised her previous estimate—there must be at least two dozen of them aboard and probably more, if they could crew the ship and serve the passengers at the same time—and knew that if she didn't stop thinking about this, she was going to start asking questions that Vivi very specifically didn't want her to.

Instead, she watched the traffic on the river as the boat beneath them edged out to join that steady procession, other vessels politely making way for the emperor's pleasure-barge, for of course even the sails were bedecked with imperial crimson. His own personal banner was flying at the top of the tallest mast, though he was not in fact aboard as that declared, and she wondered again how much trouble Vivi might be getting them all into.

And wasn't going to worry about that, no, nor about anything; so she gulped again, and coughed again, and snatched Vivi's hand again and led her astern, to where their friends were busily trying to help and of course getting in everyone's way while the master and crew were being very conspicuously patient about it all.

Vivi's plan—which she had apparently vouchsafed beforehand to everyone *except* Malance—was to sail downriver to the last point of land before the opening ocean. There she had ordered tables and lamplight to be waiting, with palace cooks and palace food and palace dining service. Everything was timed around the turning of the tide, so that when they were done the boat could tide it back to the city despite the wind in her teeth, drop her passengers off somewhere more convenient than the palace dock, "and the kids can have all the fun of taking her home by moonlight."

And you, her bright eyes added, *can have all the fun of taking* me *home by moonlight*, with all that that implied.

Mostly, to Malance on this particular day, it implied long conversations all through the night, which might not have been what Vivi had in mind but were definitely what Malance needed. Assuming she stayed sober enough to stay awake, never mind sober enough to grill her friend as mercilessly as she intended. It might not be polite to question pages about their service, but oh, she needed answers more than she needed diplomatic manners. She needed information; she yearned for understanding.

She did the best she could, to seem at least relaxed among her company of friends. These were people she had met at palace functions and private dinners, at parties and parades and solemn ceremonies. Some she had done work for, or for their families, when she was just a Veranthan interpreter, when Verantha and her own heart were still whole. Some were well-born, some were merely famous. She did have other, humbler friends—blessedly, that had been the whole drive of her first years in the city, to meet and hold on to as many people as she possibly could—but they tended to have jobs or other duties, that interfered with long nights and meticulously planned spontaneous outings.

Vivi had apparently even planned—or else, more likely, commanded—the weather: there was an offshore breeze to keep the sailing easy and the passengers warm. Also, of course, there was no easy or obvious way for Malance to flee this particular party as she had fled so many, if her mood should suddenly turn solitary. She was quite convinced that Vivi had planned for that too.

Happily she was also relieved, and excited by her company tonight, and looking forward to her company later, and yes, a little drunk. Maybe more than a little. She asked a page for a glass of water, and laughed at her friends' shock and outrage, and was quite pleased to discover that she could apparently be sensible after all, at least a little bit, at least for now.

There was even a dock at Lookout Point, to make the landing easy; a dock and an old fortification, to provide level ground for the tables and height above the water for views and even some kind of rudimentary kitchen for the cooks to work in. It hadn't been needed or manned for generations uncounted—Feremendas had nothing to fear now from any attack, here at the heart of empire—so there was moss between the stonework and some aggressive vine that climbed the walls. Dock and structure both were kept in good repair otherwise, exactly for entertainments such as this; it was a popular place for the elites of the city to play, and Malance suspected there must be some kind of privy booking system, to ensure that two parties didn't clash on the same night.

If there was, of course Vivi would be privy to it. That went without saying. She could probably simply cancel anyone else's planned party, if it interfered with her own. Though she'd certainly be apologetic, and have an alternative plan for the wounded party that offered just as much fun somewhere else. Likely she'd even pay for it, with the emperor's money. Of course she was high-handed; she was imperial kin and palace-raised, she called the emperor "Uncle". And page-trained, that too, so of course she was efficient. *Ruthless*, some might call it. Malance liked to think of her as *focused*, totally determined on her own path and confident in her choices.

One of which, apparently, was Malance. That had been ... unexpected, and was still unsettling. In a good way, though. Usually.

They'd met at the palace, one Friday after court. Malance had been walking back to the Strangers' Gate, hoping to find a cabriolet waiting there as they usually did, and suddenly here was this short dark vivid girl walking beside her, silks and jewels cut as beautifully and worn as natively as her own skin, grinning up and demanding her name, her provenance, her purpose. Which latter she all too clearly proposed to change, if Malance was willing. If Malance had ever had a choice. Vivi started as she meant to go on, always.

Of course the emperor watched over his family—his *chosen* family, the ones he kept close, the ones who called him Uncle—as carefully as he did his protégées. She shouldn't have been so startled, to learn that he had known. Perhaps she should feel doubly cared for, twice protected?

There was some inevitable argument over who got to sit at which table in the courtyard here, in company with whom; but people mostly avoided arguing with Vivi, because she was sure to win and was royal besides, though that was not why she would win. So Vivi and Malance ended up with the best seats at the best table, an unimpeded view of the sun setting over the ocean, casting a vivid red glow across the sails of ships arriving and ships departing, all the commerce of the world.

More than that, they had the company of Malance's favourite people among this group: the artists and the poets, mainly. Those who wouldn't think twice about arguing with Vivi or with anyone, but they'd argue about scansion and metre, and the difference between them; or else about meaning in a sculptural line, and where or when or whether architecture could ever become sculpture, or even be an art in itself. Those were the arguments that Malance loved to listen to, and loved even more to set Vivi loose on, because this particular—this *very* particular—imperial offshoot had opinions on everything and was always willing to be contended with. She would argue, yes; but she would always listen as well, and she was ready to be convinced. Malance had even seen her change her mind, actively and wilfully, right in the moment. She had adored that, and quietly arranged to give the young man in question a commission—through the kind and anonymous offices of the diplomatic court, because you could offer your friends anything except money—as he was stubbornly true to his vision and hence of course the poorest of the poor.

As Verantha now vested entirely in her, Malance had felt entirely justified in spending what was nominally Verantha's wealth in a good cause. The painting that resulted currently hung in that same side-hall where the court gathered before an audience with the emperor; she was in hopes of sending further custom her friend's way.

Of course he wasn't here now, he'd be working—she hoped—or else honourably starving, or both. Likely both. She'd best take a moment to check up on him. Not tonight, and not tomorrow either. She'd work of her own to do. Feckless artists would have to wait.

Those she had here were less feckless, or more willing to bend to fashion, towards wealth. Marmon had several patrons at court, and delighted in playing their jealousies off against each other, and gossiping about them on nights like this. Feralja had been acclaimed by the emperor himself, and her epics were now read avidly all across the city. Leily had invented a whole new process of glazing pots, and could not keep up with demand even with a whole studio full of apprentices, even with rivals springing up who had entirely stolen her methods. Or, more accurately, stolen her apprentices.

Food came—served, of course, by pages—and she ate it, and it was routinely delicious of course, and she was listening to the conversation and paying attention to Vivi who if she was honest was relentlessly demanding of attention, and of her own in particular, and of her in general, though she really didn't mind, so that she forgot to eat half of it before the next course came. And there was music, because of course her friends had brought their instruments and would stop eating to play because the music mattered more and there was always going to be more food and someone to bring it to them when they were ready, when they were done; and there was audible politics at another table and probably she should have been listening in, doing her diplomatic duty, but honestly what for, who *for*? And she was only a fake ambassador anyway, it was only a cover the emperor had granted her because he liked to be kind and he did like to annoy Clath. And—

And in that moment something passed between her head and Vivi's, a thing she could almost not sense at all, only the power in its passing: an expression of air, perhaps, if air were all speed and impact, a solidity too fast to glimpse in lamplight, something snatched from darkness and hurled with fury, something that neither hissed nor buzzed but something in between—

And there was a momentary flower in Marmon's throat where he was laughing, which made no sense at all, and it was black at the centre and opening to red—

And then he fell straight backwards all at once, thrown down by the sheer force of it—

And now Malance was falling too, and she had no idea why. She'd been hit, hard, from the side; and she landed badly on rough stone, which knocked the wind from her.
    And there was a body on top of hers, and the side she'd been hit from was Vivi's, and that was Vivi's perfume in her nose, and oh gods, had Vivi fallen too, and into her, and was she tangled up with a dead body now, because there

was suddenly no doubt in her mind that Marmon was dead, though she still didn't understand how?

She opened her eyes to find Vivi's head just inches from her own, ferocious and intent and no, not dead at all.

She tried to sit up, thinking to get disentangled as a first thing; and so found that she couldn't move, that they weren't actually tangled up at all. Vivi was straddling her with purpose, holding her down.

It seemed to be taking her minutes to reconstruct a second's action in her head. Something had been shot at them—an arrow? maybe?—and hit Marmon, and they'd both seen or felt or heard it happen, and almost in the same moment Vivi had hurled herself into Malance and knocked her to the ground, and...

And what now, she did not know, but—"Vivi?"

That was as much as she had breath for, so perhaps it hadn't been minutes, if she was still gasping from the jolt of it all.

"Sorry to be rough," Vivi murmured, and her voice was tempered steel, just as her body was wherever it was touching Malance's, and that was almost everywhere. "Old habits, early training. If I get off you, will you promise to lie still, just as you are? Sitting up now would be ... rather stupid, actually."

Malance nodded, but Vivi made her speak the words, "I *promise*, yes!" before she rolled away. And even then she kept a chaining grip on Malance's wrist, to be sure of her, and how in the world did she get to be so *strong*, little willow-wand girl that she was?

At least breathing was a little easier, now that she wasn't being crushed into the stonework. And she could turn her head, even if she'd promised not to lift it; so she did that, and no one had knocked over any of the lamps, which was probably just as well, but it did seem that everyone was lying flat just as they were. Quite a few of her friends were lying beneath pages, she realised, who were only now peeling themselves off with soft murmurs of instruction, and that

was so exactly what had happened to her; and of course
Vivi had been a page too, and *once a page, always a page*; and,
"Wait, you train *children* to act as bodyguards?"

"Yes, of course. They're disposable, at that age. We can
always make more, if we start to run out."

White teeth flashed in the gloom beneath the table: a girl,
one of their servers, still holding someone down till she was
sure of him, grinning cheerfully at them. No, at Vivi. Recog-
nising one of her own. That grin was positively *feral*.

It seemed oddly quiet. No music now, only the sounds of
the sea on the rocks far below. No one was screaming, blessedly—but then, they'd probably all had the breath knocked
out of them—and no one was talking either. Except for
herself and Vivi. It was a *waiting* silence, ready for someone
to take command; and almost not a surprise now, almost not,
when that someone turned out to be Vivi.

Who whistled softly, a distinct pattern of notes. Briefer
whistles of acknowledgement came back, from all across the
forecourt. Had she just declared herself in charge? Malance
did rather think so, and Vivi confirmed it with a crisp set of
instructions.

"Eyes. From the north, clockwise. Go."

"Nothing."

"Nothing."

"Nothing..."

The voices ran in brisk rotation, with an almost military
feel to it, except that some of the boys' voices hadn't broken
yet. Who *were* these children: the emperor's private army?
Effectively yes, she supposed. Like the palace gates with no
guards, no visible guards: he could surround himself with
protection and never let it seem that way.

There was nothing to be seen, no threat identifiable.

"Injuries? Speak out."

No one spoke. Malance suspected that none of her friends
would dare to, however they might have been hurt in the
throwing-down; she felt much the same way, shy to insert

herself into such an organised call-and-response. Or simply overawed, perhaps; or content to lie silent where she had no place, no right nor need to speak.

Several emperors had been assassinated, she knew. Of *course* his servants would be trained to react swiftly and efficiently. That they were children probably only affected the means of that reaction.

"Good. Just the one, then, and the assassin most likely gone. Best guess?"

One voice came back to her. "East wall, highness. Climb up by rope, crouch between the merlons, best chance not to be seen." Was that chagrin, was he blaming himself for not seeing the killer anyway? Yes, absolutely he was; he went on, "I'm almost sure I caught movement there, after." Not before. It wasn't chagrin, it was shame.

"Confirmed," another voice. "I saw it too. After."

"Go and check. Stay low."

"Yes, highness."

Malance couldn't see from here, try though she did; but she almost persuaded herself she could hear the soft sounds of two lithe bodies slithering across stone. Certainly there was nothing else to listen to; was everybody holding their breath?

She realised that she actually was, for one, and released it with an effort.

"Rope, highness, yes. And a boat on the water, sail high."

"I told you to stay low!"

"Yes, highness." He'd wanted to redeem himself, of course. Idiot boy. Vivi—this new Vivi, this girl she knew not at all, *highness*—would skin him for disobeying, for lifting his head into the embrasure. Later, though. Once everyone was safe.

"Someone run to the master, let him know."

"Shel's already gone, highness."

"Let him know about the *boat*. He can follow—oh. No, of course he can't. Not without a crew," and all his crew was here.

Malance half expected her to say "*Everyone* run to the boat"—but no wise commander gives orders that his people won't follow. The pages' first duty, she was beginning to realise, was here, was to her and to Vivi and all of their guests. They wouldn't abandon their charges now, with one already dead among them. Not even to chase the killer.

Vivi had been propped up on her elbows, to supervise her troops; now she dropped down and rolled onto her back with a sigh. "All right. That one's gone; make sure there's no one else. Check the buildings, check the path. In pairs, knives out. Go."

She wasn't expecting anyone else, or she would have gone herself; and she was checking anyway. Willing to take the risk, to make the sacrifice if need be. Malance wanted to hold her breath again, for all those kids, as if that could help in some way; but Vivi thrust an arm out blindly in her direction, so she held her hand instead.

And took this as licence to speak, if not to sit up yet, as shadows flowed away from the lamplight, pages in pairs. Some of them were holding hands too, she noticed.

Others had stayed, crouching over Marmon's body. She was glad of that. And starting to tremble, now, at last, meaninglessly.

She wanted to take her mind off violent death; all she could manage was to talk about it.

"What *was* that?"

"Crossbow bolt, I think. Yes?"

That was a call, quiet but carrying. A voice came back, "Yes, highness. In the throat. Bodkin, not broadhead."

"A broadhead would have taken his head off, near enough."

Malance wasn't sure who that comment was meant for; she hoped not herself.

What Vivi said next, though, absolutely was for her. "A bodkin is an assassin's choice of bolt. Less brutal, more accurate. A trained killer will take accuracy every time."

"But ... why would anyone want to assassinate *Marmon*?" He could be irritating, true, and he played people against each other, powerful people, but—

"Not him, fool. You. Even trained killers miss. You don't so much as raise your head until we're absolutely sure, do you understand?"

"But—yes, yes, I understand!—but why would anyone...?" And then, a sudden realisation: "It passed between us, just as close to you. And you're royal, and I'm damn sure you've made enemies at court, you couldn't not. Of course they were after you, not me. You keep your own damn head down."

She'd have reached out to make sure, held that slim neck to the stone however strong Vivi had surprisingly turned out to be, except that her hand on that side was being inconveniently, unhelpfully held, and that grip wasn't letting go; and—wait, was Vivi *laughing*?

She was, she really was.

"Vivi!"

"Sorry, I'm sorry... I'm a very *minor* royal, Malance, and all my enemies love me really. They're obliged to, they're my relatives for the most part. I told you, shockingly interbred; we're all cousins somehow. You, though," and she was abruptly sober now, glowering through the dark, "you have real enemies. Clath has had people killed within our borders before this; and if their monarchs' council didn't think you a foe worth disposal, the Clath ambassador here absolutely does. I've seen her look at you at court."

"You never come to court."

"Sometimes I do. I may not come to you, though. You're for after."

...And the emperor's pages had seen her leave the court and linger, seen her go off with Malance week after week, to one party or another; and if his pages were his bodyguards as well as his servants, then certainly they were his spies and informers too, and they were all about them here, and they still recognised Vivi as one among them as well as an authority over them, and—

"Vivi, did the emperor *know* about this cruise tonight?"

"Sweetling, he *suggested* it. How else could I have taken so many of his pages?"

"And you were going to tell me this when, exactly?"

"Not at all, if I could avoid it. But he's worried, Malance. He knows I like to go out with you and your friends into the city, and I don't know why, but he's worried about something. He wanted to be sure we had protection. Which is why"—a broad gesture of her other hand, to embrace the situation and the pages who were coming back now two by two to confirm the watchtower's emptiness, and the imperial boat waiting below—"all of this. To keep us under his eye."

"He agreed to let you come to me tonight."

"Yes, he did. I told you, I'm not the one in danger. If I'm with you, you're at least safer than you were. And—have you forgotten?—he's sent two more of us into your household tonight. They'll be waiting for us. Watching out."

She had, as it happened, forgotten. Now she remembered. Was he sending her protection, though? Or implanting his spies? *The emperor knew exactly where we would be tonight*, and that was a thought she meant to share with no one, and very definitely not Vivi. Its implications made no sense at all—but neither did the mere suggestion that the crossbow might have been aimed at her. Besides, if the emperor wanted her dead—gods, if *anyone* wanted her dead—there must have been a thousand easier chances than this. No watch was kept at her house—or used not to be, at least. Perhaps that would prove a new use for those delightfully useless boys. Or for her new pages, whom she absolutely did not need else. Watching her, spying on her, reading her messages, reporting to the emperor because *once a page, always a page* and the pages all belonged to him, body and soul. Proficient bodies, devoted souls. And Vivi was one among them, so Malance was suddenly dubious about her loyalties too, while still actually believing that Vivi must have been the target, so it would be just as well that she came home with her tonight, with those pages to protect her...

Malance was mildly aware that her thoughts were making no sense whatsoever. She was inclined not to blame herself severely, in the circumstances.

And now, at last, they were being allowed to move. Pages were helping her friends to their feet; others were here now to do the same for herself and Vivi, except of course that Vivi needed no help and she herself stooped to grip Malance's wrists and haul her up.

"All's clear," she said, bright-eyed at the end of adventure. "Master Tolt has sent a runner back to the city, just to be certain; I know Partin"—of course she did, she doubtless knew them all—"and he'll be in well before us. Long legs, that boy has, and the boat will be slow on the tide, with the wind against us. So we can expect an escort when we come to shore, but I am still coming back with you, Malance. And we're not letting them into the house."

"Imperial troops can't come into the house," she said, smiling at last, finding the feel of it strange on her face and in her heart. "It's sovereign territory. It's Verantha."

V

THREE

Once it must have been lovely, this house

They were slow indeed, tacking back and forth across the narrowing river to take what they could from a contrary breeze, depending more on the incoming tide to push them home; and the news—the boy, Partin—did run ahead of them, all the long way back to the city. By the time they crept up to a landing stage, there was a small army waiting.

Malance still thought that they were a small army in themselves, these quiet, determined, dangerous children. She'd felt bizarrely safe in their company, despite coming home with Marmon's body laid out in the master's cabin, on his chart table. She had passed most of the voyage in there with him, with her other friends, sitting silent, mourning the loss of him and everything he'd been, loud and impetuous and infuriating, delightful. One of them. His might not be the first death for any of them, but it was the first death in their actual circle, since they had found each other. That mattered. And the manner of it, that mattered too. Someone—one of the pages, certainly—had pulled the bolt from his throat and wrapped his neck in clean linen, but they still knew what lay hidden there, and if Malance was the only one who couldn't stop thinking about it, she would have been very surprised.

Vivi had sat with them for a little, then left them to mourn between themselves, aware that the palace wall raised a difference, that she had been one among them but never truly one of them, a latecomer whose privilege hid her worth. It was kind in her, Malance thought, to give them this time alone; and when a page came in to tell them that journey's end was in sight, Malance went straight out to join her in the bow, hand in hand once more as they watched the land approach.

As they saw the lanterns, and the people waiting. So many people, and all of them troops, *official* troops, drawn up in array. It could almost feel like an arrest, if she hadn't known and understood the reasons for it. If she hadn't been an ambassador to the emperor's court, and thus immune to such indignities...

"You know," she murmured, "they can't touch me. Technically, they can't come anywhere close to me."

"Oh, me neither. I'm royal; I could have horrible things done to them, if they displeased me. Horrible." Vivi smiled then, just a little, and nudged Malance with her elbow. "Let's not ruin their night, though, eh? They're trying to keep us safe."

Malance sighed. "All right. But I need some clear lines, apparent dignity. Even under escort. *Especially* under escort. Everything that happens tonight will get back to the court, and to the other ambassadors,"—*and to Clath, especially to Clath*—"and they already know me as something artificial, the emperor's whim, a playtoy. I may never win their respect, but I will have it from these." Though she was only a girl yet, and appallingly alone, and in honesty nothing deserving of respect. From these, or from anyone.

"Oh, trust me. I will make absolutely cold-stone certain of that." She might not technically be the emperor's niece, but she was a part of his chosen family, those he wanted round about him, and her eyes glinted with hierarchy, lineage, all the arrogance of power. Malance caught her breath; this was another face of Vivi's that she hadn't seen before. That made two in one night, which was revelatory in itself, and served as yet one more shift in what she had thought solid, those structures that defined and constrained her life: the court, the emperor, Clath. Lost Verantha. Vivi. Who went on, "You stay on board until we're ready for you. You'll know. This is ceremonial, not enforcement, and it is going to look the part."

And then she turned away, and whistled up one of the pages for a quick murmured conference, and left Malance standing in the bow there like a figurehead, like a trophy, like a portent. Doom to come. A chicken, home to roost. Something.

Very well: she would stand exactly there, and watch things happen. And know her moment, and step into it. Yes.

The boat nudged up to the landing stage, and no pages needed to make wild tumultuous leaps ashore with the mooring ropes, because there were men already waiting to receive them. With the boat secure and the gangway run out, Vivi was first ashore and soon in earnest conversation with the man Malance took to be in charge below. He wore a sword and carried no spear, so certainly an officer; and Vivi in this mood would speak to no one but the senior present, and she would be making her own demands rather than listening to his proposals. Malance wanted simply to lean on the rail and watch, because even at this muting distance Vivi was still awe-inspiring and a little terrifying and always a joy to the eye; but she could hardly demand dignity and then forsake it, so she stood proud and solemn in her isolation until the officer barked orders that broke his massed troops up into a formal honour guard, which honestly looked a little ridiculous at the foot of such a narrow gangway but never mind, here was her moment and she seized it on the instant.

Down that gangway, trying to be brisk and imposing, as opposed to Vivi's potent storm; and here was the officer to welcome her ashore, and here was Vivi to introduce them, "Madam Ambassador, this is Captain Ranek of the Imperial Guard, here to see us all safe home," and she and he exchanged salutes according to their ranks and the customs of their countries. Which was all as it should be, and so was this, as she took instant charge of the conversation.

"Captain, I will require some dozen of your men to convey the body of my fallen companion to—Vivi, where would be appropriate?"

"To the memorial chapel in the imperial palace," Vivi said without hesitation. "And more of your men to seek out his parents, if they are in the city; or to send messages if not. They will want to know that the emperor himself honours their son and their loss, and welcomes them to join his mourning. Marmon's friends aboard will know how to find them, I am sure."

Actually so did Malance, but this wasn't the time to say so; she had to be above such commonplace arrangements in a culture not her own. She spoke for a different land, in a different key. She said, "Also, I will want escorts for my friends, to their various homes in the city. We cannot be too careful on such a night, with one of us slain already out of hand. And the pages too, of course; the children will need guarding back to the palace"—and that was mere mischief, because it was sure to enrage all of them within hearing and Vivi too, oh yes—"though I'm sure they will want to accompany Marmon, and see him laid down with all that is proper to your people. I want your men to watch over them all the way. That should still leave enough"—and yes, of course she had counted his men, every one, before she set foot on shore—"to accompany the princess Vivyana and myself back to my embassy, where she has kindly offered to remain the night with me in my sorrow."

She had counted carefully, and he had no grounds to argue with her demands. She waited to see all the others away, and to say goodnight personally to each of her friends and collectively to the pages, one last farewell to Marmon; and then there were only half a dozen troopers and their captain remaining, and Vivi, and herself.

The captain looked somewhat at a loss, finding himself stripped down so far, and Malance was quite certain that his orders had been rather different. Nobody short of the emperor himself could stand against Vivi in this mood, though. She was imperious and commanding, the very image of a royal personage abroad, backed—Malance saw, with her new understanding—by all those years of page training and service, a deep underlying knowledge of how the city worked and all the various parts within it. Including, of course, the Imperial Guard.

She didn't—quite—give the captain actual marching orders, but it was all too obviously at her desire that they found themselves walking three abreast, guards before and guards behind but at such a distance that it must be clear to anyone that this was protective and not custody. The captain did ask if he should send for a carriage; Malance said, "No, no, not at all. Not for me. I should like to walk awhile," although her legs were still uncertain and actually she might have preferred to ride, but this was important too, another kind of mourning, a tribute to Marmon's long legs and his urgency. He had always walked everywhere, all through the city; it seemed only right—only a rite—to do the same tonight. She wondered if Vivi had anticipated that too and explained it to the captain, some sort of foreign ritual, a Veranthan way of paying tribute to the dead. If she had, Malance was sure she would have used the word "Veranthan" once at least. All her friends had taken that on as a task abiding, to keep the name alive wherever and whenever possible, and especially if Clathians were about. Vivi, she knew, was particularly diligent, and took particular delight in flourishing it on imperial occasions, and under the Clathian ambassador's nose.

Vivi had wickedness bred in the bone; of course Malance should have realised that she'd served as a page. She should have recognised the traits, even in a royal scion: the preternatural awareness, the self-confidence, the bearing, all those things that had drawn Malance to her in the first place. The mischief.

Now, though, she was quiet and alert, trusting neither the guards before nor the guards behind nor the captain at her side. Malance had no idea what weapons she could carry, if any, in that casual adorable outfit she'd worn for a pleasure jaunt on the river and a supper with friends; but she was tolerably sure now that there would be something, and that Vivi was poised against a need to use it. Malance herself was still in formal court dress, which meant increasingly uncomfortable and a little resentful that she hadn't been given a chance to change, but that was Vivi all over. Demanding, heedless, expectant. That was the Vivi she'd known till now, at any rate. Apparently, this tonight was Vivi all under: in control a wholly different way, steely, deadly. As at the landing dock, a little terrifying.

And still holding Malance's hand, determined on it. Not to be denied.

Very well, then.

There was a wall around the garden around her house. Her embassy. There was a gate in the wall. It stood ajar, as ever. The vanguard had paused uncertainly this side of the gate, awaiting orders. Vivi gave them, briskly.

"You can't come in, of course. This is Veranthan sovereign territory." Malance's words, in Vivi's mouth: it was somehow and suddenly shockingly intimate, that moment. Hand in hand. "Nevertheless," Vivi went on calmly, as though she hadn't felt the shock of it at all, "the ambassador has been the subject of an assassination attempt tonight. I am confident, captain, that you and your men are sufficient to guard the perimeter, this night at least. Until more permanent arrangements can be made."

He stiffened; he saluted. "Yes, highness. Of course."

"Thank you, captain." That was Malance herself, and almost surprised by herself, such a competent response when she felt the very opposite of anything remotely approaching competence.

Vivi heaved the gate closed behind them—with an effort, for it was never closed and never oiled, and no one ever weeded any longer in this garden—to make the point, *thus far and no farther*. Then she seized Malance's hand one more time and marched her down the gravel path towards the house. The embassy. Her home—and their refuge, this night at least. Under the emperor's protection, no less. Well, she was in any case—all ambassadors were as a matter of course, she supposed, but no others lay quite so much under his eye or under his care, or owed him so much in return—but for now there were imperial troops to watch her gate and patrol her walls. It wasn't exactly a *comfortable* safety they offered; but she remembered the breath of a crossbow bolt against her cheek, she remembered the very *sound* of it, unnameable, like a tearing in the air itself, and she was glad to have them none the less, whatever they purported. Change was coming, change for the worse. According to the emperor, who knew everything. She wasn't sure quite how things could get worse—but then, she would have said the same thing this morning, and now Marmon was dead and there were troops at her gate. Change was coming, change was *here*, and she liked this first brief taste of it not at all.

Change was here, in her house; the door opened in greeting as they approached the steps, and there was one of her sweet boys, looking rather less disreputable than usual. Looking oddly *braced*, and far from his natural manner. He had shaved, she saw, and his hair was brushed, and his clothes were—well, they were still his clothes, she knew that.

She had bought them, after all. But he had managed to put together an outfit that was almost formal, if not quite a livery. He looked almost like a respectable servant in a regular household. Which was bizarre.

He didn't grin at her, in his usual lazy, confidential way. He stood back and almost, *almost* bowed them through the doorway. Which was enough to stop her in her tracks and look more closely.

"Amil, you borrowed that jacket from your brother." She remembered now; his own was gaudier. Felid was quieter in his dress, at least a little.

"Yes, lady. Mine was ... not dark enough to please. This one barely suited, but..." He shrugged his rather wonderful shoulders, and looked somewhat abashed, which was not an expression she'd ever have guessed that he could manage.

Ah. Yes.

"Well, never mind. At least it fits." They were still very much of a size, her boys, though she made no fuss to keep them that way. Bought as a matched pair, no doubt they were losing value day by day, as she allowed them whatever little liberties they liked. Amil's hair was longer these days, and Felid did like to eat, and not to exercise. "Amil, this is—"

And she was suddenly and utterly uncertain, how to introduce Vivi to her household: under what name, what title. What reason she had to bring a guest home, which was a thing she never did.

"The Lady Vivi," said the lady herself. Not quite a *nom de la nuit*, but not quite her own self either, in all her syllables and rank.

"Yes, highness," and now Amil did bow, for all the world as if he'd been drilled in it. Which, of course, he almost certainly had. He'd been *briefed*. And scrubbed, and dressed, and stationed here to watch for their arrival.

Change. Yes.

She took a breath, reclaimed Vivi's hand, and stepped across the threshold. *Her* threshold. Yes.

68

O nce it must have been lovely, this house. High and wide and open, surrounded by gardens that must have been lovely too. Those days were past, long past, before ever Malance arrived. Verantha had been briefly under the governance of a fantasist who dreamed of glorious futures, and a Council too weak to control him. He had sent a ridiculous embassy, to the greatest power in the land; he had spent far too much money, constructing an embassy far too grand for the needs of a very small country a very long way away. No glorious futures had materialised, and they could never afford to maintain it, but even after that Council and its leader were deposed, they were still just a little too proud to sell it to someone who could. For a hundred years now, the Veranthan ambassador to the highest and wealthiest court in the world had lived in an increasingly decrepit and mouldering mansion, struggling to keep the roof watertight and the windows in their frames. Gardeners had probably been the first to go, though hers was a gardening people. Her first day here, she had found the ambassador himself on hands and knees, in rough clothes, doing his best to restore some kind of order to a shrubbery grown wild.

Malance had abandoned even that level of effort, and left her small demesne to the birds and the insects and the undoubted rats. The house alone was too much for her, and her little band of outcasts was helpless to keep the damp out, or the rats. She could have spent the emperor's money, of course, he wouldn't have begrudged it her; but she chose not to do that, except what little she must to keep them all fed and clothed and tolerably comfortable in the few rooms that they needed. She never invited anyone here, because she knew that word of its condition would spread throughout the diplomatic community, shaming her with every whisper, and so delighting Clath; and of course the emperor would hear too, and probably come to see for himself, and... Well, no. She couldn't bear that. Veranthan pride was still very real in her, whether or not there was yet a Verantha to be proud of.

She took a breath as she stepped inside, ready to apologise instantly to Vivi for the strange smell that constantly
hung about the hallway. She was tolerably sure that it was rot,
but she didn't know exactly where or what, and she really,
really didn't want to investigate. There was nothing she could
do about it anyway, so why learn just how bad it was?

But she held that breath and bit the words back sharply,
because she actually didn't smell it. She smelled scrubbed
wood, to be sure, but that was commonplace; Estar wasn't
much of a lady's maid, but she was very good at scrubbing.
It was only that the smell had proved too insidious, and
couldn't or wouldn't be scrubbed away.

What Malance smelled instead was fresh incense. There
was a stick burning even now, she saw, on the vast dresser
that was almost the last respectable piece of furniture left
in the house, and that only because it was built into the wall
and couldn't be taken out and sold without damage. By now
she wasn't even sure which would sustain more damage by
its removal, the dresser or the house. It might be all that was
holding the hallway up, if that rot were deep-sunk in the
timbers.

She only had a moment to be quite ridiculously pleased
that Vivi's first impression of her home wouldn't be the stink
of it. There was movement to one side of the hallway, and
that was Ash and Alder stepping through from the reception
room to greet them. Change personified. She didn't know
which one of them had had the bright idea of masking one
smell with a brighter scent, but she was grateful, and hoped
she showed it in her smile.

"Welcome home, lady. Highness," with a separate bow for
Vivi, long known to Alder, clearly, and possibly long cherished. Could they have been pages together, Vivi at the end
of her time and Alder just at the start of hers? Perhaps; and
the same would go for Ash, of course. Ash, who was gesturing
them through to the reception room, which she never used.
It was too big, and too much fuss, when she never had guests

and was frankly more comfortable down in the kitchen anyway, with her people.

But there were lamps burning in there against the night, which there never were. Surely someone would have told this intrusive, demanding pair that the room had been abandoned? If so, they'd taken no notice. Irritated—for she'd been planning to take Vivi directly to the intimacy of her own suite, her own little sitting room—Malance glowered at the pair of them and snapped, "Shouldn't you two have changed into some other clothes by now? Something more appropriate?"

They might have pushed Amil into a change, to suit their ideas of proper dress for a servant of the house, the poor boy; they themselves were still wearing their livery. Their *imperial* livery.

"Mal, they probably don't *have* any other clothes." That was Vivi, defending her own—but doing it laughingly, hugging Malance's arm.

"Oh—of course, your trunks are probably not here yet, is that it?"

"Felid is fetching them from the palace now, lady," Ash said gravely, "but they only hold clean liveries and our personal things. As her highness says, these are all we have."

"Pages are always on duty," Vivi expanded, nudging Malance forward with her shoulder, "so always in livery when they're not asleep or stripped. It's meant to keep them ever-ready in the palace, and virtuous in the city. They're only allowed out on errands, so if anyone sees a page in their livery enjoying themselves, it's a truant by definition." She paused then, and shared a smile with the other two, *once a page*, and went on, "Of course, that's what's *supposed* to happen, that's the *rule*. Pages have been finding ways around it for—well, probably ever since pages have existed. Of course we have. There's a very well-established tradition that when you move on, when you leave his grace's service, you also leave all your highly illegal party clothes behind you, for someone else's benefit. There's probably some girl out in the city right now, wearing my blue satin tunic. I loved that, and I mourn it yet."

"Oh—the one with the upright collar, and the silver embroidery?" Alder asked, grinning delightedly. "Yes, we still have that. I added some brocade into the seams, though, so it would fit more than just the tinies."

"I am no longer *tiny*," Vivi scowled. "I am now *petite*."

"Yes, highness," giggling through another bow. Yes, they'd definitely known each other when they both wore the livery. "Will you come through? We have set out wine and some snacks from the night market, as we heard that your dinner had been ... interrupted."

They knew. Of course they knew. The runner-boy—Partin, she was determined to remember his name, even though she had no idea which one he'd been on the boat—had come first to authority, of course, to be sure the news would reach the emperor and arrangements would be made to meet the boat on its return; and then he would have gone to his own people. Word would have spread like fire, through the pages and all their friends and contacts, illicit or otherwise. Of course these two had heard it. *Once a page.*

If they were meant to be his spies in her household, the emperor might have made at least a futile gesture towards disguising that, she thought, finding another target for her irritation. He might have given them some clothes.

It was the reception room, though, that had been disguised, and nothing futile about it. This too had been a hurried change, improvised with what they could find or fetch in what little time they'd had; but a fire roared in the enormous grate—clearly these children had no notion of the cost of firewood, nor her own impoverishment, or else were heedless of both, but she couldn't begrudge it them, this one night—and the windows that were never opened had been flung wide, all of which would lend both woodsmoke and fresh air to cover whatever smells might have accumulated in here. Not to mention leaving the mouldering curtains still bound up in their swags. The ancient sofas had been covered with equally ancient rugs—pity her poor boys, for she was willing to bet who had been obliged to beat all the dust out of those—to hide where the mice had eaten through the upholstery. A low table between the sofas had been furnished with all the things she loved from the night market—they must have asked Estar, for there was no hope of the boys' remembering, and the cook couldn't conceivably know—and some that she didn't, which she guessed had been bought for Vivi's pleasure, and did these two know *everything*?

Perhaps it wasn't the emperor after all, perhaps it was his pages.

He—or they?—had remembered the promised wine, too. A bottle lay ready, already open, in a bucket of ice. Blessing his kindness or their efficiency, both, Malance sank into one of the sofas and tugged Vivi down beside her.

"Have you *tried* this? It's so amazing..."

"Ooh, Taktarka? Yes, it's one of his grace's favourites." Of course she had. Never mind. Malance poured anyway, while Vivi went on, "He always used to demand an extra bottle, and have it opened for him, just before he stopped drinking and went to bed. So then we pages simply had to finish it for him, because it doesn't keep at all, and he disapproved of waste so very much."

"He still does," Ash said, grinning at her. "Highness, may I serve you with some of these duck gizzards?"

Definitely, those had been bought specifically; Malance couldn't abide them, and Vivi was reaching already. Even so:

"No," Malance said, "no, you may not. I will do that, she's my guest. What you two may do—and *all* that you may do—is sit down, yes, on that sofa over there, and serve yourselves."

"Lady, we only laid two plates," Alder murmured.

"In that case, very well, you may trot off and fetch two more. And forks, yes, and glasses, those too, don't forget the glasses." She had them under her thumb now; she knew what they liked. "And then we are going to talk, all four of us together. I want to know just exactly how you have corrupted my household, and what more surprises I may expect, and—"

She broke off then, because both the pages were grinning at her, and Vivi was openly laughing.

"*What?* My friend is *dead*," her first friend in the city, her first client when she was an interpreter, when she was what she had wanted to be, "and something awful is coming, and the emperor's up to something, I know he is, and all you pretty willing pages turn out to be a secret army or something, and if I can't take control of what's happening in my own life, in my own *house*, then—"

Then she stopped abruptly, because otherwise she'd be weeping, or throwing things. She was already trembling, both hands knitted together around the stem of her glass, to the grave danger of the wine within.

The others sobered quickly, and she was sorry to have done that to them. Almost wanted to apologise, except that everything was true and she couldn't just brush it all away. Ash had vanished; Alder stood patient, attendant, hands behind her back, perfect in her livery, her stillness; Vivi was the one who moved, who involved herself. Vivi who came to crouch before Malance, who was hunched over in her misery, elbows on knees, shaking harder now, so that she wondered if she might shake all the flesh off her bones and be done with it, be clean, be gone. Vivi who wrapped both her own hands around Malance's, though she was too late to save the wine. Vivi whose touch had some power to it, seemingly, even now, because Malance could feel her fingers lose the urgency of their shaking, feel it subside, feel it ebb away entire: first from her hands, that point of contact, and then that stillness spreading up her arms to encompass at last all her body, as fire reaches from its source to consume whatever has been laid ready, whatever will burn.

She would burn, seemingly. Or her sudden weakness would burn away, under Vivi's hand. That was honestly a revelation. This Vivi was new so many ways, so startlingly *more* than the playful pampered royal Malance had enjoyed so much.

For a while, for a long time, all she could do was sit there and be still, in Vivi's grip, gazing at those miraculous calming hands. Vivi didn't try to speak, she only waited; and at last Malance could take a slow, deep breath—well, something of a sniff, to tell true, perhaps even something of a slobber—and lift her head.

At first, still, all she could see was Vivi: the fresh reality of her, the *potency* of her. The eyes, solemn and insistent. She seemed to gaze deep into Malance, and whatever it was that she saw there, it satisfied her. She gave a nod, and rose, and came back to Malance's side, still claiming both her hands with one of her own and nestling in close, tucking herself up against her like a child, like a lover, like a friend.

Now Malance could see farther, could see the other sofa, where the pages had settled themselves, obedient to orders. They had plates and forks in front of them, and glasses too. All of which were empty.

Vivi passed Malance a napkin. She wiped her face, decided this was no time to be delicate and blew her nose robustly, then glowered across the table at the children.

"Feed yourselves. Drink. Now."

"Yes, lady." Two obedient murmurs, and a flurry of passing dishes, one to the other. Even helping themselves they were neat and dextrous, efficient, fast. Neither one seemed at all shaken by her outburst; she supposed that after half a lifetime living and serving in the palace, they must have seen all kinds of emotional upset, from grief through lust to fury and beyond. No doubt it was part of their training, to meet whatever came with equanimity. Perhaps if Vivi hadn't been here, it would have been one of them who came to her, who came to hold and comfort her. They might see it as part of their duties.

Speaking of which. Now was the time. They were both eating, as neatly and quickly as they had served themselves: small bites, though. Expecting interrogation, and far too well trained to speak with their mouths full. Far too well trained altogether, she thought. Vivi, too: how much of her now, of her personality, was a consequence of that training? And how much was a mask she wore, to disguise the true depths of her? And ... oh, so many questions, and now was not the time for Vivi. That would come later. After she had sent the children to bed.

There was wine in their glasses, but they weren't drinking. Yet. Nor would she be sending them off with the remains of the bottle. She wasn't the emperor, and she only had a case of this ambrosia. Besides, she hadn't decided yet whether or not to be angry with them; and besides again, she and Vivi would certainly be needing it.

"What," she said, "has the emperor actually told you to *do* here?"

Ash swallowed whatever he'd been chewing, touched his lips lightly and unnecessarily with a napkin, and said, "To serve you, lady."

"For how long?"

"Until you dismiss us from your service, or we die." That was Alder, who had gone as far as putting her plate down and picking up her glass, though apparently only to hold it.

"But as far as I'm aware, either or both of you might be lordlings, children of ambition, with families expecting to hear of you at court," not still acting as house servants, and especially not to a foreigner.

She hadn't—quite—asked them outright, and they didn't answer her. Their silence acknowledged the truth she had spoken, and no more.

It was Vivi who said, "Nevertheless. The emperor has told you to do this, and so you will. Is that right?"

"Yes, highness." Ash.

It made no sense—or at least, Malance could make no sense of it. Which was not at all the same thing. She said, "To whom is your loyalty now?"

"To you, lady." Alder, being absolute. "We are no longer in the emperor's service. We are still his subjects, with all that that implies by way of duty and submission; but he gave us to you, and we are yours, for as long as you will have us."

Spies and informants of course would lie about such matters, but Malance believed her anyway. Besides, the emperor had no need to spy on her. He need only ask, and she would tell him whatever he wanted to know.

She hadn't wanted them at the time; she didn't want them now. But—well, perhaps the emperor was right. Perhaps she had been in want of them, or someone like them. Competence and order. Her boys were years older than these two, not that much younger than she was herself; if the pages could turn Amil meek and abashed, and send Felid off to fetch their things for them, perhaps they were precisely what she needed. What the house needed.

Besides, it was rude to turn away a gift. Certainly on the first day.

"Very well," she said. "I'll take that on trust; I'll take *you* on trust. For now." Perhaps she'd turn them away tomorrow. "So tell me, what have you actually *done* here? Apart from turning my household upside down, that is?"

Mostly, it seemed what they had done was make lists— one each, separately—of everything that needed to be done in the days and weeks ahead. Nothing about the house, it seemed, met their exacting standards. Of course it didn't; they were used to a palace and a staff of thousands, including themselves and their cohort. One or both of them might very well have grown up in a palace of their own. If not, if they happened both to have been street-children snatched from desperate lives and remade to another mould—well, she had heard that those who had known another existence

were the most transformed by livery, adopting all its stric-
tures with a dedication born in fire. They'd be the more
exacting, not the less.

Oh, and they had also set Estar to clean Malance's own
suite, with Amil to help her now. "Clean" was the word
they used, but cleaning was what Estar *did*, when she wasn't
serving as lady's maid. Her rooms had already been clean
enough to suit Malance's taste. Not, apparently, theirs. She
suspected that every piece of furniture was being taken out,
every carpet lifted, every floorboard swept and scrubbed and
only not polished because there couldn't possibly have been
time. No doubt that would come, another day. Soon, probably. She was sure it would be on both their lists.

They had a list of duties for each of the servants—the
other servants, for these two seemed to occupy an entirely
different sphere. Those duties would add hours of work to
everyone's day. It was probably no bad thing in the boys'
case, but she worried for Estar, until she understood that
there was another list, of extra staff to be sought. Including
a trained lady's maid for herself, though either page could
stand in at need. Alder did manage to suggest that the need
was very evident. Malance sighted privately for poor Estar,
though even more privately she totally agreed with them.

The list included another scullery girl, a gardener with
several boys, and—of course!—a cook. She gathered that
Mechet didn't measure up. Again, it wasn't possible to
argue, but she really must talk to this pair about money. She
couldn't conceivably afford everything they were so sure that
she needed.

Nevertheless: "Tomorrow," she said, "we're going shopping. Both of you need new clothes. You can't go on wearing the emperor's livery." For a moment, they both looked
distraught. "Everyone in the city knows what it means," she
went on, determined, "and your allegiance—your *immediate*
allegiance—is no longer owed to the emperor. It would be

dishonest to trade on the power of that livery, when you're only serving me."

They steeled themselves to the truth of that, she could see them do it, and loved them just a little, knowing only that she did not know how much of a wrench it would be, to take off the imperial crimson for the last time. Vivi could tell her, perhaps, if she had the words. If there were the words.

"Yes, lady," they said, both together; and then, Ash alone, "Is there a ... suitable Veranthan livery that we could wear instead? That we could all wear?"

They couldn't bear, she realised, to be out of uniform. Not yet, not already. The livery had defined them through all their years of growth; they were leaving their cohort behind, and they needed something new to bond to.

"Veranthans ... don't really go in for such things," she said. *Didn't* might have been more proper, but she at least was a Veranthan yet. "Still, I do understand. We'll see what we can find. Though you will also need clothes of your own, of your own choice." They wouldn't be sneaking out for nights in the city, if she had anything to say about it. They would be going forth with her blessing, in pretty party clothes, and hopefully not creeping back till morning, ashamed and exhilarated, hung over and sweat-stained and worse. Sore. She had relished those days—those nights—in her own youth, most of them here in this city, and she was abruptly determined that these youngsters should know them too. That it was her task to ensure that. Let them be responsible for her house, for her garden, for her clothes and her servants and all manner of other duties; she would be responsible for their education. Even if that only came down to *run and find out.* That was mostly how she'd learned the world, after all.

"Very well." She had no appetite for food, at this long end of this appalling day. Vivi at her side had picked at her gizzards and set down her plate. If the children wanted more, they could eat in the kitchen. "Clear all this away, and get yourselves to bed. I presume you have found beds for your-selves?" The house was full of beds.

"We chose a room, lady, yes. It's airing now."

She had no doubt of that. Swept, scrubbed, waiting to be polished. Beds inspected, clean fresh bedding fetched. Her poor people would be exhausted tonight, and probably grouchy in the morning.

"One room? Between the two of them? We have so many rooms, we could spare them one apiece."

"They wouldn't want it. They're used to company. For half their lives they've lived in a pack, and they don't know how to be alone. They've bathed together, swum together, bunked together; it's what they know, warm bodies all around them and no privacy to speak of. No page could ever be body-shy. And it's what they like, that too, as well as what they're used to: whispers in the night, plots hatched in darkness. They will have rewritten all those lists by morning."

From somewhere, Malance found a smile. "They're irre-sistible. Like a mountain flood," when the snows melted and all that water came hurtling down at once, fierce and cold. Terrifying, fascinating. Irresistible. Yes. "If they share a room, do you suppose they share a bed?"

"Oh, I expect they're in and out of each other's beds at the drop of a hat. Though they might just do that for the company, too. Warm bodies are better than chilly sheets, and friendlier than pillows. As far as I remember, I rarely went to bed alone at that age, and half the time it had nothing to do with sex. You'd have to ask them."

"May I? There are so many things you're not supposed to ask pages—but are they even pages, still? I don't even know what to call them."

"They're yours; you can call them what you like. Person-ally, I intend to call them by their names, which I think are as pretty as they are. They chose well, when they went into his grace's service. No, don't ask me what name I chose. That's one of the forbidden questions. She was another person, that girl who wore that livery. Now, may we please stop talking about those insidious children? I have other matters in mind. You will have noticed, I hope, that neither one of them suggested airing out a room or a bed for me, though they knew full well that I was staying."

She had noticed that, yes. She hadn't intended to mention it. Veranthans were ... not so direct, as a rule. Even after all her years here, even thinking herself a city girl now through and through, she still preferred to let matters take their course discreetly: a glance, a touch, a gesture.

Vivi was apparently in another mood, imperious, explicit. No surprise.

Vivi's hand on her cheek. turning her head: gentle, firm. Irresistible, yes.

Vivi's eyes, wide and dark, determined.

Vivi's lips on hers: exploratory, insistent, assertive. Nothing tentative or suggestive, nothing like her own ways of seduction. No offer of pulling back, or waiting longer.

Malance could lean into that certainty and find comfort there, and support. It was too soon for promises, but tonight she'd take this gladly. Someone who could seem stronger than herself, someone who knew what they wanted. Someone to take charge, just for the night. In the morning she would need to be herself again, ambassador again, mistress in her own house. Tonight, though—tonight she could yield, and follow Vivi's determined lead, and let her choose the way.

In token of which, when they abandoned the fire below and went up to her suite, she let Vivi take her hand and draw her after, even though she was hostess here, and this her bedroom—warm with a fire of its own, laid and lit and lovely, and she really must speak to those heedless infants about the price of firewood—and this her bed, these her linens, perfumed with rosemary from her own garden, yes.

V

FOUR

Where the emperor sends gifts,
everyone sends gifts

Morning, then. Morning and all the changes, churning in her mind. Marmon dead, *dead*, and nothing resolved now, nothing clear. Threats to her, perhaps; threats to her symbolic little life, her presence here, if the emperor was right—and of course he was, even if he wouldn't say what form those threats might take. Just something to be dreaded, up ahead. And turbulence in her house already, the emperor again, disrupting everything in his kindness. Perhaps that was what emperors did, perhaps it was what empire meant.

And Vivi. Here, now, and who knew? Maybe she'd stay all day and still be here tomorrow. Malance had no idea, and no clothes that would fit her, so it didn't seem likely, but. But everyone was going shopping, so. If palace royals ever bought clothes in the market, which didn't honestly seem likely either. But Vivi was turning out to be a rather unexpected royal, so. She might think it fun, to play at poverty for a day. Or two.

"Those brats," Vivi announced without stirring, "are enjoying themselves altogether too much, turning your house upside down directly beneath us. *Noisy* creatures."

"We'd best wait up here, till they've put everything the right way up again. Don't you think?"

"Emphatically."

And this time—her house, her room, her bed, and just one night had left her feeling rather more oddly herself—it was her hand that reached, and Vivi who responded.

She couldn't remember ever lingering in bed this late, *ever*. Certainly her household was taking advantage, getting things done while she was safely out of their way. In the end, though, even the newlings must have lost patience, or grown concerned, or perhaps just curious. Not that they peeped in themselves, as she might have done at their age. They sent Estar—a noticeably well-scrubbed Estar, with her generally rather wild hair severely brushed and groomed into a tight ponytail—carrying a tray that Malance couldn't remember seeing before, with a tea service that she *definitely* hadn't seen before. When she'd searched through this rambling over-stuffed house, which was often over the years, all she'd ever turned up was rubbish. Those infants had been here not one full day yet, and they were finding treasures.

Porcelain so thin, the tea shone through it like a light, amber and scented with bergamot and rose. She'd never tasted anything like it.

"Estar, did this come from our own kitchen?"

The maid looked up, startled, from the hearth, where she was cleaning out last night's fire-ash.

"I don't know, lady. They brewed it in this old pot of ours they dug out from somewhere, but I didn't recognise the caddy either, and it can't have kept fresh in a junk room. Perhaps they brought it with them?"

They being so obvious, they didn't need naming, or else she had no better idea than Malance had, what to call them.

"Should I light a new fire, lady? The grate's still warm, it'll only take a minute to catch..."

"No, Estar, thank you. We really must get on. You've been hard at work all these hours, getting ahead of us; we need to catch up, and there's a lot to do."

Shopping, for one. If the pages were to have new clothes, then so must all the servants; that was natural and obvious, presents for all. Perhaps Ash had been right last night, perhaps they ought to have a livery. Except Mechet, perhaps, down in the kitchen. What would be the point? He could have a new apron. And something to leave the house in, if he ever did. Everybody should have something new, for when they went out and about.

All that was going to be expensive, but for once she had no qualms about it. The emperor had thrust all this mayhem upon her, no doubt for reasons of his own. She would cheerfully send the bills to the palace.

There couldn't possibly be time this morning to see everyone suited. The pages must come first; she wanted them out of the emperor's livery as soon as possible. And she would be needing something herself, for Marmon's funeral. There were as many styles of mourning across the empire as there were peoples within its eventual borders, but here in Feremendas City, white was the colour of loss. That was why she always had something of white about her, something at least. She was in perpetual mourning for her country, and could easily have assembled an entirely white costume from her own dressing room—but no. Not this time. Not for him. Funeral clothes should be new, worn once and set aside: as empty of memories as they were of colour, as her life now would be ever empty of her friend.

Now that they were finally astir, they washed quickly—hot water ready in the dressing room; one of the boys must have come up to help Estar carry, and been unexpectedly discreet, slipping in and out without notice—and dressed, and went down to find breakfast too awaiting them in the reception room. There was Mechet's familiar grain porridge, sweetened with honey and cinnamon; and there also were breads still warm from the market, fruits with the dew still on them, cold meats and preserves and food enough to feed a dozen people.

"I suppose you have all eaten already?" she demanded, glowering around at her gathered, smiling household.

"Long ago, lady." That was Felid. The pages in their liveries said nothing.

"Good, then you're safe to be hungry again. This can count as your midday meal, after we're done."

Just as she spoke the bells of noon swept across the city in their common flood, started and kept together by the great bell at the palace. At her side, Vivi cracked with laughter.

Annoyed as she was at this conspicuous indulgence, Malance couldn't keep herself from smiling too. "Oh, as you please. Our midday meal too, then. Alder, Ash, this has to stop, and stop now. You are not in the palace any longer. I dislike waste almost as much as I dislike extravagance," *and I can't afford either.*

"The emperor said we were to serve you as we have served himself, lady." Alder was not so much defensive as challenging, willing to argue the point.

"The emperor has resources that I lack."

"No, lady." Ash, this time. Did they decide in advance, or just take turns? Or signal each other, *you take this one*? "He said that his purse is your own, to open as you please."

"Yes, but I do not please. Did you think this would *please* me? Oh, and while we're on the subject, do you even know what firewood costs...?"

She might not be pleased, but Vivi was: picking at titbits, murmuring happily, "Ooh, melonberry pickles, and just the right cheese for them," ignoring the scolding altogether. That didn't help. The pages had after all been catering for a guest, and one whose expectations were clearly as much higher than Malance's as her purse was deeper.

Neither one of them said that, but Malance found herself running down in any case, embarrassed to be dealing with a

household problem—worse, a *money* problem—in front of
Vivi. Especially this morning. This afternoon, apparently.

"...Oh, never mind, then," she finished weakly. "This time.
I know you're new here, you don't understand how different
my life is. But not all the court is courtly rich. Please ask me
in future before you spend my money—or the emperor's
money, rather. At least until you've been here a while and
know how I run things. Yes?"

"Of course, lady. Though I do think the emperor sent us
here to help things run a little differently."

"Alder—don't. Don't make this more difficult than it is
already."

"No, lady. I'm sorry this is hard for you."

Oh, they were ruthless, these two. Giving no ground. How
did children become so self-assured? *When they went to the
emperor's barracks to be his pages,* of course. She was caught
between swift capitulation—which would cost the emperor
nothing but money, of which he had a plethora, and herself
nothing but a little self-respect, a little *more*, and she had
precious little left already—and a building fury.

And was interrupted by a figure, a stranger coming
up from the kitchens, where he never should have been.
Another boy, and she had enough of those already, she had
too many; and this one had a sack over his shoulder big
enough to carry all his worldly goods, which it likely did, and
a shy uncertain manner which had its appeal in this company.

"Please," he said, "the Lady Malance?"

"Well?" She may have snapped that; certainly he flinched.
Certainly she was reaching limits of patience and temper
that she hadn't known were there.

"Master Mercady sent me, to join your kitchens."

"I told... I told him not to do that," and now she didn't
know whether to yell or scream or weep with frustration.
Was she to be allowed no authority at all, in this game of
embassies? Did even Brion see her as a joke now, a whimsical

creature whose wishes could and should simply be overridden at will?

"Malance." That was Vivi at her elbow, *taking* her elbow, guiding her to a seat. "Here." A cup of coffee, pressed into her hands; a plate of pastries picked and ready for her. "Malance, things are different now. You have always had the emperor's favour, and that is known; now you have his conspicuous, his unprecedented favour, two of his own favourites—the heavens know why, but he loved these two—in your household. Of course the court noticed. Of course the court will follow suit. Where the emperor sends gifts, everyone sends gifts, unless they want to make a very specific point and risk his anger. Clath will do that, no doubt. Your friend Brion, on the other hand, will be first, of course, and the first of many. You should look for more surprises, more generosity. More welcome. Don't fling it back in people's faces. Spend his grace's money as you like, take new people into your house as they come, accept the change. He knew this would happen, all of this, and he'll have his reasons. He'll see a need for all of it, in the time ahead. He's an open-handed man, but he doesn't just … indulge people in luxuries, willy-nilly. Believe me, I do know."

Eight years in barracks, before she put off his livery and dressed as the royal she was. Of course she knew.

Malance gazed at her suspiciously. "Did he … send you, too? To be here, to tell me what to do?" *Are you another of his spies?*

Vivi laughed, and kissed her. "No, love. I am entirely my own idea. I choose to speak up for the man sometimes, that's all. And you're distressed, and that isn't what he wants, trust me. And as I'm here—because I want to be here, I want to be with you, and there's really nowhere else I need to be until Marmon's rites; my duties as a spoiled palace child are not exactly onerous—then you might as well let me help, where I can. Let me help you adjust. I do know rather a lot about almost everything."

Malance was surprised and overtaken by a burble of laughter. "You do, damn you." About bodies, certainly; about both their bodies, after this night. Right now Vivi's hands were on her neck, exerting a gentle, comforting pressure, hinting at pleasures past and to come. *Tonight, she's staying for tonight at least...*

Determined to be strict, Malance could still not be cruel. She could also apparently be persuaded. She looked at the nervous, waiting boy, and said, "You'll be his restive soul, then?"

"Lady?" Now the poor lad was merely bewildered.

She gave him the smile he needed most and tried again. "Never mind. You're ... what, his cook's assistant?"

"One of them, lady, yes," with a degree of chagrin that made her smile more naturally.

"And you want a kitchen of your own, yes. Well, you can't have that here; Mechet manages my kitchen," with a wave of her hand at the ancient behind him, above stairs for once and looking a little belligerent. "You'll work under him, of course. But at least you'll be the only one. You can be assistant cook, rather than cook's assistant," that surely sounded better, didn't it? A step up? "Ash, can you find—oh, wait. What's your name, lad?"

"Farl, lady."

"Good—find Farl a room, Ash, and see that it's cleaned up and so forth?"

"I beg your pardon, lady, but Alder stepped out to do that a little time ago."

"...Oh." She looked around and indeed the girl was gone and Malance had somehow never noticed, and Ash had understood her mission by whatever sympathy it was that they shared, and she must have left long before Malance conceded, and how could she conceivably have *known*...?

She glared up at Vivi, who might after all have given Alder some kind of signal behind her back, and said, "There is a conspiracy here, and be assured that I will root it out. In the meantime, Farl, welcome, and don't look so scared. We are none of us mad, and even I'm not usually this cross. Put down your things, and come and eat. All of you, eat. Ash, you can fetch more plates and so forth. Cups. Put the kettles on for more coffee. We're going to need a lot. After that, I'm taking you shopping."

Of course Vivi came with them, the pages and herself. The rest of the servants were left behind—with lists, though also with promises of future shopping trips—to adjust as best they could to this new regime.

Because Vivi came with them, though, the shopping was not as Malance had intended. Again, someone else was taking charge of what ought to have been her task; and because it was Vivi, who was another irresistible force, she did choose to allow that to happen, or so she told herself. Perhaps when she finally gave way, she gave all the way?

At any rate, they didn't go to the local market to see what they could find. They went to an indoor bazaar instead, which Malance knew by reputation only; she'd never been inside. Here were high ironwork arches and mosaic floors, individual shops with doorkeepers whose sole task was to open doors to customers. Malance wasn't wholly persuaded that doors would have been opened for her, if she weren't accompanied by one palace royal and two imperial pages still in livery. As she was, though—and as all three of the wretches were clearly well known here, and Vivi at least was much beloved and ever welcome—any and every door was drawn hopefully wide at their approach.

Vivi knew where she was going. Of course she did. Probably the pages knew where she was going too, although they were following very properly behind, for all the world like obedient servants and not disruptors of the world.

In at one particular door, then, though it wasn't clear what marked this one out from all the others. It was firmly closed behind them, no other customers to be admitted till they were done; and here was the proprietor to meet them, calm and gracious and thankfully not at all effusive, though she greeted Vivi by name—her full name and title, which Vivi disliked but would use when it was useful—and the pages with a nod of recognition, which they returned with a little more depth, as was only due. And then, "Madam Ambassador. Welcome. I am Lirian, and I have looked forward with hope to this day."

"You ... you know me?"

"Of course. All of Feremendas knows your courage and resolution, to maintain Verantha's name and presence here." That was obviously not true, much of Feremendas couldn't possibly know anything about it; and she was here due to the emperor's insistence, largely, rather than to any quality in herself. But Lirian did seem to mean what she said, and no doubt her notion of the city did not embrace the sections Malance was thinking of. "All of Feremendas" in this context probably meant all Lirian's clientele, which would surely mean most of the court and not much otherwise.

Not Clath, she hoped. She wouldn't want to be dressed by the same hands that dressed Clath.

Still, here they were and that was a question she couldn't conceivably ask, and Vivi was doing all the talking in any case.

"The ambassador needs a new livery for her household, in Veranthan colours. Gold and green, isn't that right, excellency?"

Gold and green were the flag's colours, yes; so they should of course be her colours, if she was to stand as some kind of Verantha-in-exile. And it would be distinctive at least, if not at all Veranthan at heart; and it meant that Vivi had done some work to learn that, at some point before yesterday afternoon, and Malance could have, would have loved her for that alone. She nodded aloofly, as a proper ambassador might, and let her pages be whisked away to be measured while Lirian sketched busily with coloured pencils on a pad, on the counter between them.

Sketched *upside down*, so that Malance could see the picture the right way up as it emerged: androgynous, because of course they would both wear the same, and she wondered if they would keep that same short haircut that the emperor demanded, or if either one of them would like to grow it out. That, she would leave up to them. Actually she supposed the new livery too had been left up to them at least in some measure, because they had actually asked for it, one dress for all her servants, and apparently she'd accepted that without ever actually having said yes. Indeed, she was tolerably sure that she had actually said no, and here she was regardless.

No matter. What emerged from those brisk, confident pencils was respectful, and a nod—no, more than a nod, a downright bow—towards the familiar imperial livery, but still something different, and rather lovely. Those two would look gorgeous in it, of course, though they'd look gorgeous in anything or nothing at all; and so would her boys, of course, with the same proviso; and perhaps she might have something of her own made to match. It struck her as odd for a moment, that she might dress to match her servants, rather than the other way around. But she was an odd mistress to start with, and no kind of ambassador; and it would be a way to fling Verantha constantly into the public gaze, if the public could learn to see this dress as Veranthan, though it never really was. If anyone could work that transition in the public's mind, or merely in the court's collective mind, she suspected it would be Vivi. She herself would need to dress the part, though. Very well, then. And the emperor could pay for it, yes.

And now Vivi was saying, "And, Lirian, this is lovely but we will also need funeral clothes for myself and the ambassador. For a friend, and soon."

"Of course, highness. This would be the young poet murdered on the imperial barge, no doubt? So shocking, and both yourselves were there, I know."

She did know. This city, this trade: of course she knew. That would be half her business, the simple knowledge of what happened, day by day. And Feremendas buried its people quickly; she would be used to designing and making the necessary clothes at speed.

"Would you wish to match?" she asked now, turning to another sheet of paper, ready to sketch: charcoal to mark the outlines of what of course would be entirely white in the making.

Malance drew a breath to say no, not to commit Vivi to any such open statement, and was forestalled, as perhaps she'd hoped to be. That really had been rather a long breath in, for such a short word.

"Yes," said Vivi, better prepared. "He was a friend to both of us, and we both were there; of course we will go together."

Together in more than one sense, then. The court would see, and know, if it wasn't known already. This was a declaration. Malance sought Vivi's hand, blindly. Found it, and squeezed it. Impossibly bad things, made somehow impossibly better: was this what lovers did? She wasn't sure, she hadn't known. Not really, not till now.

Lirian was extraordinary, Malance decided, watching her work. Vivi must have known already; why else would they be here? But the woman had wiped her mind of liveries, in the moment of taking a new sheet, and now she had solemnity in her fingers as she sketched a mourning-dress that somehow would suit both the diminutive Vivi and Malance too. It would make a public pair of them, while still accentuating, no, *celebrating* the differences between them, the height and her own foreignness in colour and gait and style, Vivi's inherent belonging. It was a statement and a confession, *we come from opposite ends of the world and we belong together*, and it was still a tribute to their friend and a grieving for his loss, all of this at once and no doubt more too that she wasn't Feremendan enough to understand. She had learned their language readily and long ago, that was her gift—not diplomacy, oh no—but not so much the language of their clothes. She hadn't been able to afford that, either as student or interpreter or of course ambassador.

To be fair to the emperor, she hadn't *allowed* herself to afford that, these latter days. But neither Lirian nor Vivi mentioned money at any point; it was understood, Malance supposed, that the reckoning was the emperor's to address. Did all the city's tradesfolk know?

Probably, yes. In a spirit of—not defiance, no, but she hoped not surrender either—she said, "I will send the rest of my household to you another day, to be measured for the same livery. They will need a couple of changes each, of course,"—those boys of hers were notoriously sloppy trenchermen, though no doubt these two would teach them to use napkins any day now—"and linens beneath. I'm sure I can leave all this with you," because no doubt the fitting-out of larger households than hers was much of Lirian's business, and no doubt the mistresses of those great houses didn't spend even this much time on it, "and if you could put together something practical but resplendent for my cook and his assistant, I'd be grateful. I don't want them feeling left out. How soon can you have things ready?"

She was assured that her own funeral garb and her highness's would be ready for a fitting here in the morning, or could be brought to her house tonight—Lirian would bring them herself—if that would be more convenient, and the pages' liveries likewise; and Malance was rather surprised to hear herself confirm that her house this evening would be preferable. *To save the tedium of another journey to the bazaar* was unspoken but somehow implicit, though she really had not intended it to be there.

Then it was their turn to be measured, tip to toe—or rather her turn, since apparently Vivi's details were known here and no doubt at every other fashionable boutique in the city. Vivi came with her anyway, while the pages waited outside; and afterwards she asked, a little plaintively perhaps, "Can we go home now?" and of course Vivi said, "Oh no, we've barely begun yet. Have we, children?"

And the pages chorused, "No, highness," at her back, the traitors. Had they forgotten who they belonged to now?

She'd promised them party clothes, though, and Vivi at least had not forgotten. And Vivi knew just where to go, and it was again nowhere Malance had been before, though she had thought she knew this city so well; and this was a marketplace more rough and raw than ever she would have brought these children by herself, or had she known. Except that they and Vivi were suddenly three pages together, and they knew this place altogether too well. Here were bales of silks and velvets that had surely been stolen or smuggled or both, because they could never have been this cheap otherwise. Hells, they could never be *here* otherwise, fabrics of this quality. This would be a market the street children knew, she realised, and brought their high-class cohorts to: somewhere that pages of all backgrounds could afford and relish. And make friends of another kind, and what could be more valuable? More than anything, she understood suddenly— more than manners, more than training, more than discipline—an imperial page would need information, knowledge of the city in all its folds and corners. Here was one of the very folded corners, and all three of her companions were at home here, and again she was only allowed in thanks to her company.

No page could ever be body-shy, Vivi had said, and she wasn't wrong. Soon enough those troublesome youngsters were stripping down, trying on, parading for her approval. It was a struggle to persuade them that no, this truly was their choice, they must pick the clothes they liked the best. In the end, she just said, "Oh, for heavens' sake. Pick for each other, then. You'll be good at that."

They took to it like ducks to water, quarrelsome and indulgent and cackling with laughter. Bored meanwhile, Malance wandered off, telling herself that she was scouting out things her boys might like, or Estar. Vivi at her side kept saying things like, "You'd look marvellous in that, if I could only persuade you to dress down for an occasion. I have exactly the right occasion in mind," which didn't help at all.

This was not the sort of market that offered to deliver. Nor did it treat in accounts or promissory notes, nor with the bursar at the palace. Vivi had a surprisingly large supply of actual money with her, though; which was fortunate, as Malance emphatically did not. And once Vivi had pointed out that it was all the emperor's money anyway, and that she could have more simply for the asking, Malance was happy enough to help her spend it.

Accordingly, they were both burdened with piles of new clothes and boots and so forth by the time they found the pages again. Who were busy baling up their own—or each other's—choices into bundles they could more readily carry. Good: if they were going to be this expensive for the emperor, then they might as well work for it. Malance cheerfully added her own purchases to their burdens, then scooped Vivi's out of her arms and added those as well.

And then stood back and watched, entirely unsurprised, as neat and nimble fingers folded and tied—and she absolutely wasn't going to ask where they'd found so much twine—until they had two heavy but manageable bales, with cloth shoulder-straps knotted in. Of course this would be another of their skills, to transform unwieldy heaps into organised parcels; why would she ever have imagined otherwise? They helped each other into those improvised straps like the closest of friends, like co-conspirators; and then caught Malance watching them and grinned at her with a private triumph, as though they read her every thought revealed on her face. Perhaps they did. She was not yet entirely sure that they weren't a pair of imps from the nether kingdoms. Wicked imps, obviously.

Vivi slipped her arm through Malance's—and yes, of course Vivi had been a page; she was another wicked imp— and smiled up at her.

"Now we can go home," she said. Which did sound good, so Malance nodded and let herself be steered away. And didn't look back to make sure that the children could keep up, under the weight of all that shopping. She had no doubts of that at all.

Coming out of the bridge's shadow, blinking at daylight, they climbed a curving flight of steps onto the road above—and found themselves abruptly face to face with the Clathian ambassador, alone and unescorted. Nothing about that seemed likely. She commonly took a companion wherever she went, except to court occasions; and she never went anywhere without guards at her back, which was nothing but wisdom. Malance might be the last Veranthan left in this city, but she was certainly not the only person to detest the kingdoms and the sway they held over vast swathes of land that were rightly not their own.

Besides which, the ambassador never walked anywhere. Her stables held some of the finest carriage horses in Feremendas, and she was ever loth to pass up any chance to exhibit them.

"Clath." Malance never passed up a chance to greet the ambassador by title, in part because it was such an ugly word and so easy to say coldly and she enjoyed flinging it out like a weapon, like a blow. Also, it meant that the other woman must either follow suit or else demean herself with a breach of manners, and generally in front of witnesses, and either way Malance felt that she came out ahead.

Also she liked to pretend, at least to herself, that she had never troubled to learn the ambassador's name. It wasn't true, of course; she knew the family and its history for many generations back. It was a part of her all-consuming hatred, an obsessional study of all things Clathian and in particular their ruling families and those who clustered around them. Occasionally she fantasised about sending assassins—or better, going herself, stealthy and strong, night-black clothing and a night-black knife—to slay them all, to destroy the kingdoms from the top down. But that was why the ambassador was always guarded, because assassination was a known danger in Clath and here too; and that was why, one reason why it was so extraordinary to find her here, on foot and unprotected.

True to form, the ambassador ignored Malance entirely, in favour of greeting Vivi with all the courtesy her royal rank demanded.

"Highness. How rare, to encounter you abroad and alone; and how fortuitous."

"I am hardly alone, excellency." Indeed, Vivi hugged herself close against Malance's arm, to make the point more clear. "I see that you truly are, though, which seems … unusual?"

"I do occasionally leave my people at home. I find air and exercise to clear my mind, and allow my thoughts to focus."

Malance didn't believe that for a moment. The woman was a diplomat these days, which meant she lied professionally; she was certainly also a spy, reporting back to her Council of Kings anything that might conceivably give Clath an advantage commercially or at the negotiating table or on the battlefield. Living inside the Veranthan embassy for years had at least given Malance a clear notion of an ambassador's work, and very little of it happened at court. The woman must be at large for a meeting, certainly clandestine, probably dangerous to someone, possibly even a threat to the emperor or his interests. At least Malance need take no action there; Vivi was safe to tell him in person.

"Of course. And you called our meeting fortuitous?" Vivi was doing this for her benefit, she knew. *My friend's enemy is mine as well*: Vivi might have felt a detached sympathy for lost Verantha before, but now she had made Malance's cause her own. It was something more to love about her, as well as a cause of anxiety, because there was no telling with Vivi, quite how far she might go.

"I did. I am in hopes that you might attend a small gathering at our embassy, a week from tonight? I had intended to send an invitation to the palace, but a personal invitation is always so much better, don't you find?"

"Actually, I don't." Vivi spoke with all the hierarchy of her lineage, dismissive of anything so crude or *outré*. "My people keep my calendar, so a written invitation is essential, really. Please have it sent to the Veranthan embassy, though; I am no longer in residence at the palace."

That was news to Malance. Not the bald statement itself, so much as the way that apparently royals could lie as readily as diplomats, with a perfect face and not a hint of hesitation. She wondered if this was another skill acquired as a page; if so, she would have to be watchful of hers.

Honestly, those two were building up to be so much *trouble*, whatever uses they might have displayed already, just in this first day. Oh, and was she expected to pay them, as well as providing board and lodging, livery and more? She had no idea. Vivi might know—but as she'd said herself, the emperor never did this, handing on his pages to someone else. Where there was no precedent, there could be no established custom. The rest of Malance's household simply lived at her expense—meaning the emperor's—and saw no wages else unless she tipped them. Imperially-trained pages might be another matter, though. They might have expectations.

She had missed the ambassador's response to Vivi's declaration, thinking about those wretched pages; but she didn't miss the woman's reaction to the pages themselves, still of course in their imperial livery, when she realised that they were tailing Vivi and Malance, and carrying a small hoard of bright and lovely dress. The emperor's own servants, seemingly helping a princess of the blood move into the supposed embassy of a country that Clath had annexed and absorbed, quite obliterated?

It was an outrage, obviously, deliberate offence; but then the mere existence of the embassy, of this girl in this role in this city, was an offence. A needle the emperor used to jab at Clath. No doubt this was a simple escalation, his moving one of his relatives into the building. In Clath, it might have meant that she had fallen out of favour at court and was seeking refuge; but the emperor did not handle his family's affairs in that manner. No, this was him, playing out some game of his own devising, seeding a further irritant into an already strained relationship...

Malance was tolerably sure of her reading; for a diplomat, this woman had very poor self-control. Perhaps that was the general, still lurking underneath. Unless she merely didn't choose to hide what she was thinking, confronted with the very cause of that offence in company with a very minor royal.

Be it intentional or otherwise, Malance wasn't alone in reading those thoughts as they marched in order across the woman's face. Vivi stiffened a little at her side, and then turned to her with a smile that was sheer mischief, while her eyes were sheer rage.

"Oh, the ambassador does have a point, my love," though Malance had missed it completely. "Perhaps we *should* actually tell my uncle about this? We both know that he will know already, his eyes are everywhere, but even so. It might be only manners. We could write him a letter, perhaps: the first from both of us together, with your embassy as our address? He might appreciate that."

"So he might," she agreed weakly, thinking that she herself might have appreciated being told too. Possibly even being told first. Or even asked, perhaps. She knew that Vivi was improvising here, building an imagined future on the sharp spur of the moment—but they would actually need to see this through now, if only for their own pride's sakes. Vivi was proud by nature and training both, while Malance was obliged to be, for lost Verantha.

"...And of course we'd be delighted to attend your *soirée* together, Madam Ambassador. I don't suppose it'll be our first appearance as a couple, but it might well be our first at a cultural occasion."

Curse her, Vivi was *enjoying* this! She was still furious, Malance could feel it in her, like a vibration just too subtle to see; but she was taunting the ambassador also, knowing that Malance would be the very last person she wanted to admit through her doors.

As it happened, Malance wanted to be there no more than their hostess would want her. And now they were all committed to this too, for the invitation could be neither withdrawn nor spurned; the niceties of court and diplomacy made either choice simply impossible, when a princess of the blood insisted to the contrary. The Clathian nodded her acceptance, spoke a frosty farewell—perhaps she too had seen the wickedness in Vivi's smile—and moved on.

"Whatever she's doing, she is not out here for the exercise of walking," Vivi said musingly. "If I could, I'd send one of the kids to track her, see where she goes—but they'd be a bit conspicuous with that bale on their back, and t'other couldn't possibly carry both."

And nor, of course, could either of themselves take one. That would be unthinkable. Sometimes Malance could love Vivi just for that, the set of her mind that laid down such absolutes, that simply couldn't see an obvious alternative.

Just now, though, she was, what—perturbed? Irate? Something of both, and dizzy besides as her life continued to spin unsettlingly around her, and all thanks to other people's choices.

"Vivi, I know you were angry, but—"

"But what? I should have let her insult you, to your face? To *mine*?"

There it was again, a glimpse of the young woman she adored, who was categorically not going to assert which was the worse insult. Even so: "She didn't speak a word to me."

"No, and that in itself was indefensible, between one ambassador and another. And then to issue an invitation, to me alone, directly in your hearing? Of course you couldn't respond, so of course I had to."

"So what, now we have to live together, just to spite Clath? Do you seriously intend to move out of the palace?" *To move in with me...?*

"Does that really sound so very terrible, my darling?"

She'd always known that Vivi was mercurial, but she'd never seen her this wild: laughing up at her, all her slight weight hanging on Malance's arm now as she stretched up for a kiss.

In honesty it sounded delightful, and perilous in every imaginable way, and what on earth would the emperor think about it? What would he *say...*?

She didn't even want to try to imagine that. Instead, she said gruffly, "I don't want to go to Clath's damn party, and she certainly doesn't want me there, so..."

"So we will both go, and be charming and witty with everyone else, and ignore her completely, as she has just ignored you; and perhaps we will learn something, for there is certainly something out there to be learned." Now Vivi sobered, just for a moment. "Someone tried to kill one of us, remember. If it wasn't you, it must have been me, and vice versa. And if Clath wasn't behind it, then she was probably in front of it: something that she wants, from me, that someone else doesn't want her to have. It might have been easier to ... remove me from the board, just take that possibility away. She doesn't usually invite me to her parties. So yes, Mal, we will go, and we will do everything we can to find out exactly what she's up to; and then we will do everything we can to poison her reputation among her other guests, and that will only be the start of our campaign. By the time we're done, she won't merely regret this day. She will regret the very day that she was *born*."

And she might still feel dizzy and bewildered, but that was absolutely Malance's cue to bend down and kiss Vivi in her turn; and then Vivi was all full of another purpose, how to move her things and her people from the palace to the Veranthan embassy, and how to make sure that the whole city knew about it, and how they should probably send one of the pages to take that letter to the emperor, but not until the kids had their own livery to wear, because you couldn't possibly send such a messenger in the emperor's own colours, unthinkable...

V

FIVE

Just don't break any actual bones

Vivi's people came with—well, probably not all Vivi's clothes, she probably had rooms'-worth, possibly even a whole wing's-worth—but enough. Wagons'-worth. Malance hadn't understood that she would even come with so many people, never mind so many clothes.

But here she was, and here they all were, and it was just as well that the house was so stupidly large, for there were so many of them: maids and grooms—oh, and horses, suddenly there were horses in her stables and they stood in need of hay and straw and stable-boys and more—and pages, of course Vivi had her own pair of privately trained pages, and oh, so many clothes.

"Vivi—what in the world do you *do* with so many people?"

"They'll find work, don't you worry. I'm a terrible lot of work, just myself, you know. Or your two will find work for them, and they know that. They'd rather find their own."

Malance's two—actually her household was up to six now, as far as she could tell, but apparently only two who counted—were already delightedly busy, distributing people and trunks and duties hither and yon. The emperor couldn't possibly have known—could he?—that Vivi was about to descend like this, with so much fuss and complication. As it turned out, though, he couldn't possibly have given Malance a better gift, or a better-timed. Her pages' authority in her house was accepted by the newcomers without a moment's hesitation. Malance alone would have been overwhelmed by this influx; Ash and Alder simply took it in their stride.

"Oh, and," Vivi went on blithely, "some part of my girls' work will be looking after you. Your Estar is charming in her own way, but not really up to the mark as a lady's maid. It'll break her heart, I know, but she should probably go back to the kitchens."

"I don't want to do that to her," Malance said. Especially not with all these new people in the house; someone among them, surely, could take on Estar's work belowstairs?

"No, but you need someone who knows how to dress your hair"—Vivi had never approved of Malance's tendency to keep her hair short and easy—"and how to prepare you for court and so forth. We can dress each other for parties," with a grin that was pure evil, and pure promise, "but there will be more formal occasions now, more invitations, and you can't walk to those in your dancing-slippers."

"I don't have dancing-slippers." She was in mourning for her land; she did not dance.

"I know. They're on the way. I sent Estar to my shoe-maker with one of your favourite boots for sizing. I do like the child, I promise. She just ... doesn't belong in our rooms, unless she's making up the fire."

Malance was stubbornly determined at least to promote Estar to chambermaid—*her* chambermaid—so that she'd be in and out of their rooms all the time. She wasn't going to let Vivi submerge her utterly. Was *not*. Estar could make up the fires, yes, and clean and dust and so forth, and not have to work quite so ridiculously hard. That would be something, at least, to set against what Vivi was proposing to take away from the girl.

Right now, though, it was true: she would be glad of some better help than Estar could offer. Now it was time to get ready for Marmon's funeral, and she needed to be immaculate.

It seemed that Vivi's maids would be sharing her with their mistress turn and turn about, rather than any one of them being assigned as her own. She supposed it made sense, in a world where you needed one gifted girl to arrange your hair and apparently have no duties else, one to care for your clothes, another to dress you, and so on. In Vivi's world, that was. Which Malance had apparently stepped into now, or been drawn or dragged into, or maybe it was entirely the other way around, that Vivi's world had merely expanded to absorb Malance's.

At any rate they were here, all these girls, and they were darting between the long-established mistress and the new, equally deferential to both while being at the same time a little familiar, a little teasing, even a little flirty with Vivi in a way that they were not—yet—with her. And it all made sense, and it was all very welcome right now, when she had to prepare—no, to be prepared—to appear beside a princess of the blood, at an occasion that must suddenly be more formal or at least more *noticed* than ever it ought to have been. And at the same time she was inwardly resentful, on her people's part and her own, at having been so thoroughly taken over, on a whim, after a random encounter, an oh-so-polite confrontation. Was this Vivi's life, or was it hers? She wasn't entirely sure any more. But it was happening in any case, and resentment didn't help. They would all learn to live with it, no doubt. She would learn to live with Vivi, for as long as Vivi chose to let that be.

Malance did try to focus on the cause, rather than the attention, but it wasn't easy. Her new mourning-clothes were … remarkable, unlike anything she'd ever worn before; and Vivi was just the other side of the room, being similarly dressed in sorrowful beauty, to be worn once and never more. Perhaps that was half her wardrobe, funeral dress and other gowns that couldn't possibly appear again...? But no, she was oddly too practical to have brought those here. She would have left them at the palace, filling rooms. Or rather, she would have expected her maids to do it. Vivi did not pack on her own behalf. That was why she had people.

Malance was learning—slowly—that this was why she too had people. She'd been accustomed to thinking of her little household as something she had to protect, above all; even her silly extravagance of boys she'd bought to save them from a worse life, and meant to give them a good one, so far as she was able. But of course their prime purpose was to serve her; and under her new pages' discipline—and under the eyes of all these strangers, incomers, critical and know-ing—serve they did.

Felid came in, unexpectedly flushing under the gaze of so many females, all gathered in one place. Her boys were simple, robust creatures, on the whole; she hadn't known that embarrassment lay anywhere within either one of them.

Malance beckoned him farther into the room, which was mean of her; she only wanted to see how long that flush could last. How long she could make it last.

"Yes, Felid, what is it?"

"Only to say that your carriage is ready below, lady. High-ness." No more running down to the road for Felid or Amil, and riding back on a cabriolet; they'd miss that. So would the drivers. So, no doubt, would she. Now that she was the chosen companion of a royal, she must ride in their own car-riage, behind new-liveried servants, as soon as those liveries arrived. Her pages had theirs already, but suddenly the order had expanded beyond imagination, and even Lirian could not apparently work miracles. Never mind. Vivi's servants had come in Vivi's livery, of course, which would do very well for the moment. For today, it would do very well indeed;

there was a discreet flash of imperial crimson on the facings of the jacket, as there was on the bodywork of her carriage. That little reminder wouldn't hurt, as Malance struggled to make another new way through the world, through the city.

Not struggling alone, at least, this time. Any more. For as long as this lasted. Whatever it was. Beset by doubts, she looked wildly across the room. She was vaguely aware that the still-scarlet Felid took advantage of her inattention to slide away, eager no doubt to return to whatever labours the pages would set him to next, rather than endure the interrogation of so many eyes. He'd settle soon enough, they all would. She hoped they would. But in this immediate moment, she was deeply unsettled herself, and she wanted reassurance.

And found it in Vivi's eyes, which were already fixed on her, calm and steady, as though she'd known. As though she'd heard Malance's thoughts from the way over there. As though there were nothing, nothing in the room, nothing in the empire more important right now than gazing at Malance in a kind of reflective wonder, interleaved with the self-possession of a thousand years of privilege. She was of the blood, and she would keep her vows. Even those made in private, in the heat of the night, in the heat of a shared bed and the lingering aftermath of passion. Of course she would.

They rode in an open carriage this day, to make clear their loss to all the world that watched. Malance had wept yesterday from sheer grief, and shouted at Ash from the same brute cause, but not now. Now she was mourning again, and all this ostentation somehow helped. It gave her distance from the streets they passed through, that she had walked and ridden through for all her years here; distance from the people, the same people who had jostled her in markets and greeted her with smiles and tried to pick her pocket. At least they'd never got away with that. Now they gawped up at her, awash with curiosity: what women, whose funeral? Why had they not heard?

They had not heard because Marmon had only been a celebrity in a very narrow field, his patrons and his clients and his friends. The manner and occasion of his death—and the nature of some of those attending, yes, obviously—would draw a wider circle to his obsequies, but not so wide that a crowd was expected either at the ceremony or outside in the street. Nor was Vivi so well known that she would draw the common folk after, even if they did decipher the livery's modest cues. Her face might be known everywhere, but not for her royal connections; she rarely exploited those, out in the city with friends. To those who cared, her name would be known better than her face; and mostly they would not yet have connected that name to the new arrival at the Veranthan house, despite so much fuss going in and out.

There were only a few running after their carriage, then, and most of those children, who mostly fell away at the borders of their own petty territories to yield their place to others, like a relay game played between rivals—deadly rivals, obviously—and only the last to play could be the winners. Some bolder souls no doubt would follow all the way, but not enough to make a difference. This would not be a circus, at least on the outside.

On the inside—well. The court, the whole palace would know by now, how Marmon died: in lieu of Vivi, or else in lieu of Malance, Madam Ambassador, Verantha. And some of the court, much of the court, much of the palace would know that Vivi had moved into Madam Ambassador's own house, to join their lives together. And some of the court would have come in any case, for Marmon; which made it respectable for others who had never so much as heard his name till this, and so there would be a turnout, yes. Possibly a large one. Lirian and her cohort might have become unexpectedly busy, creating funeral wear; perhaps that was why she hadn't been able to produce a minor miracle in the matter of Veranthan liveries for all.

The emperor would not attend, Malance knew that. Apparently he had said "Let the young people mourn their own," and the senior royals would take that as a command-ment, and the senior court besides. And there were people who only went where he went, hoping to catch his eye and thus his favour. They would not come where he did not go; that would diminish attendance at least a little. Really she would only have wanted Marmon's true friends to be there, and really she knew that was impossible, so she was stiffened to endure the inevitable. She wondered if she could hold— no, squeeze—no, *crush* Vivi's hand throughout. Best not, probably. She didn't want to hurt her. Nor to feed the gossip that must certainly be making its way around, for that might hurt her too, either personally or in reputation, in the pal-ace where she belonged far more than in Malance's house, Malance's bed, at Malance's side...

Ah. Here she was already, crushing Vivi's hand. She let it go, with a mute smile of apology; Vivi seized hers back.

"Just don't break any actual bones," she murmured. "This is hard for me too, and I do mean to claim you, yes. As we go in, and as we come out, and all the time between."

And that was the real miracle, that Vivi understood; and was willing to put up with a bruised hand if necessary, to make some things clear to the watching world.

The coachmen's backs made a liveried wall in front of them, so that they couldn't actually see ahead, but even so: Malance knew, when they were arriving. Even though she'd never been here before, she knew. The city seemed to fall away behind them, as they emerged between buildings into a broad open plaza; a hush descended, even on the cobbles where the horses' hooves came down. Straw, she saw, spread thickly and all over. No one should come noisy into the presence of death.

Through ironwork gates that were likely never closed, because who would close gates against the dead? And here was a narrow path again, closed in by trees and monuments, the markers for those dead. Straw here too, against the crunch of iron shoes, iron rims on gravel. Did they lay it fresh for every funeral? Probably, yes. There were not so many privileged to be buried here. Marmon likely only counted because of his patrons' influence, and certain of his friends. She might herself count now, she realised suddenly, when she certainly hadn't before.

Nobles lay in this place, senior figures from the courts of long ago, even a scatter of royals. Did Vivi have a place here? Or would she be claimed by the palace itself? Malance had no idea, and felt obliged to ask. Some day, sometime. Not now.

Now she only looked, this way and that, as she held Vivi's hand on the cushion between them. And now here they were, at a point where many carriages were assembled, and a few cabriolets too, she was pleased to see; not everyone here was grand. Not everyone as grand as her, making such an entrance, hand in hand with a princess of the blood, and the two of them a cynosure anyway because of that moment when the bolt eluded them both, by what chance she could not imagine, and took poor Marmon instead.

Here was an area set aside, fenced and gated. The gate was lovely, but the graves beyond were modest and crowded together. She didn't know why she'd never come up here, in her explorations. Perhaps she still had some vestige of superstition in her; a Veranthan childhood had left her wary of ghosts.

In Verantha, though, ghosts were wary of people too. No ghosts here, then, today. Many, many people. Grand people, yes; staring at them, yes; but blessed be, here were all their true friends streaming towards them, so many friends, surrounding them, absorbing them, bestowing a kind of privacy *en masse*. Even if they'd shared rides, they were still too many for the cabriolets, and only a few of them had connections grand enough for carriages.

"We walked up," Leily murmured in her ear, in mid-hug, before she'd even had breath or time enough to ask. "All of us together. Well, mostly all; all who could. We played music as we walked, and sang. You know how much Marmon did love to be sung to."

She did. He could never sing a note himself, but that hadn't mattered. He listened beautifully, as he'd been very fond of reminding people.

She kept Leily with her, an arm around her waist, so that made three of them side by side, being sheltered, being moved gently forward where a path had been kept between the close-packed graves. She knew what must be waiting for them; talk about something else, then, this last little time they had.

"What is this place, Lei?" A gesture of the head, to show that she meant this particular enclosure.

"Oh, you haven't come before? Silly goose, it's lovely up here in the summer, and the dead enjoy the company. They do, I'm sure of it. Sometimes we picnic with them. This is our place: the Artists' Colony, we call it, our own private corner, where the powers that be reward us for making their city beautiful by letting us lie together in peace. We have a view and everything, do you see? It's getting a bit crowded now, but we never did mind squashing up and getting close, did we?"

No, they never did. They were squashed close now, though people ahead were still somehow making room, so that she and Vivi could eventually come through to the graveside. Marmon's body lay atop the soil dug out beside, which had been shaped into a rudimentary table for him, as the custom was. There was no coffin, as there would have been in Verantha; instead he had been wrapped in beauty, fabrics dyed or painted with swirls of vivid colour. He would have loved that too, and would have known exactly which of his friends had created each of the cloths.

More cloths lined the bottom and sides of the grave, and Malance might have wept for him then, for the loss of him, for how much they had loved him. But with all her friends packed behind and around her, she and Vivi were exposed again: because the other side of the grave, the other side of Marmon, all the grand folk stood arrayed. Taking up as much space or more, though there were not so many of them, because of course they were not in the vein for squashing close. They were there to see—to see *her*, in the main, her and Vivi, hand in hand—and to be seen. By each other, of course; and, perhaps, by Vivi and Malance too. This might be a token towards alliance, in the hectic swirl of palace politics. *We came to the funeral of your friend, to show respect for your loss.* There would probably be a *quid pro quo*.

If it brought these people nothing else, though, they could be sure that word would get back to the emperor. He could not possibly have come himself, but he would certainly want the names of everyone who did. He was known to be fond of Vivi; he might be grateful to know who from the palace had found or made the time to support her, he might show them kindness.

Perhaps they'd be a clique now, Vivi's own, her particular friends at court. She'd like that. No: she'd *use* that. And enjoy the using of it, of course, all the plots and machinations. Vivi made mischief as birds made nests: of many separate threads and fabrics, complex and entangled, purposeful.

Brion Mercady was there, of course, though he at least would be there for her. Her clique of one. She knew and liked some few of the others, and would need to learn—and like—the rest now, probably. Well, all but one. One more she knew of old, and hated as of right.

The Clath ambassador was haunting her footsteps, as it seemed. Three times, in half a week: some god was working malice, unless it was the woman herself, sending a message that Malance couldn't fathom. Perhaps it was a warning, *I am watching you.* Perhaps it was far, far worse. Wanting to see the thing done right. Malance scanned the surrounding area, but it was hopeless; any tree might hold a man with a crossbow, come to try again. There were a lot of trees.

No matter. Vivi no doubt was on alert, and would push her into the empty grave and lie on top of her if she sensed danger. Meanwhile, this day was not for Malance, though half the court might think otherwise. She could ignore them all, whether they wanted to spite her or slay her or ally with Vivi through her, or whatever else it was they might be wanting. On this side of the grave, everyone was here for Marmon.

She turned her eyes back to the wrapped body, and—as best she could, at least—her thoughts too.

In Verantha, there would have been a priest. Here, there was none. The emperor made no rules concerning his subjects' ceremonials, though many churches did for their own believers. Like many of his friends, Marmon had dabbled with a dozen different gods—there were many and many to choose from, here in the city, gods from all across the world—and accepted none of them; so his friends would see him away in their own style, which had been his before.

There was no one to lead. Taking charge would have been ridiculous; even trying to bring a little order to the occasion was not to be thought of. He was their friend, and they would say goodbye as they had said hullo every time they saw him: noisily, chaotically, each in their own way.

Someone played a tune, a melancholy little air that took a sudden turn and went skipping unexpectedly away. Someone read a poem; the ink might not yet have been dry. Someone sang a song, unaccompanied; someone else called them all in on the chorus. Someone spoke their sorrow, memories of Marmon that could still make them laugh.

The court … watched. And did not sing along when they all sang together, except for Brion, who turned out to have a wonderful bass, rich and carrying, rolling across the gulf between them. Really he should have been on this side of the grave, Malance thought. And deliberately called for another song that she knew would exhibit his voice. He would recognise that as a message, a thank-you specifically for him.

Once they'd started, they honestly didn't know how to stop. There was so much to say, so much to sing, so many ways to wave Marmon off, when they really didn't want to let him go.

In the end—when the court grew visibly restive to one who knew them well, or so Malance guessed—it was Vivi who found a way not to end it, but to bring this segment to a close. She took a step forward to the very edge of the grave, turned her back to the court beyond, and raised her hands for attention. For the attention of their friends, made absolutely clear.

"People: sorrow requires strength. Most of you made the long march here, I know, and must be hungry now. All of us are thirsty, and Marmon wants his rest. Let him find peace now in his long home, and do you all"—*all his friends*, and that was why she'd turned her back to all the rest—"come to us, to Verantha. There we can eat, and drink, and speak of him; and sing more, and have music, and dancing too for those who wish to dance. It's never a proper funeral in Feremendas if there isn't dancing."

That raised a laugh, as it was meant to; it was a line from a ridiculous farce that had been presented at court. The emperor was seen to laugh, and so now everyone in the city had seen it and it was still presented nightly to delighted audiences in a public theatre. Vivi had dragged Malance to it more than once, and half their friends besides.

Vivi had, however, clearly gone completely mad. Malance tugged at her sleeve, hissing. "Vivi, we can't! This crowd? We can't possibly. There won't be anything to eat, and I know there's nothing to drink but tea and they won't want that."

"Neither do I," said Vivi calmly. "Don't fret so, Mal. Pages can do anything, remember?"

"...Oh. Oh, you *planned* this."

"Of course I did. All my people and yours too have been *extremely* busy, ever since we left; and they still have an hour or so in hand, because most of these have to walk back, remember, and half of them will stop to pick up a bottle or two on the way, and they'll all pitch in to help as needed when they get there. That's how this works."

It was how she and her friends had always worked, certainly; she was surprised to discover that Vivi understood it too. She was meant to be surprised, she saw, surprised by everything. She drew herself up in ambassadorial indignation and declaimed, "You have suborned my servants, in my own house...?"—and then couldn't sustain it a moment longer, against the sheer pain of sudden laughter that she couldn't swallow down. She seized the girl instead, and hugged her tight enough to crush; and when Vivi protested, squirming, she silenced her with a kiss.

A proper kiss, deep and lasting, just what the court had been waiting for. When she broke away and looked around, half of them were already heading for the gate and their carriages, the ride home and the gossip after. Spreading the news through the palace and beyond, adding it to their configurations, trying to work out what this might mean for the future, or for them. Only a minor royal, to be sure, and only a pretend ambassador—but both carried the favour of the emperor. Curried that favour, indeed, according to some, and both of them so young to be so cynical...

And there was Clath in the midst of them, taking an arm here, murmuring in an ear there, passing from one palace functionary to another in a careful choreography. And neither Malance nor Vivi had died today, so perhaps this was what she was here for after all, this casual access to high officials. Delivering more of her preferred personal invitations, perhaps...?

"Well, that'll keep them occupied," Vivi said, laughing up at her, dragging her mind back to the moment, this moment, when everyone else was thinking about a kiss. "And make a terrible tangle on the road going back, in their desperate hurry to be first."

"Don't you look so smug," Malance said, as that first consequence—the first of many, surely—truly hit her. "It'll take us for ever to get home."

"No, it won't," Vivi said, tucking her arm comfortably through Malance's. "I'll tell the coachmen to wait till the chaos eases; and meanwhile, you and I, we'll walk with our friends, and sing Marmon all the way down."

Walkers were quite untroubled by traffic. They could use footpaths, and narrow bridges, and unexpected stairways hidden under spreading trees, and all the shortcuts that an ancient city affords. Even so, it did take the hour-and-more that Vivi had forecast, and perhaps a little longer yet; and they did sing all the way, for Marmon and for company and because it made the walking easier if everyone was in step.

There wouldn't be too much singing later in the night, Malance thought regretfully; their throats would never stand it. But there was a world of talking to do, and other things besides. Hers wouldn't be a quiet house till dawn; she knew her friends.

What she didn't know any longer was her own household, never mind Vivi's. All those people, instructed in secret and sworn to silence, to surprise her on her return as much as Vivi had surprised her at the graveside. Oh, they were going to be in such *trouble*, her people, when she had time for them. Not immediately, she didn't want to spoil this night and the anticipation would be good for them, let it weigh on their souls all night long; but oh, she would spoil their morning. Those pages especially. They were safe to have been the chief conspirators, with Vivi. She had said as much, or near enough. *Pages can do anything, remember?* She'd certainly wanted Malance to think she counted herself among their number, *once a page*, but Vivi was immune to any trouble that Malance could raise. She couldn't offer that immunity to anyone else. Malance's own people, keeping secrets from her...

She fumed deliciously, theatrically, within her own head as they walked, as they sang; and at one point she glanced at Vivi at her side and murmured, "Pages may be able to do anything, but Verantha can't afford it. Can't afford *this*. I know you don't understand, but—"

"You can now," Vivi said lightly, hugging her arm. "*We* can now. I'm Verantha now, with all that that implies."

Access to the imperial treasury, or some portion thereof: that was the implication. What Vivi was offering. But Malance drew on that treasury in any case, and tried to take as little as she might, for reasons that were obvious to her.

They weren't to Vivi. "Oh, I know, sweetling: you're as frugal as a bowl of lentils. But I'm not, you see? I'm an extravagance at every turn, I push the emperor to the very limits of his generosity. He has on occasion had to administer a very mild scold in my direction. Not that he can't afford me," she added, pouting, "he just doesn't choose to indulge me. His words, not mine. The man's a brute. But I'm a Veranthan now; maybe he'll indulge me after all? He likes you, and he finds you useful; he's been heard to complain that you don't spend half enough of his money. Which also made me pout, by the way, when he was clamping down so meanly on me. He plays favourites outrageously, just not with family, apparently," which was so spectacularly and obviously not true that Malance was half inclined to push Vivi into a suddenly convenient holly bush.

She refrained, with an effort. There was more to say, a great deal more—but here was one last footpath, and here a turn into an alley that she would have sworn had never existed before tonight, and they came out onto her road, with her park before them and her house, her own house visible even from here, even in the gloom, it was all lit up so brightly.

"If those children have set fire to the place..."

Vivi laughed again, and hauled on her arm to slow her when she would have run.

"Don't *worry* so, my Mal! Look, even the trees have lights tonight, to see us on our way."

It was true, there were lanterns in all the trees guarding the pathway up. Malance took a breath, took a step into trust, and another slowly, decorously into the park, if one in a party singing raucous marching songs could ever be called decorous.

The house was ablaze, but not with fire, no. With lights alone: every window shone its welcome. And the doors stood wide, and both her boys were dressed to match in Vivi's borrowed livery, standing either side to bow her—their—guests a welcome.

That must have taken some coaching. She knew for certain sure they'd lacked any such courtly manners when she bought them, and they had learned none at all from her.

Even now, she could see, they were struggling not to grin at her as they usually did, as she and Vivi ascended the steps like royalty. Well, one of them was royalty. She smiled because she loved them both, and shook her head sternly because they were in such trouble with her and they really ought to know it, she wanted to *ruin* their peace of mind tonight; and then she stepped through into light and colour and movement and sound, a house she couldn't recognise, and forgot all about the many betrayals and perfidies of her servants.

Even the hallway was transformed. Banners hung from every wall, lamps glowed softly in every corner; there was a rug underfoot that she'd emphatically never seen before. The reception room to her right was alluring with firelight and candlelight and comfort after a long and difficult day; while to her left—

To her left was the ballroom which had not been used since her country fell, and seldom before that, at least in her tenure here. Verantha was a small land, with a modest purse. Let the grand nations throw their grand balls; Verantha would accept invitations gladly, but reply with quiet soirées and private dinners, more fitting to her scale.

Come to think, Malance hadn't been invited to a single grand ball yet. Brion welcomed her as often as she would attend, but the Outlands were as poor as her own homeland; the entertainment there would include marvellous food and wine, interesting guests, and perhaps a quartet of musicians in the gallery, no more. Certainly no dancing. Brion did not dance, and a host's obligations are paramount.

She wished she might have had a moment alone with Brion after the funeral. She might have invited him here, to this, had she known; he might have come.

That was a pang. This, though: this was a marvel. The ballroom had been opened and aired; the sprung floor had been polished; candelabra burned at every vantage point, with lamps too to assist them. There was a massive fire in the massive grate, and chairs around the sides, a raised dais for musicians, everything.

And her pages at the doors, of course, their imperially schooled unrevealing faces not even trying to hide the complacent smirks beneath.

She beckoned them and they came to her on the instant. She growled, "You two... I am going to *beat* you two, I swear. You are never to keep things from me again, do you understand? *Never.* Not for her highness if she asks"—and she would ask, of course she would, she had set a precedent now;

and she was standing right there at Malance's side, of course, and listening to every word—"nor for the emperor himself," though he—she hoped—would never ask.

"Yes, lady." Both of them as one, and both of them meaning it, as far as she could tell with such deceitful creatures; and both of them still in high delight with themselves and with Vivi and with everything they'd achieved tonight.

And now she was smiling, damn it, and they took that as their cue to smile too, in this private conversation; and she scowled at them, which almost made them laugh aloud, and went on, "All right, tell me. Tell me *everything*. What have you done for food?"

"Farl has been cooking since this morning, lady. Since *early* this morning. He ordered everything in yesterday."

Of course he did. Conspirator. She would have words with Farl too, tomorrow. "And what exactly did he—no, never mind. I am sure there will be enough, and that it will at least be edible. Mechet will have ensured that, I have no doubt. In a supervisory capacity." Poor Mechet, usurped in his own kitchen—but it was probably just as well. Her friends had eaten his food before. "Drink?"

"Wine and beer were here yesterday, lady," brought in no doubt under cover of Vivi's arrival, all her wagons, all her people; of course Malance wouldn't have noticed other wagons from other sources. "Brandy came in this afternoon, from Helforth," with a glance at Vivi to confirm that it had been her order and not their own inspiration. Malance would have known that anyway.

"Oh, did it so?" Helforth was legendary for both the qualities of his imported brandies and their price. She thought of her friends, let loose on an array of bottles from Helforth, and her heart sank. The emperor would be facing a hefty bill for this night. "Very well," she went on, a little grimly. "Food, drink. Firewood, candles, lamp oil. Wall hangings, apparently—"

"We found those, lady." Ash was suddenly eager to appease. "In presses, stowed away." *Not a penny piece*, he was saying.

"Good. That's something. Musicians?"

"No, lady. We thought you might not like that," and no guilty glances towards Vivi, so this must have been their own thought, and she could—almost—have kissed them for it, regardless of how much trouble they were in.

"No. Thank you for that." Her friends would make their own music to dance to, as they always did. She nodded a dismissal, and the pages went back to the ballroom doors, where people with instruments in their hands were already finding their way in.

"Vivi, you are going to *die* for this. Die *horribly*, I swear it. My hands and mine alone will spell your doom."

"Delightful," she said, laughing, twining herself around Malance's long body. "I'll look forward to that all night. Now, though, shall we see what your Farl has worked with the rather splendid ingredients I arranged for him?"

She suspected that Vivi had arranged the money—or more likely the credit—and little more, except perhaps the vaguest of instructions about what she'd like to see tonight. Malance would be astonished if she actually knew the first thing about how to cook, never mind what ingredients to order.

She tucked that slight figure under her thoroughly disapproving arm, and steered them both—her house, after all!— to the reception room.

Here too, everything was different. There were more sofas and more chairs, a lot less room; tables lining the walls. And on those tables—yes. The fruits of Farl's labours.

There were bowls of fruit, bowls of salads, jugs of iced sherbet. There were platters of sliced meats, platters of roasted fowls and fishes. There were breads of many kinds, heaped high. There were pies and tarts and pastries.

At last, she simply had to stop looking.

"How...?"

"Perhaps he started yesterday," Vivi murmured. It was good to see her taken aback, for once. Even she hadn't expected this. "And he might have had the breads fetched up, perhaps?"

"I doubt it. No, this is his chance to show what he can do. He's been aching for this, Brion said." Now she really did wish she'd invited Brion. "He will have done it all himself. And now I'm not sure I'm even hungry."

"Yes, you are," Vivi said firmly. "You're starving, just like everyone here. We'd best start eating before everything's gone. Come along."

Food, wine, music. Friends eating, drinking, dancing. Everyone stopping to talk with her in ones and twos, all evening long. Watching the colour and the light and the movement, battered by the noise of it all, she felt overmastered, at least a little. She had given no parties in this house, before tonight. She had no money and few friends at court, so imperial functions, ambassadorial functions were out of the question; and this was her mourning-place in any case, she wanted to keep it private. She'd never even invited these people, her friends, not even by the handful. And now they were all mourning together, and they were all doing it here; and of course that was right, it was a masterstroke of Vivi's, and even so. She loved them dearly, and she didn't want them gone, and yet.

And here was Vivi, hot from the dancing, just a touch less than immaculate for once; sitting beside her, flushed and breathing hard, saying, "Tired, Mal?"

"No, not really. Just sad, I think."

"Good. Come up to bed, and let me make you happy."

"Vivi, we can't! *I* can't! This is my house, and my party. Our party." *Your creation.* "We can't just ... leave. These people are our guests."

"They are; and you have a houseful of servants now, who are all showing themselves to be very good at looking after guests. Our guests are actually pretty good at looking after themselves and each other, come to that. They'll notice we're gone, of course, and they'll be sorry; and then they'll carry on playing, drinking, dancing. They'll talk the stars to sleep. And eventually they'll start going home. Some of them will, by themselves or otherwise. Some of them will stay; I had a whole floor of bedrooms cleaned and laid ready for them. This house is *huge*, Mal, I still haven't explored it all."

Neither had she. They should probably do that, some-time. Not now.

"Some of those who stay won't be sleeping alone," Vivi went on, grinning. "I'd lay money that both your sweet boys will have someone to help them off with those awkward liveries. Assuming you're willing to lend, of course."

"Of course." It wouldn't be the first time. Permission could be assumed by now, where the boys were willing.

"Good. So, there's nothing left for either of us to do down here, so we might as well go to bed. Before we're too tired. Yes?"

"...Yes. Please, yes?"

V·

SIX

The infinitely familiar shape of her

Waking up with Vivi was a process, and one to which Malance had in no sense become accustomed. To be fair to herself, she really hadn't had time—Vivi tended not to allow a person time to settle—but in truth, she wasn't sure she'd ever grow used to this. Some significant part of herself wasn't sure she'd ever want to.

First there was opening her eyes, opening her mind to the reality of this: the comfort of companionship, the luxury of touch. The perfume of Vivi in the morning, which was herself and the night and a little bit of Malance too. The tangles of her hair, the impertinence of her fingers. The way she had of chuckling deep in her throat, even when there was nothing overtly funny. The self-content of her at her own cleverness, having brought herself and her people to this house, herself to this bed. On what had been honestly little more than a whim, a flash of temper, but it seemed to delight her yet. Malance hoped strongly that she could hold on to that delight, because the loss of Vivi now would break her.

Then there was the necessity of pulling apart—eventually—in order to get out of bed. Late, indulgent, probably outrageous. She was sure Clath rose with the sun to attend

124

some austere service before sitting down to a drab bowl of gruel and some hateful paperwork. She hoped so, anyway. She hoped the ambassador's life was entirely disagreeable in every way.

Herself, she scrambled into a robe for decency while Vivi—who didn't bother, of course—rang a bell. That started a procession of people into and through their bedchamber, such as Malance had never experienced. First came the maids, and pages with great pans of bathwater slung between them, hot as hot. A hot bath every morning was one of those things Malance never wanted to take for granted, she wanted to relish it just as much each and every day—though she might never grow used to being attended while she took it. *No page is ever body-shy*, and Vivi naturally took it for granted, but Malance had never been a page and lacked those advantages, and these maids were strangers to her yet.

Still, it was nice to have her back washed with the softest, kindest soap imaginable; and it was nice to be engulfed in hot towels and vigorously dried after. And then it was back into her robe and back into the bedroom and oh, so many people waiting for them. Dressers and hairdressers and Estar, yes, making the bed now as she'd already kindled a bright little fire in the grate, greeting Malance with her usual smile, seemingly glad to have at least this hour in their rooms before she went back to the kitchen.

Vivi was predictably hard to satisfy, in matters of hair and dress and footwear. At least she didn't swear, or slap her girls, or throw things; rather she seemed to enjoy the fuss of it, trying one outfit after another to see what best suited her notion of the day ahead. Her maids were either extraordinarily patient or they too loved dressing and undressing their mistress, as though they were little girls yet and she their beloved and somewhat contrary, somewhat arbitrary doll.

Malance was by contrast the most undemanding mistress imaginable. Whichever girls might come to her in a morning, she would happily let them bully her into their own notions of what would suit the day, from the still-narrow selection that her dressing room afforded. And her hair of course needed no more than a brush pulled through the curls. She could be dressed and done in ten minutes, though she tried to remember to let it take twenty, just to give the girls some sense of achievement. Then she'd sip a cup of tea and watch Vivi being dramatic and demanding, and be thoroughly quiet and content.

Until her own pages came back in, at least, to organise her time for her. She had become one of their lists, she felt, drawn up anew every morning: every duty, every engagement written down in order. She used to have few of either, and her day required no listing, and certainly no busybody authoritarian pages to keep it in order on her behalf. But now she lived half in Vivi's world, and Vivi half in hers, and both made such a difference.

She was privately grateful for the pages' efforts to keep her on time, in place and informed, and secretly delighted to watch them struggle with Vivi's rather more eccentric notions of timekeeping and schedules. Nevertheless, she'd greet their smiles with a scowl of resentment every morning, and growl her way through these meetings, purely to mark the transition from night to day, from bed to work.

When Vivi was finally done, they'd go down to breakfast together, and she could greet the rest of her people and bicker with her beloved over Vivi's very different ideas of how they should spend their time, and—again, secretly delighted—watch her scribble all over the pages' plans and quite rewrite their day.

So far—though that was really not far at all, and she did worry how long Vivi would accept the necessary formalities of an ambassador's life—they would end up in a compromise: official functions interleaved with fun and friends and frivolity. Vivi's long-legged youngsters, rested from their labours with the bathwater, would run messages all over the city: changes of plan, invitations, instructions. And eventually, *eventually*, they would leave the house and climb into a carriage—she always made the pages get up behind, not to give them ideas above their station—and actually begin.

So it had been, at least, those few days that Vivi had been in residence, and all her retinue besides.

Today began no differently: the waking, the bathing, the waiting. No pages came, however, to bring a list. Malance waited and waited. At last Vivi cocked an eyebrow at her through the mirror she sat before, and said, "Have those rogues decided you deserve a holiday?"

"I ... don't know. I don't suppose so. I'm sure they had plans for today. Maybe they're nursing hangovers, and running late?" One could only hope. Life with imperial pages was a constant struggle to get ahead, she found; it would make her extremely happy to scold them—loudly—and dose them for the headache and the upset stomach, and feel her moral superiority in every smug bone of her smug body.

"Never." Vivi dashed her hopes with a reflected grin. "I'm sorry. We're immune to the evils of alcohol. Our training burns out any trace of susceptibility."

Certainly it was true that Vivi could drink anything and everything and show precious little sign of being affected. Malance might begrudge her that, occasionally; she would begrudge the pages more. Still, they were manifestly not here, where their self-ascribed duties demanded that they be. Whatever the reason, she could still hold out hopes of a scolding. Yes.

"Shall we just go down, then? If you're ready?" She was apparently eager to get to it, if the opportunity was there.

"Just another minute, Mal. I'm *not* sure of this fichu, if we're going *anywhere* near the palace today; whereas I'm *totally* sure of it if we're going anywhere close to the river. It's a quandary."

It was a quandary that took another ten minutes of consideration, before she decided that she could deploy one of her own pages as a fichu-carrier, either to deliver it to her at need or else run it back to the house, depending. Her pair might lack the imprimatur of imperial training, but she had had them for years and trained them herself, so they actually had a number of uses beyond tagging at her heels, running her errands and serving at table; even so, she was always finding opportunities to keep them busy, preferably busy and bored both at once. Bearer of the Royal Fichu was ideal; she'd probably use her boy Falen, just to watch him squirm.

"You torment those children."

"Of course I do, it's good for them. It builds character. I was tormented, in their place; and see me now. I have lots of character."

Laughing, she tucked her arm through Malance's and waited with the merest hint of impatience for one of the maids to understand this signal and open the door for them. The mistresses of this house did not open their own doors, apparently. Malance supposed that she could grow used to that, at least, if never quite comfortable with it. She'd once seen Vivi approach an unattended door and hesitate a moment, as though expecting it to open by itself in the radiance of her presence. *Exactly* as though. Malance treasured the memory, and intended never to share it. Vivi's high expectations of the world around her were a part of her infinite charm, and Malance would never risk bruising that.

Along to the landing, and down the staircase, and—oh. Yes. Of course. This, no doubt, was what had distracted the pages. Her house was full of people.

People? Friends. Guests. The ones who didn't go home last night. Which at first glance looked to be most of them, though that was probably only the shock of seeing them all at once, when she'd wholly forgotten they would be here at all.

They were milling in and out of the reception room, in various states of dress, carrying plates and mugs, filled or empty, meaning needing to be filled again; and talking in low voices—for them—about no doubt everything under the sun. As she and Vivi came down, those in the hallway looked up, and there was a sudden shout of welcome.

"At last!" added Vold, in a stentorian bellow. "They're down at last! We can talk at a normal volume, without having pages jump down our throats! Ash, we need more coffee!"

Well, that explained why they'd heard nothing in her suite—their suite—and nothing even as they came down the stairs bar a murmur that might equally well have been the servants trying to make inroads into the mess left by last night's party.

...Except that there was apparently no mess left by last night's party, though the furniture still stood in its rear-rangement. It needed to; people were breakfasting all around the room, while the tables that had held last night's banquet held—well, another banquet, if breakfasts could be banqueted upon. There were steaming platters and chilled bowls, urns of tea and coffee, even if the latter were allegedly all in need of refills. She didn't know how many if any of her friends had slept last night, but she was sure that Farl had not. She'd need to go down and have a word with him about that. Give him a present and send him to bed. Alone for pref-erence, because he'd surely need sleep more than company, whichever he might actually prefer.

She wondered if all her other people and Vivi's too had similarly been wakeful all night, cleaning up. And decided not to ask, no. Presents for everyone, though, and a quiet, easy day today. Perhaps the pages had already made that decision for her? Vivi might have been right after all.

Here were the pages, a little dishevelled for once—which thrilled her soul: they should have presents too, and she would relish their separate resentments—as they chivvied servants and placated guests. "Yes, sir, the coffee's coming; no, lady, I'm dreadfully sorry, but we're out of ham entirely," with *because you ate it all last night* as a clear if unspoken rider.

Well, it had been excellent ham. She remembered it distinctly. And to be fair they were earning their presents, managing both her friends and her new and enormous household, keeping the former fed and the latter busy. Her boys were back in livery, being cheerfully familiar with the guests, fetching extra treats to their favourites, refilling juice glasses, lingering to laugh at their jokes. She wondered if the undeclared game was to guess which particular one—or more—of her friends each boy had bedded down with last night.

Perhaps she'd leave that to Vivi, though, who was bound to win the game anyway if it were ever declared. For the moment, she was happy to see them happy, her people and her friends both. Even the pages she thought were happy in their own way, exhibiting their usual terrifying competence, being themselves. *Big* presents, definitely. And let the emperor pay, of his kindness, for having foisted the wretches upon her in the first place.

Half a dozen voices demanded their company; a dozen bodies shifted up on numerous sofas, to make room. For a wonder, Vivi glanced at Malance before making a choice; she shook her head to all of them, and shrugged at the predictable chorus of complaints. Ignoring everyone, she filled a plate for herself and made sure that Vivi at least took something solid, and led her out of the reception room and across the hall to the ballroom, where there were chairs to sit in and at least a chance of peace if not a likelihood of privacy, and—

O h.
    "Triman? What are you *doing*?"

He had built himself an unsteady-looking scaffold of tables and chairs and ladders and planks, and was high towards the ceiling, marking thick lines in charcoal—scavenged from a cold fireplace, to judge by the thick awkward nature of the stick he held—on the ancient faded silk of one wall.

"Oh." He swivelled around to see her, and his whole con-struction rocked dangerously beneath him. "Sorry, I thought you'd be a while. I wanted to have this done, before you came down."

"We have been a while," she asserted, with the clocks of the city striking noon all around to back her up. "Again, what are you *doing*, that you wanted to have done?"

Vivi had moved quietly to the foot of the scaffold, antici-pating catastrophe. Malance was caught somewhere between curiosity and annoyance, glowering up at her friend. Triman was a cartographer of art, he liked to say; he made fanciful maps of the city, which emphasised some features beyond their worth and diminished others unjustly. He took com-missions, so that merchants could pay to have a chart hang-ing in their office that would stress the significance of their warehouses over their rivals', or the benefit of their particular delivery routes and so forth. He only got away with it, she knew, because he was such a dedicated cartographer at heart; you had to be good before you could break the rules whole-sale, subtly to twist the whole meaning and measure of a city.

In answer, he drew one final line across the wall and said, "It's done enough, I guess. Let me just come down, and—"

And his just coming down was exactly the catastrophe that Vivi had foreseen, because his weight shifted the lad-der and the ladder's movement jerked the trestle so that it slipped from its support, and—

And Vivi was there, somehow untouched by the general collapse, and in exactly the right place to catch Triman as he fell; and apparently her body had been trained to catch falling men significantly larger than she was, or else it was just luck—except that Malance did not believe in that kind of luck, not after spending nights with Vivi, learning exactly how elastic that body was, how kept in trim, how strong—and she let his weight carry her down to her knees, and she laid him on the floor quite gently, and he wasn't apparently hurt and neither was she and Malance took a moment to wonder at that, at Vivi and all her doings, before she lifted her eyes to the defaced wall of her ballroom and—

O h.
     The scaffold's fall had revealed the whole of Triman's design; and that was her own beloved Verantha there, the infinitely familiar shape of her, all her borders clearly and accurately marked and a start made on her mountains, her rivers, her county lines.

Oh...

W hen her eyes were dry and Triman was sitting on a chair against the other wall, flexing his shoulders and feeling for bruises, still a little pale and breathless, Malance went to sit beside him. She felt pale and breathless herself, from a different kind of shock.

"Triman... *How?*"

"You showed me a map, back awhile, and talked me through it. Remember?"

"Yes, of course"—she'd been aching for her lost land and talked about it at every opportunity, trying to keep it alive in her head and make it live for others—"but..."

"I never forget a chart," he said, shrugging. "I *can't*. If I've studied it once, I can reproduce it. I thought you'd like this, and obviously you were going to stay in bed for ever, so I figured I'd have time. Your boys helped me build the scaffold." He smiled wryly. "They're charmingly cute, and Amil was a very good friend to me last night, but don't let them build anything you want to last. I'll hire proper craftsmen next week, to raise me a real one. You'll need to pay them, mind. And you're going to need to buy a lot of paint. I'll choose it, you pay. Sorry."

What he'd done was just a sketch, and she loved it already. She tried to imagine it as a full mural in bold colours, and her heart failed her.

"We'll pay you too, of course," she said, meaning *the emperor will pay you, through me or through Vivi.*

"No. I'm not taking money for this, only what I need to make it right. It's a, a love-gift. For you, for Marmon. For everybody."

She took breath to argue with him, just as Vivi appeared again with two steaming mugs. She handed them one apiece, and said, "Drink this. You both look appalling."

Malance wrapped both hands around the hot porcelain, and inhaled the steam—and spluttered, almost spilled it, set it down very carefully before she raised her head again. "Vivyana Feremend, did you put *Helforth brandy* into *coffee*?"

Vivi shrugged lightly. "It's all we have left, after last night. Yes, of course I did. You need it. Drink."

Triman was already gulping his, heedless of sacrilege, heedless of the honour being done his mouth. Malance supposed that she might as well join him; it was too late to save the brandy, after all.

She chose to sip, regardless. If you were going to put one of the world's finest brandies into somewhat-suspect coffee—Farl was too busy, surely; he would have delegated such a mundane task to Estar, perhaps, or one of the boys, or else left it to Mechet, with whose coffee she was long and painfully familiar—then you should at least give the spirit a chance to find a path through the medium and speak to you.

There. She had drunk none of it last night, but Brion—of course!—had introduced her to Helforth brandy, when it had been nothing but legend to her before. She could find it now, and feel it; she knew its touch, dilute as it was. Potent as it still was, a glimpse of fire through a thick dark curtain.

Was it possible that Vivi was right? Again? She felt it reach into her marrow, and ignite what had been failing before. She lifted her head and gazed again at the sketch of Verantha on her wall there, and wondered about citizenship, whether she could grant it if she was the last surviving authentic official Veranthan, as recognised by the most powerful empire in the world; and said only, "Triman, would you like to come and live here?"

He blinked at her, no more. She was merciless; she said, "I happen to know you struggle to afford your rent, more months than otherwise." The cartography of art was not famous for rewarding its artists well. Its artist, rather. "If I give you a room here, that's no longer a problem; and you'd be right at hand to work on this until it's done, and to keep me company then and afterwards." The one thing was not related to the other, and she needed to make that clear. That it was also a way to pay him for his work without actual money changing hands was actually and honestly minor; she would very much like a friend in the house, whether or not she could grant him honorary Veranthan citizenship. Amil might like it too, apparently, and she did want her boys to be happy.

"To keep *us* company," Vivi said pointedly.

Oh. That was right, of course. Perhaps she should have checked with Vivi, before issuing the invitation. She glanced up a little anxiously, and found a smile waiting for her, so all she said was, "Yes, that. Us. It would be good for you so many ways, Trim. I bet we could find you clients at court, for one thing. They'd all love to learn that their holdings were more important than their rivals', and you could do that for every single one of them."

Triman looked from her to Vivi and back again, and blushed abruptly, when he had been so pale before. She thought it likely that this was his first taste of Helforth brandy. Also, that he too was thinking about Amil. He said, "I ... think I would like that? Very much? But you can't know if you'd like having me around, so if we could just say until I've finished here, and see how we all feel then...?"

"Of course. Though this place is so big, you could live here and we might never see each other at all; that's not going to be a problem. Vivi and I keep dragging each other out anyway, to one thing or another. I'll have my people find you a room of your own, and a studio too, you shouldn't have to work where you sleep," *or where you sleep with Amil, if that's what Amil wants to do.* She didn't at all mind lending her boys out for a night or two, but a longer relationship was another matter. Perhaps she'd ask Vivi to test those particular waters, if it seemed that Triman wanted that. Amil would feel obliged to say yes if she asked herself, whatever his true feelings.

To be mistress in her own house had been a dream of hers, once. It was turning out a lot more complicated than she'd thought. She was even obliged to worry about pretty boys she'd bought at market on a whim.

Still: that was for another day. Triman might not want any such thing. He'd conspicuously chosen to live alone thus far, though he slept with any boy he could lay his hands on. Once, at any rate. He was a legend among her acquaintance. Privately she'd wondered before this whether it was simply that he couldn't afford a boy of his own, never mind an actual boyfriend, with all the costs that entailed. She wished she'd thought sooner of offering him a place here in her house; it was a resource she possessed, and she could have made so much better use of it, offering him a haven and bringing herself a friend.

And now she was thinking about it, the same must be true of others among her cohort. Not all of them would want it, but some she was sure would welcome the offer of a home, shared with their own circle. She had stupid amounts of space here, and she didn't have to hoard it all to her own misery, her mourning. With Vivi here, she probably wouldn't have the chance anyway, so why not?

...Though she'd need to discuss it with Vivi first, of course, before she flung her doors open to her ragtag polity and declared this an Artists' Colony of the living. That was something else that was new, something to learn. Assuming that Vivi chose to stay. Malance was still very much not taking that for granted, despite all the fuss entailed in moving all her things and people here. She could just as readily move them all out again, and enjoy a whole new level of fuss.

Meantime Malance glanced over her shoulder, confident of this one thing, that she would find one page or the other in attendance, waiting for her notice.

"Ash. Did you hear?"

"Of course, lady." That was his job, apparently, except where it was to anticipate, before she need take the trouble actually to say anything. "If you'll come with me now, Master Triman, we can look at what rooms might be suitable; and I'll send Amil to fetch your things from your current lodging immediately," because he knew that would give Amil the chance to unpack Triman's things in his new room, which would at least give Triman the opportunity to say, "No, that goes there, and by the way, why don't you move your own things up here too, if you'd like that, if your mistress would permit it...?"

It might be premature, but she loved Ash for setting that up so gracefully, just in case.

Triman was dazed and delighted in equal measure, as far as she could tell, as Ash led him away. Vivi grinned down at her and said, "So. Are you planning to open our house to all your wastrel friends now?"

Our house. She liked that. And said, "Yes, maybe. To *our* wastrel friends, if they want to. If you will allow it."

"Oh, do I get a voice?"

"Yes," emphatically. "It's your house too." *Our house, you just said so.* "You get a voice in everything. Of course you do." *So long as you're here.* She still didn't dare trust her luck; Vivi was notoriously mercurial. Or, no, *deliberately* mercurial said it better. Malance was convinced that her every whim was thought out ahead, and flourished for a purpose.

"Good." Vivi dropped down into the chair Triman had vacated, and reached for Malance's hand. "Because my voice thinks this is a lovely idea, for Trim and for anyone else who'd like to live here. This house needs company, Mal, as much as you and I do; and these particular wastrels will fill it with music and colour and *noise*, and it'll be glad of that, it's been solitary too long, and so have you. Anyway, it'll be fun; and you were worried about giving our people enough to do. That lot will bring plenty of work with them, I guarantee it. My people will be outraged, and yours will adore it, so it'll be good for everyone."

Even so, Malance wasn't issuing an open invitation. Not yet. Let Triman settle in, let the mixed household get used to that. Meantime, she had other things on her mind.

"Vivi?"

"Yes, Mal?"

"What can we—you—actually *do*? At court, and otherwise? I mean, I know the emperor looks kindly on us both, for different reasons," and she was delighted that Vivi at least had no qualms about spending his money, because she herself was suddenly doing rather a lot of that, "and he's given me so much already," this house, this opportunity to keep Verantha's name alive at the heart of empire, "but how can we *use* that, to help my people and, and, oh, whoever it is you want to help?" She realised suddenly that she had no idea whether Vivi had any pet projects, any notion even of supporting people less lucky than herself. Apart from Malance herself, of course, and apparently those friends that Malance brought into her purview. Really, for two people sharing a bed and now abruptly a life together, they did know very little about each other.

Vivi took Malance's hand between both of hers, and started to work the fingers carefully, from one bone to the next. "Mal. Your people are my people now, and I will work to help them all. I even like most of them, though we are going to have words about one or two. And yes, I have my own people whom I help where I can, and I hope they will become your people too. We will visit them, in the days ahead. But none of this is urgent, and it all needs thinking over. Talking over, you and me and others." Their people, their other people, the servants who kept this house running; did they need consulting, or just instructing? Vivi wouldn't hesitate, but she knew that Malance would. "What is urgent, right now, is that you either eat that plate of food you brought in here and forgot about, or else go back to fetch something fresh and hot. I put enough brandy in that mug to drown a merchant ship, and you'd better get something solid inside you soon or I'll have to put you to bed again and you'll be no fun at all for the rest of the day. I expect Ash is doing exactly that to Triman, in whatever room he's chosen." Ash would have made the choice, of course, not Triman. Triman would just accept what he was offered. "And then, once I know you're not going to fade out on me, we can talk about the court, and the city, and all we have to do."

The house was too full of people. That was so strange, to feel there was nowhere they could be comfortably private, to talk without someone overhearing. To have to chase servants away—Alder had appeared in the ballroom the minute she'd sent Ash off with Triman, and she had no idea how they did that—and fend off importunate friends. To close the front door behind her, shutting them all in, so that she and Vivi could be alone out here in this ruin of a garden. That felt ... inverted, after so many days and nights of closing the world out to retreat into herself, in her huge and empty home.

Also, she wanted air. Nothing to do with the brandy, no; she wasn't light-headed at all. Nor feeling any effects from last night's party. She just wanted to breathe awhile under an open sky. And walk hand in hand with her *amour*, at least a little way. Perhaps they'd go out into the park, beyond the gate. Maybe they'd go all the way to Outlands to share a second breakfast with Brion, and let him send them home in his carriage.

But she didn't want to be evasive, and she didn't want to put off the serious questions of the day; so first, just this short walk halfway down the wide gravel drive. The garden itself was a hopeless tangle, but just here was a little stone-flagged area with a pond—long dried up—and a bench that had not yet rotted or rusted entirely. She intended to sit there with Vivi, and look at her rather than at the dereliction all around them, and think about the future rather than any part of yesterday. Try to find some way forward, perhaps: a path to follow that would make sense, and bring some sense of order into the chaotic swirling of her life right now, and hopefully bring them at last into a better place. Yes.

And—

And just as they arrived at that helpful bench, her eye was caught by movement down by the gate, which of course had been left open for the party. Vivi said, "I think we have visitors," and she might feel a little surge of warmth at that *we* but before all else this was the Veranthan embassy, and she the ambassador here.

It was as Verantha, then, that she walked down to the gate, bearing all the weight of her country on her shoulders, determined that they should be broad enough. Not holding Vivi's hand now: formal and correct, perhaps overdoing it a little—the people hovering uncertainly at the gate wore rough clothes and carried bundles—but nevertheless. Madam Ambassador, accompanied by a princess of the blood.

A very curious princess, murmuring to Malance all the way: "...straight off a ship, by the look of them; probably we should have sent a page down to talk to them first, to learn whence and how and wherefore—but why let the kids have all the fun? How many do you make it, a dozen, give or take? Oh, and children: they've got a few little ones with them, see? They're travelling together, they didn't just meet on shipboard. I'd say the tall man is the leader, yes? What is it with you tall people anyway, always taking charge?"

"Vivi, hush." She was all Verantha now, as though she had stepped further into the role with every measured pace. Somewhat to Malance's surprise, and probably somewhat to her own, Vivi actually did hush.

"Good morning," Malance said, stepping up to the very edge of her territory, that line in the gravel where the gates had closed. None of the newcomers had yet stepped over that line; they seemed anxious and uncertain. More than one had been weeping, she thought. "I am Ambassador Malance Hermentine of Verantha," in case there was any doubt. "May I know your names, and why you have come to visit me?" She wasn't inviting them over her threshold, not quite yet, though there was no sense of any threat about them. Sorrow, rather, and exhaustion, perhaps desperation. As though she might be their last hope, perhaps? Had they trailed from one embassy to the next, all through the park, only to wash up on her doorstep at the last?

No. No, they had not. The man Vivi had identified as leader bowed in a way that sang to her, unexpectedly; her breath caught in her throat.

"A good day to you, madam. I regret arriving in this manner, in all our dirt, but—well, we have come a long way in a hurry, and have almost nothing with us. Nor could we find anyone to help us here; we went to the First Light temple, of course, but the priests turned us away. So we came on here, to see you. To ask for your kindness, if you will."

"Where,"—she was finding speech unusually hard, all of a sudden—"where have you come from?" She knew already, from his voice and his manner and their dress and more, but she did need to hear someone say it.

"Why, from Verantha, madam. Your home and ours."

And he said it in Veranthan, of course; and that was when she realised that the whole conversation had been in her mother tongue, and she had slipped into it so readily, unthinkingly, that she hadn't even noticed until this.

Now she really was light-headed, and she did need Vivi's hand merely to root her, to keep her fixed in the world, not to let this shake her off her feet. It was as much as she could manage even then, merely to stay upright; she knew she was staring; she couldn't talk at all. Not in that tongue, not in any.

Vivi was equal to everything. "Good day to you all. I am Vivi Feremend," which should tell them all they needed to know of her lineage and significance here. "Please do come in; you are very welcome here. Perhaps you'd like to bathe and change your clothes? I'm sure we can find you fresh things to fit—or have you not eaten this morning, would you rather have a quick wash and then go straight to table? You do all look so weary. Please, come this way."

She almost had to turn Malance physically, and then give her a little shove in the small of the back to get her feet moving in the right direction. The mazement hung about Malance's head like an aura, all the long walk—and how had it grown so long, when it was short before?—back to the house.

By the time they reached the door, it had opened wide in welcome and Alder stood there to greet these unexpected guests and learn what was needed. For once, Malance was unequivocally glad of her. And of Ash, too; between them, she knew, they would take all of this out of her hands. For now. Much as Vivi had done at the gate, and that too had been a reemergence of Vivi the imperial page, she thought, as much as it was Vivi of the imperial house.

Indeed, it barely took a minute before Alder was sweeping all the newcomers away to see them settled. Malance didn't know where—she hadn't even registered which they had decided on, baths or breakfast—but no doubt a place would be found for them, comforts brought to their doors. Bustle bustle. She only wanted to sit down.

Vivi read her mind, steering her directly to a chair and then crouching down in front of her, resting one hand on her knee for balance.

"Mal, I have to go to the palace. I really must tell the emperor about this. I mean, he'll know already, of course he will; but I need to tell him anyway, he'd expect that. And I think he'll offer to help. We've always been good with refugees. I'll take the carriage with my own pages up behind, so they can run back with any news or messages. I'm concerned about you, though. Can you manage, on your own? Just for a few hours?"

"Yes, I can." Ah. There was her voice, come out of hiding. All it took was outrage, apparently, a deep offence. "I am these people's ambassador; they came to me for shelter and protection. This is their land, and my house. Of course I can manage." And, to be fair, she was very much not on her own. So many people here, both hers and Vivi's, and half their friends besides. Between them all, they'd leave her with nothing at all to manage, if she allowed it.

Which she would not, no. These were her guests, hers, and her compatriots too. A bolt from the blue, which had shaken her so; but a blessing above all, survivors. Hopefully a blessing.

"Go," she said, rising to her feet, shaking her head at Vivi's mute offer of assistance. "Talk to the emperor, and whoever else you need to at court. Send me word, whatever you can arrange. When I know what's happened to bring these people here, I'd like to see him myself; but we will need clothes, supplies—oh, everything. You saw how little they had. Toys for the children. I'd like a doctor here to check them over. And—"

And she didn't know quite where that sentence was headed, what she needed more, there was so much. Vivi smiled, stretched up to kiss her, and patted her lightly on the shoulder.

"You'll be fine. Say all that to Ash and Alder, and see how quickly they can magic everything together. Then say it again to our friends, let them enjoy themselves running around the city to gather up what they can. I'll do the same at court, because too much will be better than not enough, and something in my stomach wants to tell me that there will be need for more, whatever we collect today. I think this is a beginning, not the end of a journey. Not even for those poor people."

So did Malance. She nodded, and watched Vivi walk away, whistling uncouthly to summon her pages to heel. Those weren't imperial prodigies, just the children of family friends that Vivi had taken under her imperious wing; but to be trained by Vivi was probably the next best thing, on the whole.

Of course Vivi had to go. Malance had understood that much from the outset. Nevertheless, she would miss her presence badly. Vivi was a daily revelation, constantly uncovering more facets to her character, always with a steely core beneath. Without her—well. Malance didn't lack for steely-cored people about her. She looked around, and there was one of them now, waiting to be used.

"Ash, good. Tell me, did our guests opt for baths, or for breakfast?"

"Baths first, lady, and breakfast after. They are hungry, I believe, but they have been hungry for many days now, and can wait. They do very much want to feel clean again."

"Good." She would have made the same choice. "What about a change of clothes?"

He smiled. "Alder is rummaging, lady." Which seemed to be a way to say *Everything's under control. Where Alder rummages, there is no need to follow.*

"Good," again. "Tell her to ... rummage ... in our suite, if there is need of anything in our sizes. Vivi has a ridiculous number of clothes," and her own collection had been growing steadily, these latter days.

Again, that soft elastic smile. It came and went. "It's always easier to ask forgiveness than permission, lady. Your apartments will have been the first place she raided."

Malance laughed, unexpectedly delighted with them both. "When they've bathed," which would be some time yet; that was a lot of water to be heated and carried up, a lot of bodies to be scrubbed, and she wasn't sure how many tubs she had, "they'll want a quiet room, where they can all be together. What state is the conservatory in, I wonder?" It was her favourite room in the house, and the most perilous: one she never went in. She'd had it locked last night; it was too alluring and too dangerous, especially for drunken young adventurers. Built of wood and glass and iron, it had been least protected from the weather and neglect, first to rot. Already a number of the higher windows had crashed to the tile floor, during winter storms. As far as she was aware, the shattered glass was still there.

One more time, that smile; she couldn't quite tell if he were more pleased with himself or with her. "It's being swept and cleaned as we speak, lady. Only with cold water, I'm afraid; all the hot has been spoken for."

"I'm sure it has. Oh, but what am I thinking of? You can't serve them there. That's the point, it isn't safe. Nor for the servants, either. Call them out of there, Ash."

"Lady," and this time the smile was some part for himself and some part for Vivi, seemingly, "her highness told us days ago that she wanted the conservatory back in commission. It wasn't ready yesterday, or I would have told you then; but I did have men up on ladders, working from the outside. There is much more to be done in there, but no more glass is going to fall, that much I'm certain of."

Imperial pages, retired or given away or still dogging the emperor's heels: they were all conniving creatures, wholly given over to working behind people's backs and holding secrets. "Didn't I tell you to keep nothing from me, ever again?"

"Yes, lady, and we never will again. But the ... holding ... happened before that, and there really hasn't been time since to tell you everything that we've been doing with the house, or to consult you about what else you might desire, if we can achieve it. And—well, her highness does love to surprise people."

"I know she does. But you two are *mine*, you answer to me first and her highness second. If she tries to involve you in any more schemes and stratagems, tell her that I have forbidden it, unless she discusses it with me first, whatever it is. Is that clear this time?"

"Yes, lady."

Malance laughed, and boxed his ears lightly. "Oh, don't look so forlorn about it! I'll let her talk me into allowing one surprise on my birthday, and one at each solstice, and you two can conspire with her all you like. If you're *very* good, I might allow the equinoxes also. But right now, I do want to know everything that's going on in my own home. Even if Vivi would rather keep it to herself." She would swallow Malance whole, otherwise. Her and all her people. *Hers.* "Now," she went on, "let's go and see how much you've done in the conservatory, and whether it truly is safe yet. Think of little children, running about all over. I do *not* want accidents and blood. Especially blood."

"No, lady. Especially with the grouting in that condition. It would soak through to the beams beneath, and the whole floor could go."

She snorted, considered swatting him again, understood that he had certainly already squirmed through all the underspaces to confirm that the floor actually was safe, and merely said, "Bad boy. Heel."

And heel her he did like a trained dog, like a page, as she stalked ahead.

V

SEVEN

You're going to need more wine

"**M**adam, we failed."

This was ... she didn't actually know quite how long later. She had inspected the conservatory after her poor weary boys were done with all their sweeping and scrubbing, and pronounced herself satisfied: the exiles could have this space for their own, as long as they needed it. Until they were ready to confront the world again. She had no idea how long that might take, or what form it might assume. What did you do, when your life and land were lost to you? How did you start again? She had simply stayed where she was and let things happen to her, of the emperor's kindness. These people had fled across half the world to be here; she wouldn't blame them if they didn't want to go out of the door for months. Or ever, in all honesty. Well, at least there was plenty of room.

Once the conservatory was furnished with tables and chairs and extra cushions for the children, places laid and everything ready for what might be a protracted meal, though it could hardly be called breakfast any more, Malance had asked for a pot of tea and settled by the stove to wait. Not that the stove was really necessary at this time of

146

year, as the city turned towards its summer heat. Ash had felt that the warmth and glow of hot coals would be comforting to travellers worn almost past bearing, so he'd burned some paper to be sure that the flue was functioning, then had Amil clean out the grate and fetch kindling, fetch coals, build and light a fire. She'd been inclined to tell her boy to take a nap afterwards, he looked so dragged down; but that was doubtless half his own fault, revelling half the night with Triman when he should have been sleeping. And she was beginning to understand that the pages now stood between herself and her other people; it would be bad for discipline and bad for tempers, bad for the whole house if she started undercutting their work. Sending boys to bed in the middle of the day, that sort of thing.

So she'd let Amil go with no more than a smile of sympathy and a pat on the arm, and sat down, and had really done nothing since, except stare through fresh-washed glass at the garden's wild rampage, her mind churning uselessly over things she didn't know. Why were there refugees here, so far from home? And why now, what had happened to drive them all this way? Nothing good, she was certain of that. They hadn't come to fetch her back in glory.

The emperor had warned her, to some extent. *News from home, that may go hard with you.* Whatever it was, he'd known it then, or at least anticipated it. Now she thought these people had brought it to her door.

In twos and threes—family units, she supposed, more or less—Ash and Alder brought the newcomers down to her. She rose to greet each as they came, in their wet hair and borrowed clothes—she recognised a few of those, her own and Vivi's and the boys' best party clothes too, looking somewhat foolish on a somewhat older man—and a sudden shyness that was like a breeze from home. She too had been this way when she first came here, a country girl in the city of the world.

Well. She had learned, and so she hoped would they. And if not, they could simply shelter with her and avoid the city entirely. This was sacred ground; here if anywhere, they should be safe. They must be safe.

The children, she thought, would be first to settle and first to explore. There were three of them, bright-eyed little things, tired now but even so, sitting up and staring around, asking whispered questions that their parents couldn't answer.

She made sure that they all ate well, helping the pages serve the food herself, despite their outraged glances and murmured pleas that they could manage, lady, thank you very much, and perhaps she should sit and eat a little herself, they could fetch a plate to her if she only...

Malance ignored them haughtily, treasuring this moment: a tableful of her own people, talking together in her own tongue, needing help that she could give them, with her own hands, yes. She practised remembering their names, and made guesses at their trades and status, winning soft laughs once or twice, which she counted as a victory from people as exhausted as this.

And when they were done, when the last satisfied trencherman pushed their plate away, she gently extracted their leader from the table, "Master Richmont, come and speak with me awhile," as she and he and all of them had been waiting all this time for her to do.

She settled him next to her place by the stove, in a chair that Ash had fetched already. Alder brought them a light and fruity wine, tingling gently on the tongue, and a plate of biscuits that she placed expressively by Malance's elbow with something that could almost be called a glare, an order, *eat those*. If such a thing were not unthinkable 'twixt page and mistress. Malance glared back, and took a biscuit. At court they would be dipped into the wine, she knew, and swallowed whole; she preferred to crunch and chew them dry, for the crisp tart bite of them between her teeth, and a sip of wine to follow.

"Now, Master Richmont. Your people will prefer that we leave you all alone for a while, I know," and her pages had better do the same, or trouble would ensue, "so please, can you tell me briefly what has brought you here, to Feremendas, to me?"

"Madam," he said, though it sounded odd when he was twice her age, "we failed."

And then said nothing more for a minute, till she thought she'd need to nudge him again; and then lifted his head though he still wouldn't look at her, and gazed into the fire, and said,

"We built an army of exiles, we who had escaped the country. We had help, money, shelter, even men from the lands around, who feared the same treatment our fair Verantha had. You do not know how bad it's been there, madam, horrendous; but we were determined to take it back. Aye, even from Clath. We thought we could drive them out. It was our land; we knew it, hill and rock and gully; they knew nothing. We thought the people left behind would rise to help us when we came. We thought...

"Oh, the heavens only know what we thought, madam. We were dreamers, not soldiers. Clath won Verantha because they had real fighting men, in real numbers; we were few, ill-trained, ill-armed. They destroyed us, of course."

"And so you fled," she murmured, wanting to take his hand, except that she couldn't possibly, "and came in search of refuge, which you have found with me and mine."

"Madam, there is more," and his gaze dropped down to his hands again, where he held them clenched between his legs. "We ... scattered, more than fled. We thought we could hide among the people, in the mountains, in the city, and fight them little by little: burn their stores, kill their leaders, make their soldiers frightened to leave camp. Let them have nothing good from their conquest, and so unsettle them till they would want to leave. We would even burn our own crops and go hungry ourselves, to deny them bread of ours.

"We did this, all of this—and in response, they burned the city."

That was it, that was all he had to tell her. It was enough.

There was only one city, and she had loved it all her life, except that she had loved the idea of Feremendas more.

Verantha-city—they were not an imaginative people, hers, at least when it came to names—sat at the joining of two river valleys, a city of bridges and views and wild rushing waters. There were fine stone buildings, to be sure—the Council chambers, and the First Light temple, and the houses of their most prosperous merchants on whose behalf she had supposedly come to the seat of empire, although really it had been all and entirely for herself—but most of the city was wood, old wood. It would have burned like tinder.

"Did they, did they *warn* you?"

"Oh yes, madam. That they did. They told us a day previous, so that everyone had just time enough to panic and abandon everything and flee far enough, just far enough. And then they waited for the mountain wind in the morning and set fires all through, on every bank. We hadn't got far enough away, not to see that. Not to stop and watch. All Verantha watched Verantha burn. There was ... nothing left. Nowhere to go. The gods alone know where everybody went. We," meaning his little group at last, "found our way to Nieman-port in Harl, and there was a ship ready to sail. I think we would have gone anywhere, but it was coming here, and we knew that you were here, still keeping our name alive—that had been heartening news, madam, and thank you for it—and the master proved willing to give us passage although we had no money. He was coming anyway, he said, and if we could provide for ourselves he could make room for us, and so he did."

And so they'd come here, in some cramped malodorous hold, with precious few stores to their name; and so arrived hungry and filthy with it, nothing but seawater and no soap to wash with. If he'd been more generous, she would have seen that the master and his owners were recompensed a fair price for the voyage. As things stood, though, they shouldn't see a penny piece from her. Perhaps a letter, though, to tell them so.

And one thing more: "You said you went to temple first, and they sent you away?"

"Yes, madam. That was a bitter turn, where we had looked for succour. But the priests were all Clath, and would have none of us."

Oh. Of course. That was one problem with sharing a religion and a history with neighbouring kingdoms that had become an empire in all but name, young and dangerous and acquisitive, hungry for land. Like any Veranthan, like everyone that side of the mountains, Malance had been raised an observant First Light devotee. The day their fellow worshippers had invaded her country—or at least the day the news had spread through Feremendas, though no doubt the emperor had known it first—she had gone to temple one last time, broken her medallion of faith and cast the shards of it on the high altar. She'd never crossed the threshold since. Even then, even here, the bulk of the priests had been from one or another of the kingdoms of Clath. No doubt they had been quietly annexing the religion as they more brutally annexed their neighbours, working to insert Clathians in key positions all across the world.

Of course they would have turned Veranthans away. They would have done it anyway, no doubt, but—oh! *Oh!* The First Light temple stood hard by the bridge where they had encountered Clath; and one traditionally went to temple on foot and alone, if one had a commission for the priests, a plea to the heavenly powers, a bargain to offer either one. Did she beg the priests, or bully them, or instruct them? It didn't matter, it hadn't mattered. Clath had known Veranthans were coming, and she had gone there to ensure their unwelcome, knowing where they would find their way first thing.

"Some kind soul told us how to find you, and a few more kept us on the right path, though the way was long."

"And so you are here now," she said, "and have come home. This is Verantha, now." Had she lost all hope of recovering her country? Yes, probably she had, she thought. There was a terminal sorrow building in her chest. "Rest, and recover. Eat and grow strong again, teach and treasure your children, hold Verantha in your hearts as I will in mine. Thank you for keeping faith in a time of despair, and for bringing all these with you. I want to talk to all of them, and learn their stories, and I will; but I do have other duties,"— was that a joke, or simply a lie?—"and must leave you for a while now. Sit quiet and be comfortable. Tomorrow will be a better day to think about your future. Anything you want, any time, you have only to ask," and one or the other of her appalling pages would be here on constant duty, to see to that. She had no need to tell them so. They were apparently lurking within earshot, even though she had spoken softly; and they could always lurk with purpose, gathering up used crockery or playing peek-a-boo with little children. At any rate, they both glanced across at her and nodded as one, to say they would take care of that. Really, there was something distinctly troubling in their synchronicity. She must remember to ask Vivi if there were some occult practice involved in pagery, or if they all merely learned to think so very alike that it only looked like mind-reading.

Just now she was annoyingly grateful, not to have to issue orders. She nodded back as she rose, with Master Richmont lurching to his feet beside her.

"No, please, do sit. We are dreadfully informal here," *and you are twice my age, sir.* "It's such a relief, after the rigours of court. Vivi is of the blood royal, and I swear you'll find her down on hands and knees playing hide-and-seek as readily as Alder there. Oh, on the matter of court: the emperor will wish to see you, I am sure, when you've recovered from the journey. He'll want to hear first-hand," even though he knew already, "just what Clath has done in Verantha. You will need better clothes than these, but I'm sure those are incoming already"—if her pages had had anything to do with it, she was sure, not to mention Vivi; and if not, another visit to Lirian's was certainly in order and she could buy them clothes that were actually made to fit and hadn't been worn before, and make the emperor pay for those too, oh yes—"and I promise I will be there with you," in case it was an ordeal, "and the princess Vivyana too." The emperor wouldn't dare be difficult, not in both their faces. Hah! Moral superiority was apparently a thing that could work not only with pages, but with emperors too.

When she left the Veranthans to themselves, she found that Vivi had indeed sent one of her own pages back, as promised. He had sweated through his livery and was still panting, slumped in a chair, newly arrived and full of news.

"Lady, her highness desired me to tell you that his grace is fully aware of recent developments and new arrivals,"—of course he was—"and that he was taking steps to assist you in your current needs, and those which may develop in the days and weeks to come." Oh. That meant something more was on its way. Of course he knew more than she did, even now; and of course he wouldn't tell her directly, but at least he was willing to help. "And that her highness will be kept at the palace a while longer, and may not be home until nightfall or later," making things happen, no doubt, sweeping through the palace like a whirlwind, like an imperial page, to ensure that all his grace's requests were met forthwith and in

153

full measure, "but that, uh, she loves you and misses you and wishes she could be here with you instead."

The poor infant—what was he, fourteen? maybe?— flushed scarlet as he delivered that, no doubt word for word as Vivi had meanly screwed it into him. She was a brute, and he didn't deserve that. She didn't deserve him, and Malance would tell her as much when she finally came back. *Home*, she had said, had told him to say. That was lovely in her.

Malance ruffled the boy's wet and sticky hair, beaming upon him in affection with all pages and messengers. "Thank you, Falen. Now you take yourself off and—no, wait." There was Estar, passing through the hall; and she had Vivi's own word for it, that no page could ever be body-shy. She wasn't quite so sure about Estar, but the girl would need to learn. "Estar, take Falen here down to the scullery, strip him raw and rub him down with a rough towel. He's run a long way fast, and he's near done now. Treat him as the stable lads would treat a horse who's been ridden hard, don't be gentle with him. Let him sip some water, but beat him if he gulps. Then when he's cool, leave him to wash himself—warm water, mind—while you fetch him a fresh livery and put this one to soak. And after all of that, see if Farl can turn up something nice to eat. He's a boy, he's bound to be hungry."

"Yes, lady." Estar looked a little overwhelmed, but Malance did very much want to integrate Vivi's people with her own, and they had come from vastly different backgrounds, so she hoped that making them awkwardly intimate with each other might help hurry things along. Falen seemed to take it in his stride, even when Malance personally hauled him to his feet and pushed him into Estar's grip. He was probably used to being manhandled—womanhandled—and treated like an overheated horse. She was tolerably sure that Farl would make the process worth the pains, for both of them. She was also tolerably sure that Estar would scrub the boy down herself, rather than trust him to do a thorough job while she was busy elsewhere. It was all good. Though she did still want Vivi back, and making free with one of her pages was a sudden reminder of that.

She wanted—no, not that: she *needed*—to mourn Verantha-city that she had loved, where she had been a child and a youth; and she would do that, alone and in the company of her fellow Veranthans. And she would help them come to accept that this really did spell the end of their homeland, and they would do the same for her, and they would weep together for all that had been lost.

At the same time, something in her was a constant gentle thrill, at having even these few of her compatriots in the house. She was thinking in her own language again, easily, instinctively, after years without. Perhaps she might dream in it tonight.

She went into the reception room, and found what remained of last night's party, the small cluster of friends who had still not gone off in search of their own lives. Matti was playing music, of course, his fingers still quick and sharp even if his head was dull and heavy; others were talking, lounging together—Colan lying full-length on a sofa with his head in Sherra's lap, while she played with his hair: that was unexpected and interesting, news to be passed on later, when Vivi came home—or simply sitting quietly, being alone in company. Felid was still ferrying coffee up from the kitchens; this crew had a limitless capacity, she knew.

"People," she said, and everyone was abruptly sitting up, looking at her, paying attention. They'd been waiting for this. "I need your help."

"We know." That was Sherra, smiling at her. "That's why we stayed, those of us who could. What can we do?"

Stay longer. That was her first thought. The Veranthans would need time alone, to come to terms with where they were and what now lay ahead. So would she, private time with Vivi, and also time alone. Just now, though, she wanted people about her, support: people to plan with, people who'd have ideas of their own. These people.

Aloud, she said, "Vivi is out scouring the court and the city, so I expect we'll be inundated soon with clothes and bedding and such. Even so, anything you can spare—but more than that. There are children who need playing with, and teaching. Adults too: none of these people speak more than a few words of Feremendan. They'll want music,"— Matti nodded—"and company. They'll need guides around the city. They'll need to *do* things, and they won't know what to do. They will never have lived with servants before," *like half of you,* "they won't know how to ask for things; they've certainly never encountered a city like this. Verantha was a, a jewel, but Feremendas is a crown. They'll need everything *explaining* to them, how things work here. They need rest now, time to settle, but they'll need to have *fun,* and they won't know where to find it, and, and..."

She wanted to make things perfect for them, now that they'd arrived; and of course she couldn't do that, but she was trying to anticipate their every need before they found it out, and of course she couldn't do that either, and—

And there were strong hands on her shoulders pushing her down into a chair, impossibly strong fingers digging into muscles that had forgotten how to yield; and that was Matti, who had more than one magic in his touch. He could make music from anything, anything at all, and he could also make a person melt into a puddle, he could take her whole body apart from the outside in and then put her back together again, new-made and dizzy with it.

Even he couldn't do both at once, of course. She hadn't noticed when the music stopped, and she hadn't seen him move from there to here. She really should try to stay alert.

If she wasn't careful, he'd put her to sleep right here under his hands. He'd done it before. She let him manipulate her knots a minute or two longer, for the sheer relief of it, and then shook her head and shrugged him off. He chuckled and went back to his seat, to his music. The others had been quiet while Matti worked on her; now those first strummed notes acted like a cue, *your turn now, I've done my bit.*

"Got it, Mal. We're the entertainment, the colour, the interest." Sherra again. Colan's head was still in her lap, but now he was facing the room, facing her, bright and engaged.

"Do what we do," he said in that deep bass voice that could still surprise her when he was all bone and whipcord and none too tall and surely the powers must have meant him for a tenor. "That's what you're saying, isn't it? Do what we would have done anyway, but be here more, to do it more? Of course we'll take them out and about, of course we'll show them what the city has to offer, as soon as they're ready for it. If they're anything like me—"

"—no, petal, don't worry, nobody's like you," Sherra interrupted, petting him on the head while he ignored her magnificently and carried on regardless, and why in the world hadn't Malance seen this coming, how could she have *missed* it?—

"—then once they've got their feet under them they'll want to see everything, try everything, taste everything. This is what we're *for*, Mal, this is what art *means*. It's the interaction between the viewer and the maker and the piece, and in this instance the piece is a few hours of time and the raw material is the city itself, and—"

And he'd drawn himself up in his excitement, and Sherra reached out a long and lazy arm to pull him down again, to settle him again, to say, "There now, petal, people don't want to hear your nasty dreary lecture on what art means, they want to discuss having fun with new people." And then, to her, "He's very sorry, Mal, and he promises not to go off like that again. He actually does know how to enjoy himself, I find."

At which Colan blushed awkwardly, and they all made a very conspicuous point of looking away and not laughing or cheering at all, just to fire him up a little further. Because they were his friends, and they loved him, and it was a treat to have the chance to do so.

Malance had actually blushed a little with him. She was still Veranthan under all her city veneer, and more so today than yesterday—still thinking in Veranthan, yes, for all that she was talking in Feremendan now; it was a trick she'd acquired early, switching inwardly and outwardly as needed—and Veranthans didn't so much as hint in open conversation about matters of the bedroom. They weren't pious, particularly, but they were as shy in the world as they were sheltered from it, quiet and industrious and keeping close to home. For the most part. She'd always been an exception to that last.

"He's right, though," Sherra continued, earning Malance's silent gratitude and another blush from Colan. "This is exactly what we're for. We'll take them out and we'll bring them safe home again, until they're ready to go out on their own; and meantime we'll try to spend as much time as possible here with them, swapping languages and stories, crafts and songs. We'll practically live here, those of us who can, and you'll be thoroughly fed up with us before we're done. It'll be like a constant rolling party."

"You're going to need more wine," Hern said drily from the hearth, and they all nodded earnestly and started to list what else they'd be needing, most of which seemed to be alcohol in quantity. Wanting to put on at least a show of taking them seriously, as they were putting on a show of being serious, Malance glanced back in certain knowledge that there would be a page—Alder, meaning that Ash had stayed with their guests for now; no doubt they already had a roster, communicated with a bare glance of eyes and perhaps the twitch of a finger—standing behind her taking notes and nodding solemnly. Even though they were all of them playing a game here, Malance had a sudden suspicion that everything on that list would be in the house by nightfall,

158

and the bills sent to the palace. When the pages played, it was that kind of game.

Well, good. Her friends deserved reward for what they were proposing, and he entirely deserved to pay for it. He'd known what was coming and decided not to tell her, for whatever complex reasons he held in the labyrinth of his mind, weighing this against that in a thousand subtle permutations. Everything these days—her days—always, always came back to Clath, Feremendas and Clath, the old deep-rooted empire and the greedy young pretender. Just now she was an element in that struggle, and possibly a weapon to his hand although she couldn't quite see how. He would offer his protection to her and to her people, for as long as it was expedient; if he saw a necessary sacrifice in this long game, he wouldn't hesitate to make it. Very well. Let him pay her bills, then, so long as he was using her.

Now she did feel supported, with her friends around her and her household at her back. She sat back and relaxed at least a little, listening as they tossed suggestions back and forth, where they might take newcomers, what they might do together. What to bring the children, how best to teach Feremendan to them and to their elders. In groups, or one-to-one? In separate lessons, or just ongoingly? Perhaps they could make little signs of useful words, write "mirror" on the mirror and "door" on all the doors, so they could learn what those words looked like subconsciously, before ever they were drilled in all their letters...

Malance didn't contribute to the discussions. She told herself vaguely that she was holding herself in readiness for when they wanted her, when they had questions or more demands. Really, though, she was only sitting, letting all this wash by her, letting the morning go. Her world was new now, new in all directions, and she needed to encompass that and didn't quite know how.

A table appeared at her elbow, a tray was set firmly upon it: a glass of her favourite bittersweet fruit juices, a plate of bread and sausage and cheese, olives, tomatoes, fruits. Apparently she was required to eat more than a couple of biscuits. She looked up, expecting to see Alder, but it was Ash now.

"I didn't ask for—" She gestured, twitchily.

"No, lady. Her highness said we were to make sure that you ate, and we were to be the judges of how much was enough. She said your judgement wasn't to be trusted, when you were upset. And his grace had told us much the same, before he gave us to you. He said he'd be angry if we let you lose more weight. Of course we look to you now, not to him, but..." An eloquent shrug said the rest, that he was still emperor and the ultimate authority above them. Not above her, not technically—but in practice, of course he was. She was subject entirely to his whim. He could close this house, revoke her status and give her over to Clath with no notice, if he chose. She didn't suppose that he would, she thought he found her entirely too useful a tool, but even so. He still could.

And the pages knew it as well as she did, and they had a careful path to tread between her wrath and his, between duties owed and service demanded. She was no longer quite so sure that they served as his spies here, or not at least his willing spies; but any commands given them while they were still his own, those would still have currency. So they would assert, at least. Moral superiority, yes.

She ate an olive.

And then another, because in fact they were rather good; and a slice of cheese against the sharpness, but the cheese was sharp too, so then a slice of bread.

And then she paused, glowered up at Ash and said, "All right, but we'll need the same for—"

And cut herself off abruptly, seeing her boys already bearing up platters from the kitchen. And sighed, and went back to eating her way through this delicious plate. To please Vivi, and to please the emperor. Definitely not to please the pages, though. No. They were mere instruments of authority. Vivi used them as blithely as the emperor did, as blithely as he used Malance and no doubt Vivi too. So should she.

Well, perhaps not Vivi, no. But she would use herself, she would use herself up entirely if it came to that, and certainly she would use the pages. She only needed to decide just what to do, and what to have them do.

Except to fill her plate again, from Amil's platter. That was a given.

It was apparently a day for unexpected meals, at unexpected times. Later in the day, she and the boys were sorting through a cartload of used clothes that had manifested unexpectedly in the stable yard, courtesy of Vivi, when Alder appeared at her elbow.

"Please, lady, the Veranthans ask if you would be so good as to join them for their dinner? They'll be sitting down in half an hour, so that does just give time to wash and dress." Meaning, clearly, that it gave time for Malance to be scrubbed and groomed to Alder's exacting standards, if she went up right this minute.

Malance gave one startled glance at the sky. "It can't even be six o'clock yet—oh. No, I'm an idiot. Of course they'll want to eat at sundown, we always do. Always did." Even in Verantha-city, they had kept country hours. Here in Feremendas, Malance had grown slowly accustomed to dining later; in the company of her friends, that could mean very late indeed.

Perhaps she shouldn't have eaten so much, earlier. Perhaps she should have *thought*.

"Very well, Alder. Please tell them I'll be honoured, of course—and have Estar take a jug of hot water up to my rooms, will you?"

"It's there already, lady." Of course it was. "I'll be up in just one minute to help you."

"Oh, but the maids—"

"The maids are busy, lady. There was a delivery of new bedding earlier"—courtesy of the pages' own contacts, no doubt, since she didn't say so—"so all our guests' beds are to be made up again." There was a satisfaction in her voice that she made no effort to hide. Neither page had been happy with the previous hurried, haphazard arrangements, ancient linens embroidered with the arms of ambassadors of long ago and stored in dusty presses all this time. "You go ahead"—*right now, no dallying, lady*—"and I'll attend to you myself."

That sounded rather grim, in all honesty. Still, there was clearly no help for it. She was being managed, she knew; it was probably just as well. So she laid down the silk waistcoat she'd just been admiring, and gazed sternly at Amil and Felid. Especially at Felid.

"No trying anything on as soon as my back is turned, do you hear me? These are for the refugees, not for pretty boys to play in." Two submissive smiles in return, and murmurs of "Yes, lady". They did like it when she called them pretty. And she did understand the temptation; she'd been *fondling* that waistcoat, rather than assessing its usefulness or setting it aside. That was the trouble, inevitably, with rummaging for clothes at the palace., The fabrics and craft were often astonishing, and equally often the garment would be hopeless for day-to-day wear, which was what her newcomers most needed.

"You'd best hurry; her highness is safe to be sending more, and I would like everything sorted by tonight, so that our guests are clear about what there is available." Indeed, Vivi was safe to overdo her commission by some extravagant measure. She'd be enjoying herself hugely, no doubt, bullying friends and relatives into stripping out last year's wardrobes. And of course giving up as much on her own account, no kind of hypocrite she.

The Veranthans would be astonished by some of the clothes given up; they were like to be repelled, she feared, by

at least as many. They were a modest people, disliking gaudy
display and excess. She remembered how shocked she'd
been herself when she came to Feremendas as a gawky teen-
ager with a trunk full of sober woollen dresses, first by some
of the streetwear common throughout the city, and then
again—a different kind of shock, but shock none the less—by
the luxury and indulgence of court dress. She had eventually
found or else developed in herself a taste for bright colours
and silky fabrics, but that had been sheer self-defence. With
friends like hers, and a life like hers—oh, and Vivi, above
all with Vivi about—she'd been given no choice else. And
she could buy the clothes she loved cheaply in the markets,
and her needle-wise friends were never loth to make adjust-
ments for fashion or for length, or even take garments apart
altogether and rebuild them into something that would just
about pass at the palace, with the addition of a few jewels
that looked better than they were, so long as she kept to the
shadows.

Malance hurried up to her suite now in a sudden panic,
because Alder was sure to have chosen already what she felt
her mistress ought to wear, and if it wasn't wrong in one way
then it would surely be wrong in another. When she came
into her dressing-room, though, she found the promised
hot water waiting on the dresser, a cozy little fire burning in
the grate—and the oldest, her favourite, the very *best* of the
dresses she'd arrived with so long ago, laid out ready on a
chair. Kind and clever-fingered Majoli had rooted it out of
her trunk and made it anew for her a couple of years back,
retaining its modesty while reshaping it by some witchery of
stitching until it moulded itself to her full-grown body like a
sheath, so clingy that it ought to have been indecent and yet
somehow was not. Some muted ribbon at the seams in the
same dull rich green, embroidery at the neckline, a length
of gold chain at the waist, and it was abruptly a masterpiece
of innocent allure. She had meant to change into it after

court, that night she set out to seduce Vivi, if she hadn't been abducted and borne away.

She was still standing there caressing it gently, remembering its every best occasion, when Alder blew into the room like a strong and urgent wind.

"Lady, we need to hurry. You'll be late else, and they want to say a prayer as the sun goes down, but you know they won't if you're not there to share it."

"How did you—?"

"I asked, of course," with busy fingers already at her buttons.

Passively Malance suffered herself to be undressed and washed, dried before the fire and dressed afresh from the skin up; and as Alder dropped the dress over her head and helped ease her into it, she tried again. "Alder, how did you know...?"

"Know what, lady? Oh—the frock? It seemed ... suitable."

"It's perfect. I think I'd hug you, if it wasn't bad for discipline. And if you honestly didn't terrify me just a little bit."

Alder had her in front of the cheval glass now; she peeped over Malance's shoulder so that their eyes met, and grinned widely as she smoothed the tight wool to banish the least hint of a wrinkle. "That's my job, lady. Sometimes we even have to terrify his grace, just a little bit. But actually I think the frock is lovely. It's so discreet, and yet..."

"I'll pass that on to Majoli, next time I see him. He'll be delighted it's still at work, and still working. Discreet, and yet... is exactly what he was going for. Exactly what I asked for. What I thought I needed," she added, a reminiscent smile tweaking at her lip. Then, briskly, for the child did not need an opportunity to ask about that, never mind an invitation, she went on, "Shoes, then—the soft boots, yes, those are Veranthan too, how in the world did you—no, never mind—and I think I'm ready. Am I ready?" She'd already learned to defer such decisions to a page, either one.

"No, lady. Not till I've done something with your hair."

Alder thoroughly disapproved of her hair, just as Vivi did. Perhaps that too was part of their training, the appropriate stylings for ladies of the court? Or just a general aesthetic sense that permeated the palace? If necessary, Malance would put her foot down, with the pages as firmly as she'd had to do with Vivi. She would not, would *not* be growing it out as they wished, so that they could play with it as they wished. It was her hair, and she meant to keep it convenient.

Still: a minute's work with brush and cool, confident fingers; a rather lovely cabochon stone with green marbling, set in gold with a brooch pin, which it had never occurred to Malance to clip into her hair that way, just behind the ear; and she was obliged to admit that she did look exactly as she wanted to: a holder of high office, yes, in a great city, yes, and yet very, very Veranthan.

"No, no more jewellery." The dress didn't need it, her compatriots wouldn't like it, she didn't want it—oh, except that one ring that Vivi had given her, which she snatched up belatedly and worked onto her thumb. Yes. Better now.

And so downstairs, and through the back hall to the conservatory, with Alder at her heels except when the girl slipped ahead to open a door for her so that she needn't interrupt her steady pace for a moment. One last door, and this one Alder bowed her through ceremonially before following her within. And there was Ash too, waiting by the sideboard, and no servants else because they would make these guests uncomfortable and the infants thought of everything, bless them.

And here, now, here were her people, her own people: dressed in borrowed clothing to be sure, but they had managed to find sober and sensible garb among all the glitter. They were standing at their places at table, waiting for her, waiting still—thank all the gods, or no, better yet, thank Alder—for sunfall, for the sunfall prayer. She wasn't late.

One chair stood empty, the place of honour, at the table's head; another at the foot, next to the children. Malance smiled, and took that one.

"Madam, please." Richmont gestured from the farther end of the table. "Take this."

She smiled, and shook her head. "On such a night as this, when I am privileged to welcome my own country-folk at last, and speak my own language, before I forget it altogether? No, Master Richmont. Not tonight. It's still our custom, here as at home, to leave one place empty for our friends missing or lost; tonight we must honour them all, and nowhere else at the table will suit. Besides," she added, with a very different kind of smile, "I have talked with you already, and shall again, I know. Tonight I want to talk with these," little awed faces blinking up at her, smiling cautiously, one by one, "and tell them about Feremendas and the fun we're going to have now that they're finally here, and learn their names, and try to teach them mine." She refused to be Madam Ambassador to her own people, and even Madam was too much. She had decided to infiltrate from the bottom up: once get the children calling her Malance, at her direct and public insistence, and their parents would follow suit soon enough.

The pages made friendly but unobtrusive serving staff, hitting just the right note for people accustomed to nothing grander than a tavern meal, and that not often. The food too was absolutely right. Not quite Veranthan—her own people didn't use so many spices, and someone would have to teach Farl how to make proper panbread—but it almost could have been. A stew rich in vegetables and beans, with meat for flavour more than bulk: venison, she thought. Certainly something that had lived wild, before the hunt had found it. Again, absolutely right. Even city Veranthans ate a lot of game from the mountains, and these people had probably not had the chance to taste any since they fled.

And then a plate of sweet pastries, which delighted the children, and Malance too. Nuts and honey, and the cardamom wasn't Veranthan but was delicious none the less, and apparently Farl too had uncanny knowledge he never should have had the chance to learn, because this was exactly the kind of way they liked to end their meals.

Well, she could interrogate her cook as to his sources later. Already she half expected "Lady, your pages told me what to do," or something similar. For now, she sent the children off with a cousin to have stickiness washed away, and consented now to move to the other end of the table. Ash brought coffee and Alder brought Helforth brandy, which more than made up for the one false note of the meal, that there had been no wine on the table. One thing the pages didn't know, at last: she scored that up as a victory, and looked forward to telling them later that Veranthan wine might not be known beyond its borders, but that was only because they never exported any. Their vineyards climbed the foothills of their land, and thrived in the late summer sun; like their favourite foods, their wine was rich and dark, a little gamey. People liked to claim it carried notes of juniper and thyme, from higher in the mountains, but Malance had never quite seen how that could be so, and lacked the palate herself to taste them. All she really knew was that a Veranthan table was rarely without a jug of wine constantly replenished, or else beer if they'd drunk all the wine.

Still, she'd decided not to destroy the pages utterly by asking for it, by having to ask. They would have shrivelled up from shame, and she didn't think she could do without them now. And here was the brandy, which they had thought to bring, and glasses for all who wanted; and now she and her compatriots could drink solemn toasts to what was gone, and toasts too to the future, unseeable as it was. Surely it must be better than their recent past.

Malance made a superstitious little sign under the table, which would have shocked the newcomers extremely.

Averting ill fortune was a matter of survival for the street children she'd learned it from, and sometimes for her too—the sound of a crossbow bolt: she had felt it physically against her skin as it ripped the air apart—and there was nothing more unlucky than assuming something better had to be on the way.

Now she sipped brandy and coffee alternately, and asked the questions she could not possibly have asked the children. About their journey, how long it had taken, how bad it was. Almost longer than they could bear, and almost worse than they could endure. That was what she'd been afraid of.

"Why here, though? Why come so far? You could have stopped so much sooner..."

"At first there seemed nowhere safe to stop. If Clath could swallow Verantha, they can swallow more. They want to swallow more. We only wanted to keep going. And once we were into Feremendan waters, well. There was only one place to come."

"Perhaps. You might have been made more welcome at First Light temples closer to the border," where Clath might yet be seen as a threat rather than the natural power in the church.

"Aye, but would we have found Verantha? At the last, madam, we came to you. We had heard that you at least were here," and it was a place to start. Yes. Now she had more than an embassy. Now she had, in its ridiculously small way, a country. Right here in her house.

V

EIGHT

A reminder of what is to be gained, and what lost

The city had known and loved Vivi long in all her aspects, page and princess and party girl.

Malance too it had taken to its expansive, appropriating heart: the sole survivor, the sad ambassador, the loneliest girl in the world. Empires rarely pity, but Feremendas could afford to sympathise, and so to cherish. And to watch, that went without saying. Even great imperial cities can relish their own kindness, take pride in their generosity, scrutinise the objects of their charity and welcome.

Malance did know this, aye, and understand it too. She had felt the eyes of the city on her, warm and complacent, ever since the emperor's appointment. She'd learned to live with it, and then to use it, to keep Verantha's name alive in all the city's news and rumour. She hadn't yet learned to ignore it, nor actively to enjoy it, as Vivi seemed to do.

Now, though, now the beloved and the cherished were together, and all the city was on fire with it. Verantha's sorrow eased, Vivi's passion embraced and satisfied: it was a story for the ages, and it had happened here, and Feremendas had seen it all. More, Feremendas had brought it into being, for how could it ever have happened else? Elsewhere?

Some bright spark decided early on that the new livery in the ambassador's household was a declaration: the green of Verantha married to the gold, for what other colour could represent the empire of the world, here in the city of the world, without trespassing on the emperor's prerogative? Vivi of course was actually entitled to a little imperial crimson, but all praise to her for choosing not to use it, not to seem to set herself above. Mere truth mattered nothing, in such a fever; already green and gold were the colours of the season. Those who couldn't afford whole new outfits—or even whole new wardrobes, for the more extravagant who loved to lead the throng—bought ribbons of both, and wore rosettes of them on their shoulders or their belts, and had their servants' tunics hemmed with them, to show the allegiance of their house to the couple of the moment.

Children seized happy hold of that same loyalty, highborn or low. Ribbons appeared everywhere, almost overnight, adorning everything from lamp-standards in the emperor's private gardens to bollards on the wharfs. Someone—they were assuming children again, but who knew?—had intertwined a lattice-weave all through the bars of the embassy's ironwork gates, which delighted Vivi so much that Malance told the pages to leave it there.

"And if it gets soiled, lady?"

"Replace it, of course. Embellish it, if you like. You can have both gates enamelled green and gold, if there's someone who can do that"—of course there was someone who could do that, and of course these two would know how to find them—"but put the ribbons back up afterwards."

Their colours might be suddenly indivisible and universal, and might mean *Verantha* now in a way they never really had before, but Malance felt that she hardly got to see Vivi in person from dawn to dusk and later yet. They were both of them not busy so much as overwhelmed, Malance at home and Vivi mostly in the palace, being a second voice for Verantha, exploiting all her contacts, all her wiles and all her charms. She was ruthless with herself, accepting every invitation that came her way, taking tea with a visiting delegation or wine with a court official, flattering royals and deceiving diplomats, sliding in and out of parties, almost as universal as a ribbon herself, and soon worn just as thin.

Really she was doing Malance's work for her, or the better half of it. Malance could hardly bear to tear herself away from the embassy, more days than not. Here was Verantha now, here were her Veranthans; much as she'd like to be at Vivi's side, being here simply mattered more. Besides, there was so much happening, so many changes daily, the mistress of the house really ought to be on hand. She was interpreting again, sometimes half the day, or so it seemed: her people's arrival had stirred more than her own small precious world. Visitors came daily from the court, from the palace, from other embassies; merchants came up from the city, and tailors, and craftsmen. Her friends did intercede as much as they were able, and she was grateful for it, but she was still the only one who could translate for either side. By end of day her tongue was tired and her throat was sore; she wouldn't have wanted to join Vivi at those parties even if she'd had the energy. And Veranthans were early to rise and early to bed, so of course the whole house was tilting that way now. More often than not, Malance was already in bed by the time Vivi came home at last.

Not tonight. Tonight the sun was barely down and already Vivi was home and here, in their suite, and all Vivi's people were fussing about the pair of them, dressing them, dressing their hair with jewels. Even Vivi's toes were adorned tonight with green and gold lacquer, where they peeped out from her sandals. She'd offered the same to Malance, and laughed at her when she declined.

"Vivi, I *can't*! I have to be all dignity tonight. You can make mischief, and needle people as you like. Not me."

"No, you're right. Fine. You be the spirit of Verantha, solemn and suffering and proud; I'll be the spirit of the empire, courteous and contemptuous and savage as necessary. Help Clath understand what she's facing here, and what she could bring down on herself."

Tonight was the date of Clath's soirée. Her Highness the Princess Vivyana had duly received her promised invitation; there was none for Verantha, inevitably, but the single invitation was for "Your Highness and Party," so *Party* was getting dressed alongside her highness, and wondering quite what the purpose of the evening was. Malance knew her own purpose, which was—as so often before, at court—merely to be there, to exist within that context, to represent her country. Even in the invader's own house, she would do that. She knew Vivi's purpose, which was to use her royal status and consequent invulnerability to act as an irritant in every way she could conceive. She still did not know Clath's. Nor who else had been invited.

Well, the shape of the evening would reveal itself, no doubt. And she did know that it hadn't been intended to wound her directly, for she hadn't been on the original invitation list. It might still be about Verantha, one way or another—or it might have been repurposed, once Clath knew that she was coming—but at least it hadn't been set up as an assault on her.

And they were going in as a team tonight, and making that point clear by dressing alike for the first time since Marmon's funeral. They had identical gowns, delivered by Lirian herself this morning. They had matching everything, toes apart, and all of it of course in green and gold. Malance wondered if she'd ever be allowed to wear anything else now. She knew the pages liked it when they matched her outfit, or rather when she matched theirs; and what the pages liked did tend to become the norm, sooner rather than later.

Apparently she need only think of them now, to have them appear out of nowhere. Here they were, smiling in quiet pleasure at everyone's uniformity, discreetly check-ing the maids' work to ensure that their charges would be a credit to the house. Embodying a sullen spirit of resist-ance, because she really didn't want to go tonight although she really had to be there, Malance made a gesture at them that was *extremely* rude in Verantha. Alder giggled, and Ash blushed. Ah, so they'd already learned that one, then. She'd need to be more inventive.

Wondering mildly just who in her house was introducing her pages to Veranthan obscenity—there were no teenagers in the group, and the children were still too young, surely?—she batted the last of the maids away and reached for Vivi's hand.

"Ready?"

Her lover nodded brightly up at her. "Ready."

"Damn you, you're actually looking forward to this, aren't you?"

A shrug of slender shoulders and, "Why not? Mystery and intrigue, good food, interesting company, an enemy to chal-lenge and bring down—it could be a splendid evening."

"It could be appalling. Dangerous, even." It occurred to Malance that Vivi had probably never felt unwelcome, any-where she'd been, in all her life.

"Perhaps. But if it is, we have each other for support, and all the city at our backs. If Clath makes a move against us, in her own house, with the city in this mood? I think she will regret it. And if she does it in the court, I think she will regret it even more. The emperor does *not* like his favourites being toyed with from malice. Nor his family either."

"I'm not really one of his favourites, though."

"Sweetling. Don't be ridiculous. Do you *know* how much we're costing him? Daily?"

As it happened, she did have a tolerably good idea. She was keeping a careful record of her own expenditures, and casually assuming twice those for Vivi.

"Yes, and do you know *why* he's paying everything? Daily, so that the merchants love us and keep on coming and coming? He's using me for something, Vivi," and his motives were frankly even more opaque than Clath's intents this evening.

"I know. He uses everyone, and yet we love him anyway. Come on, let's go and learn what tonight is all about. The more you need to hold my hand, the better. Make it obvious."

Hand in hand, then, they went down to the carriage in the yard. The pages jumped up behind, because no person of repute could go to such an event unattended. Malance sighed a little for the days when she could walk through the park or the city, quite alone and unconcerned, entirely unimportant. The emperor had put a first stop to those days, when he called her ambassador; a crossbow bolt had finished them entirely.

The Clathian embassy was quite uncomfortably close to her own, easy walking distance should she ever have a mind. Could she ever slip her multitude of watchers. It took almost no time at all by carriage, barely time enough to catch her breath and stiffen her spine, and try not to look as though she dreaded this quite as much as she did.

The pages leapt down, opened their doors and bowed them out. Malance regarded them suspiciously.

"Can I keep you two at my heels all evening, where I'll have you under my eye?"

"No, Mal, you cannot. That would be a shocking breach of etiquette, and a deep insult. One *brings* one's own people, but they hand one on to the host's people, who then attend one till the affair is concluded. Keeping your own servants with you is as good as saying you neither trust nor respect your host's service. Which in this case happens to be true, but nevertheless. You can't *say* it, even obliquely."

Malance sighed. "No, I suppose not. But—well, what *are* the infants going to do?"

"They're going to infiltrate the lower quarters and make themselves useful if they can, and talk to everyone and open every door and learn whatever there is to be learned. Don't worry, they've been fully briefed."

"That is exactly what I'm worrying about," and she was not actually joking in the least. An ambassador under the emperor's protection should be safe enough, even in a house that hated her; her servants belowstairs, on the other hand... Anything could happen, an accident in the kitchens, a rumpus in the servants' hall...

"Mal, they're imperial pages. They're untouchable."

"They're not, though. They're my pages now. And I don't trust them to keep out of trouble. Can I tell them just to stay in the carriage until we're ready to leave?"

"No, you really can't do that either. It would be another way to insult your host, and annoying for the stable lads besides. What you can do is stop fretting over a pair of imps who are perfectly capable of getting themselves out of any trouble that, I agree, they are liable to find themselves in. I trained them myself, you know, when they were babes in arms; I've trained with them since. I promise you, they're both carrying knives, and they're faster than a striking snake and more vicious than a cornered rat, though I'd hope they were smart enough not to need to fight. Hop back up, you two, and let Kinner carry you around to the yard and see to his poor horses. We," she said, tucking Malance's arm firmly through her own and heading for the stairs, "are not going to stand around in the cold any longer, quarrelling over nothing. Pride and dignity, remember? If you can't say something proud and dignified, just say nothing at all. I'm willing to do all the talking."

Side by side and arm in arm, then, they marched up the dozen steps to the tall, imposing door. This was her first time anywhere near the Clathian embassy, she hadn't even spied from the woods before; and she was disappointed to discover that the whole building was equally imposing. It was built in what she understood to be Clathian style, probably by Clathian craftsfolk, just as men and women had come from Verantha to build her own. Which was why hers was mostly wooden, and unnecessarily rambling, and somewhat plain, though it had been a masterpiece of their craft before it was allowed to decay.

This one by contrast stood bulky and angular, four-square against the world, brick walls with stone facings at the corners. Naturally it was larger than her own, too—which was no longer feeling quite so large, actually, now that she had her community of exiles living with her. She counted three upper storeys above the ground floor, no doubt with levels of kitchens and storage below. They could house an army, it seemed to her. Clath was expansionist, aggressive, demanding; perhaps they did. With or without the emperor's consent. Certainly not without his knowledge, though. If anything happened, he would be prepared to deal with it.

She didn't feel prepared at all, to deal with Clath tonight. Vivi was unstoppable, though, hustling them both past flaming torches and gentler lamps, past bowing servants at the door. Clath livery was white, apparently, entirely white, and she pitied their laundresses—unless it was just for tonight, just for her, because white was the colour of mourning and she had lost so much and Clath would lose no opportunity to remind her of that, whatever else this gathering was for.

Not that she needed reminding. And her mere presence here would remind Clath—not that she needed reminding—that in Feremendas at least, Veranthans were gathered in a place that was still Veranthan territory. It might be ridiculously tiny, but it was a needle under Clath's nail regardless. It was all Malance had—or, no, she was Verantha tonight; it was all Verantha had, then, so it had to be enough.

Apparently she had needed to remind herself about this. She nudged Vivi as they advanced into a grand hallway, and hissed, "Call me Verantha tonight, yes?"

"Already in hand," Vivi murmured, smiling sweetly. "No detail overlooked. They train us well, in page school."

They do, I know. You're always up to something, all you pages. Nevertheless: they were brought to a door, which was promptly opened to them by another liveried servant. He held out a silver salver; Vivi laid a card upon it. Malance held her breath.

The man took up the card, read it—and hesitated, turned his head a fraction, back towards Vivi. She nodded, marginally. His eyes focused on the card, he drew a deep breath and announced the new arrivals.

"Her Highness, the Princess Vivyana Feremend; and her consort, Her Excellency Malance Hermentine, Ambassador of Verantha!"

He bowed them through the door, stepped back, and closed it firmly behind them.

"They'll kill him for that," Malance muttered, believing it entirely.

"Not they. He is already making his way to the kitchen door. Kinner and the pages will be waiting for him in the stable yard, with a fresh livery: one of ours, of course. He is now our second coachman. They won't start a search for him till after we're gone, or they know we'd spread news of it all across the city. So we'll take him away with us, and give him sanctuary in Verantha. Don't worry, we'll find a use for him."

That wasn't actually what Malance was worrying about, just then.

"I can't believe that you, what, bribed a Clathian?"

"Extensively. Bought him, rather, I'd have said. But he has a girl, locally; and she has an elderly father under her care, which made him very interested when I spoke with him. And we're taking them both in too, obviously. They should be at the house by now."

"Vivi..."

"Hush. Here comes our hostess. She can't ignore me, and she can't swallow you. I told you, we're going to have fun tonight."

Here indeed was Clath, looming above Vivi.

"Highness. So glad you could come."

"Oh, we wouldn't have missed it. I am so very looking forward to finding out who else is here, and what we're all up to." She smiled innocently up, then inclined her head slightly and blinked encouragingly at Malance.

The two ambassadors were much of a height, so they could meet each other eye to eye, these rare occasions they could bear to meet at all.

"Clath." She couldn't help it, the name sounded like gravel in her mouth and felt as dreadful. As though it made her bleed every time she was obliged to utter it. It was as ugly as the allied kingdoms for which it stood. Once those had warred with each other; now they made common cause, to war on all their neighbours.

The woman's lips tightened. She couldn't demean herself in her own house, under the fascinated gaze of all those gathered here; nor could she let the name *Verantha* pass her lips, when her masters had declared it anathema, non-existent, gone from history as from the face of the world. She would flog her man to death for doing exactly that, if she caught him. In no conceivable case could she do it herself.

"Miss Hermentine," she managed at last. And then, "We are both ... unofficial, tonight."

"Verantha," Vivi said emphatically and loudly, "sees no way to be unofficial, within the very doors of the Clathian embassy. She wears her office wherever she goes, but here particularly. Here she can do nothing other than bear her proudest title."

"I ... see. Well, that title shall not pass my mouth; it is forbidden here. The man who announced you thus was ... misled, and shall be disciplined." There was something merely nasty in her, Malance felt. Perhaps it was the spirit of her country leaking through. It could be Malance's own prejudice, of course, she was honest enough to admit that— but she was certain too that she had measured a degree of pleasure in the woman's voice, at the prospect of the man's punishment. *Well, good luck finding him,* she thought. With her pages taking a hand, she was tolerably sure that man would simply vanish, as far as Clath was concerned.

"Moreover," Clath went on, "I am in hopes that you'll find my other guests too ... civilised to insult their host."

"By all means," murmured Vivi at her most honeyed, unless that should perhaps have been *honed*, "let us find out your other guests, and perhaps the reason for this gathering."

There was a step down into the room beyond the doorway, presumably so that everyone could see the newcomers as they were announced. Vivi had timed their arrival, Malance guessed, unfashionably late, safely the last to arrive, so that Clath would have been on edge all evening to know if they were coming at all, and so that the man Vivi had bought would have his best chance to get away unnoticed.

Vivi took the step, taking Malance's hand now to draw her after. This was certainly not the embassy's great hall, neither its grandest dining room. Formal, yes—witness the step, and its meaning—but almost intimate in courtly terms, room for two or three dozen at the most, and then only if there were no tables laid. Tall glassed doors at the far end offered a courtyard garden beyond, greenly glowing now with scores of lamps among the foliage.

Between Vivi and Malance and the garden were—not three dozen people, no. Not if you discounted the servants, passing among the guests with trays of drinks and little plates and napkins over their shoulders. Probably not even two dozen. But a significant number, oh yes, and all of them significant people in themselves. Malance could recognise perhaps half of them, from court; Vivi would most likely know them all. She was already murmuring under her breath, a list of those who weren't here: "Why Tolch and Sireon, but not Malach? Where's Bront? He'll be livid, not to be here when all these are... Why, Dolans, my very dear! How delightful! Have you met my, ah, consort, the Ambassador? Verantha, this is, ah, I forget your actual title, Dol, I'm so sorry, but he manages all the monies for the emperor's fleets far and wide..."

"Treasurer of the Maritime, lady. Dolans Mevere. A delight to meet you, whom all the city has taken as their own," and he bowed charmingly over her fingertips, to the point where for a moment she thought he would actually kiss them.

"Dol, behave. Those are mine to nibble and mine alone," Vivi asserted, proving her claim by seizing that hand even as she released the other, thus turning them both around to view the room from another angle. "Who else is here, Dol?"

Oh, she knew exactly who else was here, and so no doubt did he; but she wanted them all spelled out aloud, so that nobody could be denied later.

"Finn and Kars from Finance," the older man listed obligingly, "Marrion of the Treasury—oh, and Sireon and Tolch, but they don't matter if Marrion's here and Malach is not, she made an error there—and Ballamen in the corner yonder. I don't suppose he'll emerge; it's his task to observe from shadow. She will have invited him specifically to carry word back to the emperor, as someone was sure to do it anyway and she wants it clear that there is nothing secret here and nothing underhand. Pharli from Trade—"

"Wait. Why Pharli without Wharre, I wonder?"

"Because Pharli's always the voice in court that worries most about our border security, and she's noticed that and passed the word upward. She's under orders here."

"...All of which being self-evidently true," Vivi murmured silkily, "then why in the world am *I* here?"

"Because she's under orders, and because news of the recent ... change in your circumstances," with a bow to Malance, which she returned as graciously as she knew how: this man was worth cultivating, clearly, "has not yet reached her masters; and because you have access to the emperor himself, and might have been willing to speak to whatever it is she wants, privately in his ear, before she raises it publicly in court."

"Damned if I will. Not if it works against Mal's interests, Verantha's interests; I'll do the opposite, of course."

"Yes, and she's counting on that now, ever since she understood that you would bring ... your consort ... with you. Because that presents your countervailing testimony as mere prejudice, support for your beloved, regardless of the truth or the merits of the question; and so she hopes he will ignore whatever you say against her. She has been forced to improvise, but none the less: there is a double play here. If you speak for her, she is lifted; if you speak against her, you are cast down. Choose carefully."

"How if I just don't say anything about whatever it is? I don't tend to bring politics to the emperor, only gossip. I'm a frivolous soul, just ask the city."

"Highness, I know exactly what you are."

He bowed to them both, and walked away smiling.

"Well," Vivi said musingly. "I wonder what we should do now?"

Malance shook her head. "These waters are too deep for me."

"Mal, I'm sorry; these are the waters we must swim in now." Vivi turned slowly in a circle, surveying the room one more time.

"What—who—are you looking for?" Malance snatched two glasses from a passing tray, barely noticing that anyone was actually carrying it.

"I'm looking for who's not here, mostly. No other family, and no one from any other embassy—unless you've spotted someone?" *From your helpfully superior height* was all she meant, not that Malance might know people that she did not. Naturally, Vivi knew everyone.

"Not I."

"So: palace officials all, apart from us. Treasury, border security, land administration. Hmm." Vivi tapped her fingers against her lips, as she always did when she was thinking hard. Malance sipped from her own glass—Clathian chilled spice wine, and the only good thing that ever came out of Clath—and held the other ready, until Vivi would be able to take it without spilling. Sometimes she became quite agitated by her own ideas, though those were usually notions for wild or wicked ways to occupy their time.

"Oh. Ohhh..." Vivi blinked up at her, looking quite startled by the results of her own thinking. "I know what she's doing. What Clath is up to. I think I do."

"Here. Drink. Explain."

"Clath and the empire share no common borders, which is just the way the empire has always liked it. There are no serious rivals between us—we have no serious rivals, Clath and Feremendas—but a dozen smaller independent states make a handy buffer, to save any trouble springing up if we had to rub together, hard against each other. Yes?"

That seemed a little disrespectful of the states squeezed so uncomfortably between the two great powers, but she had to admit the truth of it. "Yes. I've always supposed that's why the emperor wanted to keep me at court, to keep even the notion of an independent Verantha alive, because Clath had just eaten away a part of that buffer and he wanted to suggest that they not do that again, that they not come any closer to his borders."

"One reason why, I'm sure, of course. This, now?" A gesture at the knots of people gathered in conversation around them. "This is Clath's counter-suggestion. A gentle nudge towards the notion of, ah, a fair division of the spoils. Claiming all those territories between us, establishing a common border after all, with a firm treaty to ensure it."

"Feremendas hasn't shifted its borders for I don't know how long, though?"

"Not for centuries, no. We are content as we are. Clath is not. It needs to expand, if it's ever going to match us for power, for influence, for reach; and the Council of Kings wants that above everything. They have to keep pushing outwards, or they'll fall to fighting between themselves again. This may be a warning too, as well as an invitation. If we decline the offer and stay where we are, they'll go ahead in any case and swallow everything, right up as far as our current border. Which I'm sure is what Clath would actually prefer, but they're being conciliatory, bringing this to the table first, not to provoke the sleeping giant. Which is unexpectedly sensible of them, honestly."

"...What will the emperor do?"

"I actually have no idea." Vivi frowned in chagrin, disliking that intensely. "The man is annoyingly unguessable. But I do suddenly have another idea why we're here, we Veranthans." For that, Malance wanted to hug her, right then and there; which she knew, of course, and there was laughter in her eyes again as she went on, savouring the words in her mouth again. "We Veranthans, we are here as an example, an object lesson. A reminder of what is to be gained, and what lost. Verantha was small enough to be swallowed down easily, and rich enough in ores and minerals, coal and timber to be worth the swallowing. So are all the other little states that lie between us, that's how they've survived so long: no kind of threat, and good neighbours to trade with. Either we let Clath have them all, with all the economic advantage that brings to them and all the loss it offers us, or else we negotiate and cut the cake between us. This might even have been why they invaded Verantha in the first place, as an opening move in exactly this discussion."

"Which they are now bringing openly to the emperor's attention, knowing that everyone here will report to him on exactly what's being said here and what suggested."

"Oh, the emperor knows already. He always knows. What he'll do about it, though..."

Vivi shook her head, and turned to snare a handful of blistered crabcakes from a servant's tray. "As we're here, being that highly visible example, we might as well enjoy ourselves. Let's raid a few more trays, top up our glasses and go and lurk with Ballamen for a while. He's always good company, and the best source of gossip that I know. For the emperor's spymaster-in-chief, he is *amazingly* indiscreet about things he's decided don't matter."

They kept a weather eye on the Clathian ambassador, and saw how she moved from one small group of officials to the next, being the perfect hostess, while no doubt playing the perfect diplomat also, in so far as she was able, insinuating her masters' message into every conversation with as light a touch as she could manage.

Perfect hostess, perfect diplomat, in this one particular at least: they were the only two guests she didn't approach again. Once it was clear that they were to be spared that particular ordeal, Malance did almost start enjoying herself, as Vivi steered her between her particular favourites among the assembly. These were easy in their conversation, witty and perceptive; Malance invited them all to come to Verantha— she would use that term and no other, *Verantha*, now and hereafter—at their convenience, to meet the exiles. "Purely informal, you understand; just come and share a meal with us. They're interesting people, and I would like them to feel that they have a few friends at court, beyond myself and Vivi." Treasury, and border security, and land administration: really none of those touched on any Veranthan interests, except how much money they were costing. Still, it couldn't hurt.

Even so, despite warming to her company and trying to spread her networks wider, Malance was relieved to leave at last, to draw deep breaths of clean cool night air, to see their carriage waiting, with both her pages ready and the coachman on the box.

She and Vivi climbed in, the pages closed their doors firmly and leapt up behind, Kinner shook his reins and clicked to his horses, and they were away and intact, and better informed than before. Which was something, at least.

Once they'd passed the guards at the gateway and were safely on the road home, Malance said, "I thought we were expecting mysteriously to have acquired a second coachman?"

"He was too afraid to wait with us, lady." Alder sounded disappointed in him, for ruining a perfectly excellent plan. "He did take our livery, and leave his own—just as well, too, that white would have shown him up like a lamp—but he knew a back way out of the stables, through the hayloft. There always is one," she added, with the air of one who had reason to know it. Vivi snickered agreement. "So he went off as soon as he'd changed. I told him just to run to our house, before the cry was raised behind him. I hope he made it."

"It's as well he did go, though," Ash put in. "Kinner says they searched the stables for him, not long after. I don't know if a simple change of livery would have been enough disguise; and if they knew him, then we'd all have been in trouble."

Indeed. Malance doubted that her imperial favour, even Vivi's imperial connections would have covered servants too, especially not on Clath territory. She smiled in the darkness even so, understanding that it had been Alder's plan, and Ash had never believed that it could work. Perhaps he'd even urged the older man to run, under the guise of helping him change liveries. Perhaps Alder suspected that he had, whether or not it was true. The two of them had always

185

seemed so very much of one mind, before this; it was interesting, even a little reassuring, to find that they could actually pull in different directions. If they would be growing up with her, she wanted them to grow up as two independent creatures, even at the cost of an occasional falling-out. Even if that meant a cost to her, in the form of slightly less than perfect service now and then.

Should that happen, though, she guessed that Vivi would be ... less than content, and would not hesitate to make that clear. The youngsters already had a healthy respect for her, coupled perhaps with a touch of worship. Even they might fear to face her in her wrath.

Looking forward to a lifetime of perfect service, then, she secured Vivi's hand like a promise, and said, "So. Do we need to take this to the emperor ourselves? If everyone else can be relied on to do that?"

"Oh, I think so, yes. Everyone has a different perspective. And it'll annoy him, probably, to know that we were paraded about like a pet example of what could go horribly wrong. Sound *extremely* hurt, when you tell him. I shall have been too proud and too offended to share that particular snippet. Between us, we can wind him up like a clockwork toy. Or he'll let us believe that we can, if it suits him to do so. You never can be sure, with Uncle. Either way, it bodes well for Clath facing consequences. We'll go tomorrow. Ballamen will see him tonight, and some of the others will be early in the morning—but we shall have woken up in high dudgeon at the appalling way Clath treated us, *in* her own house, *when* we were her guests. Guests she declined to speak to: and me of the blood imperial, and you an ambassador to boot! Also she threatened one of her own servants with death, merely for showing us the respect that she denied us. All of that, just *flooding* out of us, turn and turn about. He's a monster, if he can resist us both. Well, he is a monster, and of course he could if he chose to, but we should definitely afford him the opportunity to choose another course and be outraged on our behalf. He'll enjoy that."

Malance's intentions, as soon as they arrived home, were first to find Clath's runaway servant, assuming he'd made it that far, and to ensure that he was settled and comfortable and secure; and second, to sit her pages down with Vivi and herself, with a bottle of something nice and a plate from the kitchen because she suspected that they'd eaten no more than she and Vivi had, and she for one was hungry still and they were adolescent yet, with all that that implied. Vivi could eat or not, as she chose, but Malance would see that the youngsters did. And while she fed them, she meant to interrogate them, with Vivi's help. She wanted to know anything and everything they'd learned from the evening: how Clath treated her servants—poorly, at a guess, if this one could be so easily found and so readily bribed—and what they said about their mistress, what they knew about her purposes. Servants knew everything that went on in the house, that was axiomatic. The one they'd poached would tell all he could, no doubt, but Ash and Alder were devious and quick, sharp-eyed, sharp-eared. Like the emperor, apparently, she favoured more than one perspective.

Only, when they came out of the last stand of trees and turned the corner that would bring them home, they saw the house ablaze, when it should have been quiet and sleeping. For a moment—as on the night of the party—she thought it ablaze with fire, that Clath had lured them away to burn her embassy behind her; but Vivi's hand on her shoulder reassured her. That was lamplight again, not firelight; the house was awake, but not noticeably imperilled.

Even so, she urged Kinner to hurry; and found Estar waiting in the yard to meet them.

"Oh, lady, I don't know if I should have sent one of the boys to fetch you when they came, but—"

"When who came, Estar?" Clathians, to make trouble in her absence? That had to be her first thought. "Is anybody hurt?"

"I don't think so, lady, and the doctor's here to check—but another ship came in on the evening tide, lady, and there's ever so many more of your people turned up now, and where we're going to put them all, I simply do not know."

V

NINE

He always likes to play with lesser pieces

The most Malance could manage in the chaotic rush that followed was to snatch a moment with the new man as he hauled ancient straw-stuffed pallets down from some obscure storeroom in the attics. She knew who to thank for having found them, and remembering where they were when they were needed. Quite when the pages could have found the time to explore and evaluate the contents of every last corner of the house, she wasn't certain. They hadn't been hers for two weeks yet, and every day had been hectic, and even so. She was quite sure that they knew it better than any of the other servants by now, and certainly better than she did herself.

The new liveryman's name was Breck, she learned. She did her best to reassure him that he had reached safety here, and that she would have a thousand uses for him; and she remembered to ask if his family had arrived at the house yet.

"Lady, yes, and I owe you thanks for that. I'm afraid Sine's father means yet more work for a busy household, but—"

"Don't worry about that for a moment. With all these people here, we're hardly going to notice one more. I'll want to meet him tomorrow, and Sine too," when she was done

189

meeting everybody else, perhaps. "Meantime, you make sure they're comfortable and have all their wants attended to. If they need anything more, tell one of the pages. Say I said so, whatever it is." She wasn't sure if any of her people would be going to bed tonight; she was quite sure that those two wouldn't. They'd work till every last newcomer was settled and asleep, then they'd go down to the kitchen, where Farl would already be baking bread for the morning. They'd beg another pot of coffee from him, then settle themselves in a corner somewhere and start making lists: what needed doing, what fetching, what ordering. Who at the palace would need to be told. Which of them should run down to the harbour and interrogate the ship's master, to learn where he had picked up these passengers and whether there were more still there, some perhaps who couldn't afford their passage. Whether he'd heard from other captains, of other Veranthan refugees.

She might be able to forestall them on that last interview, she was happy to do it herself and felt that perhaps she ought to—but first thing in the morning, she really did have to see the emperor. And she knew already how hard it was to get one step ahead of her pages, once they were focused on a task. She wouldn't be at all surprised to come back from the palace and find a complete report waiting for her.

An extra servant and his hopefully willing girl would prove a help, of course, but more so were her Veranthans. They had turned out of their beds *en masse*, to greet their countryfolk and help make room for them. The new arrivals outnumbered the old, and there were still rooms either crammed with junk or else too filthy to use. Every occupied room would have to double up, and some beds would be shared tonight, necessarily. Well, Veranthans were a practical people, above all; they would accept what could not be helped. And there was a buzz of quiet, unspoken happiness all through the house, despite all the disruption. Verantha had more than doubled its population overnight, and they

were delighted to welcome their cousins home. Malance felt
much the same way herself. When she found one of the new
mothers and one of the early arrivals singing long-familiar
lullabies to settle a roomful of restive children packed two to
a pallet—so many children! what in the world could she do
with so many children, start a school?—she lingered awhile
to join in, although she really could not afford the time. If
there'd been any space between the pallets, she might have
made her way around the room and kissed every one of
those kids goodnight. Veranthans might no longer have a
land to return to, but as long as they had a new generation,
they did have a future. She needed to talk things over with
Vivi. If a Veranthan married a citizen of the empire, say,
then certainly their children would be Veranthans born, as
well as imperial citizens themselves. Could the non-Veran-
than spouse be granted citizenship as well, merely by fact of
marriage? Was that allowed, within the ambit of the empire?
And if so, if it was a commonplace, then did she have the
authority to decree it for her people? They had always been
an insular folk, in their mountain valleys; there were few
incomers in old Verantha. But this was new Verantha, and
the rules would have to change. Aye, and the customs too.
The young folk would have to marry out; far better that than
marrying each other...

She was getting ridiculously ahead of herself, she knew.
Her new Verantha was a house, no more, however full; Veranthan citizenship was an idea that survived by courtesy of
the emperor. Oh, how she did need to talk to him. Vivi first,
though, she should definitely...

A cool hand closed on her wrist, and there was Vivi herself, with a familiar determined look on her face.

"Malance, I love you. Come to bed."

"Impossible. I haven't even talked to all the newcomers
yet, I can't remember their names, I—"

"Malance. I am not taking you to see the emperor until
you have slept. And I mean proper sleep, not just a cat-nap

in a corner while all the house is still dashing madly all about you. You will need to be sharp and rested, or that man will walk all over you."

"No, but—"

"Malance. I love you. Come to *bed*."

She went to bed. Their suite was the only restful place in the house, or so it seemed that night, unless she could go and curl up with the children and be sung to sleep by watchful mothers. Here there were no extra people squeezed in—Vivi had insisted on that—and only a minimum of maids waiting to attend them. Vivi couldn't conceive of going to bed without at least one apiece to help unbutton, to carry discarded clothes away and bring hot water back, to brush their hair and turn out the lamps when at last they were in bed.

Malance lay back with a sigh, remembering that one night when they had managed just fine with only the two of them and no maids at all. But she was learning to enjoy the ease of it at the end of a long day, and her every day was a mountain these days, and her every night too short. This night would be shorter than any, and the day to follow more precipitous, she guessed. She turned to reach for Vivi, and was met by, "Malance. I love you. Thank you for coming to bed. Now go to *sleep*."

"I was only going to tell you that I love you too," she said poutily. And nestled her head into Vivi's shoulder, and her long body against as much of Vivi as would reach, and was asleep almost before she could finish the thought that—given that she wasn't going to be able to sleep, obviously—she might as well be comfy.

And was roused too early by a treacherous page, to find Vivi already gone from her side, the turncoat.

"Damn you, Ash. What's that, and why would I want it? And where's Vivi, and—"

He spoke over her, the impertinent creature; he said, "This is coffee, lady and you need it desperately. The rest of the pot is by the window, and your maids will help you to it as you wash and dress. Her highness has been up since the sun," which meant Vivi could have barely got any sleep herself, the infidel, "and is enjoying herself immensely, telling everybody what to do."

"You mean she's usurped you two," Malance growled.

"Yes, lady, exactly that. She's better at it than we are," he admitted, astonishingly. "*Even* better, I should say, perhaps. Alder is with her, though, and taking lessons. Taking notes. Her highness told me not to wake you until you'd have time for nothing more than a quick wash and a quart of coffee; she thinks you'll manage the emperor better if you're hungry."

He delivered all of this deadpan, wearing his imperial -palace face, but his eyes were dancing. She could just exactly hear Vivi's voice behind those words, and she was half inclined to kiss him in lieu, except that he would be so extremely shocked and it wouldn't be fair. She smiled at him in any case, and said, "Very well, Ash. Consider your hair ruffled and your ears boxed, to remind you one more time that you belong to me and not to Vivi. I know it's hard to remember, that's why I ruffled your hair. Give me that cup, and send in the maids." Not that she was ready, but the day was upon her in any case. There was never any point in trying to stand up to Vivi, she was finding.

Washed and groomed and dressed again in Lirian's finest—which had somehow been pressed and refreshed overnight, despite all the turmoil, which was just as well for the pages, as she certainly hadn't been intending to wear anything else to the palace today—though without the jewels today, she went down to find Vivi of course in matching glory, and entirely ready for her, the carriage at the door.

"You know my mind," she grumbled, following her out.

"Naturally. I've been paying attention all this time."

This time it was Vivi's pages who held doors for them and swung themselves up behind; her own were under orders, she gathered. Vivi's orders, which galled her just a little, perhaps. This might be what marriage was like, she thought, learning to share even your most intimate possessions, even your pages. Certainly, she was learning, it would be what life with Vivi was like. The girl was a tempest, overtaking everything. She would have long overtaken Malance, except that there was something else in her life. Sometimes Verantha could loom even larger, a mountain rather than a storm.

We Veranthans. The two together ought to be undefeatable.

She hoped. But Clath was a maelstrom, and the empire was static by long choice and practice. She had no idea where any of this might lead. All she knew was what she had, right now. A house, just house enough to hold her people and be a territory, Verantha. She thought again about fire, about how a simple fire could destroy it all. She should have warned the pages to be watchful. Perhaps she had. She wanted to ask them, but of course she didn't have them at her back just now. For the first time, she regretted that.

She smiled to herself, thinking that they were growing on her, the wretches. Deliberately, no doubt, manipulating her as readily as they served her. If she wasn't watchful herself, they'd turn her into the mistress that they wanted, the insinuating beasts, rather than the mistress that she was.

"What?"

"What?"

"You smiled. Which was nice. What were you smiling about?"

"Oh, nothing. Just a private thought."

"You don't have private thoughts any more, silly. Now you have me." Vivi snuggled closer. "Never mind, though. I'll get it out of you later. Are you ready for the emperor?"

"Is anyone, ever?"

"No, of course not. If you'd said yes, I would have spent the rest of this journey explaining to you in terrifying detail just how wrong you were. But as long as we're equally unready, and know it, he'll likely treat us kindly. I'm hoping for snacks."

Malance would have liked rather more than just a snack, though she could never ask for it. Well, she'd gone hungry before. "How soon do you expect he'll see us?" Maybe there'd be time to ask his pages to bring something to eat, if he was caught up in important business. A plate of bread and cheese would be exactly the thing. Or just bread, she wasn't greedy.

"He will see us," Vivi said darkly, "the very instant we are at his door, or I will know the reason why. Good uncles do not keep their favourite nieces kicking their heels for hours in an anteroom."

"You're not his niece, though. Not really."

"Niece by *appointment*, which counts more. And that's not the point, anyway."

She supposed not, in Vivi's mind. Even so, she was still not expecting to be shown through to the emperor's apartments the moment they turned up unannounced. As indeed they were not; for when Kinner brought their carriage to a gentle halt in the particular courtyard that offered easiest access to those apartments, fewest hurdles to leap between, suddenly and quite impossibly there was the man they had come to see, the emperor himself, at her side and opening her door with his own hand.

Two simultaneous gasps of horror from the pages up behind, which he kindly ignored. Instead he smiled and said, "Verantha. I'm so glad you came. May I join you? I've been in meetings all morning, and I feel more than ready for a ride around the grounds."

"Your grace! Of course! I—slide over, Vivi, give his grace room..."

"Uncle, isn't this a little eccentric, even for you?" Vivi slid over none the less, but kept up her litany of complaint. "We would have come to you, we *did* come to you—"

"And I'm delighted that you have, though an hour earlier might have been better yet," which earned Vivi an elbow in the ribs, *you should have woken me sooner*, "but I had my people watching for you, so that we might escape the palace for a little. I can't go far, so just around the carriage-road will be fine." This to Kinner's stiff and anxious back. A mumble returned to him, which might just have been *Yes, your grace*, to a mind inclined to generosity. Poor Kinner; he was one more who would stand in need of a present, after all this was over. If it ever ended.

The carriage-road was a track laid down to wind all around the palace, in and out of his grace's numerous gardens, passing the best of each. One did not butt in on the emperor; when he sighed and leaned back and seemed just to want to watch the flowers, the shrubberies, the fountains and the woodland groves go by, Malance and Vivi waited. No more than that. Tense, expectant, anxious, but waiting merely, until he spoke again.

"More of your people have come to me, Verantha."

"To me, I think, your grace." Which might be impertinent, but she was Verantha now. He had acknowledged that.

After a meditative pause, he laughed, and she breathed again. "Under my aegis, at least—but yes, to you. Can you manage?"

"This many, yes, I think we can manage." *So long as you keep paying.* If necessary, she'd say that aloud, but she didn't suppose it would be necessary. "If more come…"

"If more come, we will think again. Very well. Vivi knows whom to ask, for whatever you need."

He would keep paying, then. That was a relief, but not a surprise. She produced a genuine smile, and said, "So do those scamps you sent me, your grace. Vivi has nothing to do now, they take care of everything."

Vivi gave a self-righteous snort, as one who had laboured mightily this morning while her inamorata merely slept.

Malance's elbow worked its way a little into her ribs again, *let me handle this, until I make a mistake*, and she subsided.

"I'm pleased. I did find them … immaculate, when they were mine. I trust that you will do the same. You are to keep them as long as ever you want to; they are sworn to your service as they were to mine, and no call of family can override that. Am I clear?"

"You are, your grace, and thank you." She was still determined never to ask what families they had, that might be looking for their return. They had come to her anonymous, with no more than their page-names; very well, let them stay that way. She did actually want to keep them now, so long as they didn't do anything too atrocious. They were more than useful, invaluable, in this new dispensation.

"Good. I hope my niece receives equal service from you two, hmm?" For a moment he tipped his head back to address the pages behind, clad now in their new Veranthan livery. The poor infants looked terrified, but managed somehow to stutter a promise to try.

"Good, good. Let me see, Falen and, and … ah yes, Mathri, isn't it? Yes. I don't forget, you know. My respects to your parents, if ever my niece or the demands of the day allow you a chance to write to them." In his kindness he turned his head away, to a mutual mumble of "Yes, your grace," and a relief so profound it practically shook the carriage.

Vivi leaned across Malance, to fix her emperor with a steely eye. "Uncle, you are a wicked man, and you are not to torment my people, do you hear me? They'll need a day in bed on nothing but bread-and-milk if they're to recover by tomorrow."

Mutters of "Oh no, highness, truly, we're fine," came down to them from above. The emperor beamed mildly back at Vivi's scowl, and she relented, laughing. "Oh, all right. I'll give them a treat and they'll do well enough, so long as you don't scare them again today. What was it you actually wanted to talk about, Uncle, away from the court and all its ears?"

The emperor nodded thoughtfully. "I'll send them a treat too, that is well thought of; I seem to remember needing to send you one or two in your day, O my niece of wide repute. Very well; you attended a meeting with Clath last night. Tell me your impressions."

Perspective, yes. What they'd come to offer; what he'd come to ask. Perhaps even insights, if they had any. They thought they did, though it was probably *lèse-majesté* of the worst kind even to imagine that he had not already thought more deeply and learned more, even if he hadn't actually been there.

They told him everything they'd heard, everything they'd surmised. It took a while. He listened without interruption, though they interrupted each other constantly, finding as they did so that they too had slightly different perspectives, which could afford a slightly richer narrative of the night.

When they were done, when they thought they'd said it all, he mused for a little and then said, "Yes. Ballamen reported in much the same vein. I confess it, I am ... not altogether pleased with Clath for displaying you like a trophy, like a symbol of their power."

He didn't say quite who he meant by *you*, but presumably Vivi; she was his blood, after all, his acknowledged niece, who had chosen to attach herself to the ruin that was Verantha and thereby share the humiliation. Sometimes in this last year Malance had felt like nothing more than a pet to him, an amusement that he tinkered with.

"Uncle, I was furious when I realised. It was an insult to all of Feremendas." Yes, definitely Vivi, then, if Vivi felt it so. "What will you do about it?"

"Oh, I don't think I have to do anything, do I? It's not as if anyone were questioning my power."

"...No, of course not. They wouldn't dare. I do still think it was a message to you, though, that if you won't negotiate they'll simply take everything they want."

"Of course it was a message to me. I shall ignore it. A message to me can be a lesson to you, girls: most of the time, it's better to assert hegemony by doing nothing. Power abides in stillness, in confidence, in patience. Those who rush about making noise and grabbing only show their own weakness."

That was all very well, Malance thought, but nothing of the emperor's had actually been grabbed. She remained grateful to him for everything he'd done for her and his promises of more to come, but did he mean he would sit and do nothing while Clath swallowed every other little country between their borders and his own?

It was not a question she could ask, obviously. Vivi might, but that would be perilous even for her; Malance held that useful elbow at the ready, to nudge her into silence if such a thing were needed, if such a thing were possible.

Vivi said nothing, though, and they were coming to the end of the circuit, approaching the emperor's courtyard again. A group of officials was already waiting for him; Malance recognised a couple of faces from last night. No doubt they were here to bring their own perspective, perhaps to offer counsel if he asked for it. If he ever did. He'd offered none to her, which was a disappointment.

Kinner brought the carriage to a neat halt, and this time Mathri was swifter even than the emperor, hurling herself down before the wheels had quite stopped rolling in order to pull his door open and bow him out. Unless he'd lingered long enough to let her; Malance wouldn't put that past him. He ignored the girl magnificently, which was kind in him. It was a page's task to be unobtrusive, instantly present when needed, otherwise invisible to the great.

As they drew away:

"I wonder what he expects of us?"

"Of *us*? Vivi, what can we ever do?"

"I'm not sure yet, but didn't you catch the intonation? He said he didn't think *he'd* have to do anything. Which means he has it in mind that we'll do something ourselves, to forestall any need for action on his part. That's how he works, haven't you realised that yet? He always likes to play with lesser pieces. He's the great brooding power at the centre, moving us minions about hither and yon to perform his bidding."

"But he didn't tell us what his bidding was?"

"No, I noticed that. He often doesn't. Sometimes he likes to start a ball rolling and then sit back to see what happens; sometimes he just leaves you to work out what to do on your own account. And then to sort out your own mess if you make a mistake. I think it's supposed to be liberating. Actually it's exasperating. Like when you're a page and he releases you from his service but wants to keep you at court, and you have absolutely no idea what you're supposed to do with yourself now after half a lifetime of being told, of having every minute regimented..." Her fingers fluttered against her lips as she pondered; then she said, "I need to stay here, I think. Talk to some people, see if together we can deduce what he might have in mind. Kinner, take me to my own apartments, will you? I'll keep Mathri; Falen can ride with you, and then run back to me once you're home."

"Vivi, I don't need to drag your page all the way to the embassy, only to have him run all the way back again. That's ridiculous."

"No, it's not. It's essential. You absolutely do need him to do exactly that. You're Madam Ambassador now, every time you step out of our gate; you're *Verantha*, and you absolutely must be attended. One page isn't really enough, but I need one at least, so he'll have to do. Falen, try to look big and imposing, please, and stay alert. I don't expect trouble in the street, but I've been wrong before, and Clath can be ... surprising. Seriously, Mal: if you leave the house, you take the carriage, and both your own pages up behind. Promise me."

She'd rarely seen Vivi so very much in earnest. "Of course. I promise. Two brats at my back and wheels beneath me. Though I don't suppose I'm going anywhere, with the house turned all upside down again." She yearned for a walk to Brion's house in search of that long-delayed breakfast, just to escape both inner and outer turmoil for an hour, but that had to be out of the question now. Perhaps she'd send a runner, invite him to come and eat with her. She'd ask him to bring the meal, except that Farl would die of shame, or more likely apoplexy. Except that she'd probably be too busy to sit and eat anyway, let alone have time to talk with a friend.

"Good. Thank you." A kiss was her reward, and then Vivi was slithering across her to reach the door that Mathri had already unlatched for her, rather than making Falen jump down on her side. Unless that was just the excuse for the slithering. Probably it was; Vivi wasn't noticeably interested in saving her pages work. She rather preferred to keep them on the hop. "Kinner," called back over her shoulder as she walked purposefully away, "remember to go out at the Strangers' Gate, the same way we came in."

It must have been the first time he'd ever come that way, the first time Vivi had even thought to use that gate. Malance had let it pass unmentioned, but privately hugged it to herself. *We're all Veranthans now.*

When she arrived back at the house, at *Verantha*, her carriage couldn't even turn in at the gate. The way was blocked by a wagon bearing long baulks of timber, which was itself waiting behind another, laden with bales of what appeared to be oiled canvas. More bewildered than annoyed, though somewhat of both, Malance reached for the doorlatch, only to hesitate when she heard a soft voice from behind: "Lady, no. Let me."

He was down in a flash of green-and-gold, and had the door open probably faster than she could have managed herself. She smiled at him and said, "Did Vivi remember to feed you this morning?"

"No need, lady. We always have breakfast with the household, before her highness wakes."

"All right. That must have been an early start, though; I expect you could do with something more, yes? Run down to the kitchen, and see what Farl can find for you before you head back to the palace." She was not going to make the poor lad sweat halfway across the city without something in his belly. He was too thin in any case, and she was tolerably sure he'd grown an inch or so, just this last week. It was as well he had the new livery, made to his new measure; his wrists and ankles had been left naked by the last.

Also he was already numerous inches taller than his mistress, which amused Malance entirely too much.

He grinned, and thanked her, and scudded away. She squeezed more sedately past the timber-wagon, giving the frustrated driver no more than a nod across the broad backs of his oxen; her attention had already been pulled away from the obstacles, towards some hints of a cause.

To the left and right of the drive, teams of her Veranthans—men and women, young and old, known faces and new—were starting to clear stretches of the gardens, hewing at thick rough turf with mattocks and spades, attacking overgrown shrubberies with sickles and axes. The pages—it was sure to have been her pages, even with all these people here—must have uncovered a cache. No doubt there was a shed secreted somewhere within the walls, where long-departed gardeners would have worked and sheltered; and no doubt someone among the Veranthans knew how to use an oilstone to put an edge back on long-neglected tools. She was actually glad to see her people finding work to do, so long as they hadn't been pressured into it—idleness hung poorly on Veranthan hands and minds, as a rule—but even so:

"Gardening, Alder? This is what you set them to?" It hardly seemed like the first priority amid the house's current tumult, and she still didn't understand the wagons.

Alder turned from where she had been supervising the unloading of those great bales of canvas. "They asked to do it, lady, I promise. We just made it easy for them."

"With the tools, yes. I deduced that"—and indeed, there was a Veranthan squatting in the sunlight amid a scatter more, sharpening industriously—"but I don't quite see why you'd have them tackle the garden. It gets them out of the house, I suppose, so there's room to breathe and work in there; but it can't have been top of any of your lists, surely? And what's all this for?" A wave of her hand encompassed wagons and delays and inconvenience and all.

Alder beamed. "Pavilions, lady. As soon as we've cleared and levelled the ground, we can erect pavilions. Only tents on wooden frameworks, at least at first, but they'll give us so much more room. Until more people come, at least." She chewed distractedly on a pencil, considering that problem, and Malance could have hugged her. One of these days, one of these moments she might even do that, just to see what resulted.

Not today, though. Not right now. Today, right now, she was going to do no more than urge the girl to work harder, to get these wagons unloaded and out of everyone's way, so that poor Kinner could finally get his horses to their nice comfortable stables. And then she was going down to the kitchen, to snare a breakfast for herself and find Falen again and ask him to stay until she'd finished a letter he could carry back to the palace for her; and after that she was going to go up to her suite, find pen and ink and paper, and write to the emperor. She had, she thought, found something to do. Something to ask him to do, too, if he would allow it to be done. He couldn't sit this out altogether, she wouldn't allow him to.

When Vivi came home with the last of the light, she came with both her own pages and half a dozen more in imperial livery, all crowded into a coach that should never have sat so many. Those, she supposed, were the answer to her letter. Which brought both relief, as the answer was clearly *Yes* on all counts, and dismay, a panic in her chest, because she had never expected that he would mean now, tonight, all unannounced. Or that he would think that was what she'd meant; she couldn't have implied that, could she, even unconsciously? She wasn't usually careless with words, they were her stock-in-trade both as interpreter and mock-diplomat. No, she thought this had come from the emperor himself, a definite assertion of his prerogative to make things happen at his own chosen pace. Swiftly, as it seemed, on this occasion.

Vivi slipped down from the coach and came to her side, pressed cheek against shoulder in greeting, and murmured, "What have you *done*?"

"Exactly what you said I should, of course. I'm nothing if not obedient to your every whim." Somehow, she kept a straight face for that, even with the various smothered laughs and escaped snickers from Vivi's pages and her own. "I formed a plan, and acted on it. Why, do you think I was wrong?"

"No, I think you were perfect. But, to make the *emperor* stand witness..." She shook her head in awe. "You do know I would never have dared ask, don't you?"

"You? You can twist him around your finger. I expect he's only coming for your sake, it's certainly not for mine."

Vivi shook her head. "Wrong again, Verantha. This is all for you. You've stepped forward exactly as he was hoping you would do; and honestly gone further than I ever would. I can prattle at him and make him smile, and he'll pat me on the head and give me presents—though never two of his imperial pages, let me remind you , I had to grow my own—but he won't look to me when things are serious, and he won't shift one iota from his path just to please me. You, though? There are very few people who could persuade him out of the palace right now, while he's practically on a war footing, and apparently you're one of them. I'm in awe. Also I adore you, and also we don't have time for this right now. Kids, you have work to do. Make sure everyone knows everything you need, and buckle down. There's not a minute to spare."

So again the house was turned upside down, and her poor people set to work when they had worked all day already. Every fire in the house was put to heating water, in every vessel she possessed that could be wrenched away from Farl, who was frantically busy down below. The ballroom floor had to be polished again, as no one had had time to do that since the party. All the Veranthans were assembling the best costumes they could, out of all the donated clothes. Children were washed and dressed and told to stand quite still and out of the way, not to need washing and dressing again, on pain of extreme pain. Malance needed both of her pages constantly at her heels, so she stole one of Vivi's—Mathri, because Falen had done enough running for today, and had only just had a chance to wash and change—to dash down to Outlands and invite Brion up to join them, with as much spare food as his house possessed and his carriage could carry, and let Farl die if he must; tonight was more important than one cook's pride. When she went down to tell Farl that directly, she actually said "than one cook's life," which made him smile—slightly, through his indignation—and promise not to die, even if she had decided to serve leftovers at the most important banquet he'd ever have to serve.

She smiled, and thanked him, and had his name added to a lengthening list. Presents, more presents, ever more. Was running a household always this complex? Perhaps when everything was over she would dismiss all her servants, sell her boys and take Vivi to live in a little cottage somewhere, just the two of them, where they could look after themselves and each other and not worry about a single other soul.

And then she mocked herself silly over the very notion of Vivi living without a train of attendants at her beck and call, and went up to see what else needed her personal attention, and was seized from behind and practically frogmarched to her suite by her two reprehensible pages, on the ridiculous grounds that everything was under control except herself and she above all needed to be bathed and dressed and ready for the occasion when it came.

She found Vivi already in their rooms, being bathed and dressed and groomed herself, with barely a maid to spare. Vivi nodded her thanks to the pages and let them go; and when Malance protested that there were still a thousand details to be overseen, she said, "That's why I brought a phalanx of the emperor's favourite brats. They know what needs to be done, and they are doing it. You and I are now superfluous, sweetling, so let my girls preen and pamper you. We both need to be gorgeous tonight, and very, very Veranthan. Oh, and by the way, have you actually written it yet?"

"Written... Written what?"

"The ceremony, Mal. What he's coming for. Do you have the first idea what you're going to say?"

...No. No, she hadn't. She turned to snatch up paper and pen again, and found that her mind had gone entirely blank. What would she say, what could she say? What was there to be said...?

And then Vivi was there, taking the pen from her hand, taking that hand herself, tugging Malance out of the chair again.

"No, I thought not. Now is not the time to get ink on your fingers, though. And you don't want to be reading it anyway, it needs to come fresh from your mind, fresh from your heart. Come, your bath is ready; hot water and gentle hands will do you more good now than sweating over an empty paper with an empty mind. Sit back, relax, and you and I will talk quietly about what you ought to say, to him and to us and to your people."

"Oh, but—" She gazed down at herself as the maids started to unbutton her and ease her dress away. "I, I really wanted to wear this tonight, I think it's important, and I've nothing better suited; but I can't put it on again now, in this condition, and it can't possibly be washed and pressed in time, and... Oh, but you're wearing yours again, and you've had it on all day, and it looks like new. How...?"

"Mal, my precious, I knew this was going to be our livery for a while. The pages get upset, they don't think we look smart if we don't match them. Do you imagine that I only asked Larian for one of each? Your next is airing now in the dressing-room, waiting to embrace you, green and gold and speaking of home. Bath now, go on. Shoo. Girls, you have permission to push her if she stalls again."

An emperor is a treacherous beast, Malance learned that day; he came far too soon, allowing them far too little time to prepare.

Nevertheless: his own pages were lined up sprucely either side of the steps to greet him. Malance and Vivi were in the doorway, a matched pair, shimmering with jewels. Malance saw that Vivi greeted him with that same deep nod that his pages used—*once a page*—and wondered why she'd never noticed before. Oh, yes—because she herself was always preoccupied with offering her own salute. Which tonight meant dropping into a deep curtsey, in the way that she never would at court. There she stood and bowed, greeting him on Verantha's behalf, two independent nations; but this was her own home and Verantha to boot, and he was her guest here, and so tonight she could yield him all the respect he was owed.

Tonight he raised her with his own hands, and kissed her on the cheek in greeting, and that was a first. Vivi, of course, kissed him. Her eyes sparkled. "Welcome to our home,

Uncle; welcome to Verantha. And thank you for coming. We do know that you're busy."

"Well, I do have an empire to save," he said drily. "On a daily basis. And a family to feed, that too. A costly one." She grinned at him, and took his arm affectionately. "Even so," he went on, turning back to Malance, "I would not have missed this."

"Your grace, it could not possibly have happened without you." In every conceivable way was that true: without his consent, without his help, without his pages, without his presence. Put all together, "Without your kindness" seemed to cover it, so that was what she said.

"Uncle, come along in and chat with Outlands while we dash about madly behind the scenes. You know what these occasions are like, and how much work it takes to make them happen smoothly."

"No, I don't; that's why I have pages. That's why I have you, to know these things on my behalf, so that I never need to bother with them. All my life is one smooth passage from one event to the next, and I need know no more than that."

She snorted laughter against his sleeve, and hugged his arm a little tighter. "Liar. I happen to know you served as page to your grandmother, so you're intimately familiar with this level of fuss."

"Well, but much of the art of being emperor lies in learning to forget inconvenient details. No matter. Is Brion here? I'm delighted."

"So is he. He's brought some obscure fruit from far away that he wants you to taste, and a host of other treats besides. Our own cook is a little put out, so please be sure to try his dainties too. Don't you dare try to poach him away from us, mind you, the way you did with Tarlan's dancers. He was a gift, and he's ours now, and we intend to keep him."

The next minutes, Malance's brain mainly spent swirling between two thoughts which were actually the same thought, it was only that they couldn't quite inhabit the same space at the same time; and the first of them was, *Is the emperor truly in my house?* and the second *Has the emperor truly come to Verantha?* Each of them was overwhelming, each in its own way, one personal and one ... revolutionary, she thought, perhaps.

When at last there was nothing more that either she or Vivi could usefully achieve by way of preparation—when their pages finally massed against them, hers and Vivi's both, the youngsters just as determined as their seniors, which was a joy to see—they left their household to its proper work and went to see to their own. They found their guests sitting cozily in the reception room, with a vast array of foods and drinks to pick between and apparently an ocean of conversation to navigate. Vivi gave her little page-bob bow again, so Malance curtsied once more, before going to sit with them before the glowing fire.

Normal rules didn't apply. Even here in their own house, it was the emperor's pages who served him, and so them too. It should have been Veranthan wine they served, but not even Ash and Alder had been able to find it; so this was one of her country's traditional punches, fruit and spices and wine backed with brandy. Malance knew fine well that Vivi had used the Helforth brandy again, and didn't blame her at all. So long as there was some left for afterwards, when everything was over, she wouldn't blame her at all.

A boy approached with a tray, and Brion beamed at the contents. "Sea-snail larvae, your grace, with jellyfish tentacles, on a bed of kelp. My man rinses them in vinegar and then bathes them with an emulsion of egg and oils. They are slightly messy, I'm afraid, but deft use of a napkin, see, the boy has brought plenty..."

"Brion, are you *laughing* at me?" his grace enquired mildly, taking a fork none the less, and a napkin from the boy's shoulder too.

"Never in the world, your grace! Would I lead you astray? Oh—but you are laughing at me, I see. I confess, it does sound outlandish; but I would hope that after all this time you would trust me when I say it is delicious. Redolent both of the natural world and the artistry of civilisation..."

"Mmm." His grace chewed, perhaps a little sceptically, and swallowed; and looked briefly surprised, and then said, "Malance, Vivi: where your emperor treads, you may not linger behind. One each, please. I came here to witness, did I not? I shall witness this. It is ... a remarkable mouthful. And then, Romal, you may take this away and share it among your cohort. I want you all to understand what your master endures, at the urging of his friends. It will be good for your souls. Meanwhile, will someone please take this napkin—oh, thank you, Lala, yes," as another page was instantly there at his side, "—and bring me something to cleanse my palate? Ah, crab-ice, yes. Perfect. Thank you, Serren. No, leave those here; I think my hostesses might appreciate them too. Really, Brion: I know you seldom lead me actually astray, but sometimes your chosen path is ... a little dark, shall we say? A once-in-a-lifetime experience, perhaps. Though I might make that a yearly rite of passage for my pages, if your man can guarantee to supply me...?"

It was all nonsense, of course, Malance understood that. Both men were playing on a long acquaintance to tease each other, tease herself and Vivi, take a little tension from the night. It was kind in them, and valuable, and actually working at least a little against her nerves. What worked better, though, was the sudden reappearance of her own two pages. In fresh livery, she noted, and immaculately spruced; no doubt they groomed each other. She'd still like to know whether they did anything else with each other, or whether they even liked each other, come to that. It wasn't her place to ask, though, but rather theirs to tell, if they ever felt moved to do so. Come to that, it was none of her business anyway—except that no, everything in her household was her business. Probably.

Those two behind her chair meant that everything had been done that could be done, all was in place, she could go ahead when she chose. Not yet, not quite yet; she wanted to sit and entertain her guests a little longer. Soon, though. Soon...

Soon enough, she led the way across the hall and into the ballroom, curtseying to the emperor one more time tonight, as he came in behind her. Here were all her people gathered, her own household and her countryfolk, all who had made it this far, thus far. All in their best clothes and on their best behaviour: the children variously peeping out from behind mothers' skirts or fathers' legs, or else being sternly held back from rushing the actual emperor of actual Feremendas, where they actually were now, except that everyone said this was Verantha but of course it wasn't, they had *come* from there...

There was a chair for the emperor but he refused it, choosing to stand instead among her people, where one determined child did manage to wriggle free of parental control and hurtle to stand beside him, to grip his trouser-leg and gape upwards and have her hair mussed by the imperial hand, much to her discontent after so much ruthless combing.

Malance was aware enough of the byplay to smile at it, and try to remember the child's name. She was more aware of Vivi at her side, squeezing her hand gently before releasing it to go and kneel before her, in a group with so many others, all their joint household gathered together at the centre, at the focus of this ceremony. And she still hadn't written a speech, and she barely knew what to say at all, except this:

"Your grace, excellency, my fellow Veranthans, friends: a country, a nation is more and far more than an area of land. It has to be. Land ... changes hands, more often than we might like. Land can be bought and sold, or seized at sword-point, overrun. It can be devastated, even destroyed. And yet we remain citizens of that country, we keep our homeland in our hearts, even when we are far away and it can no longer call us back, for want of any voice. Verantha endures, even though Verantha is lost; we are all Veranthans now. In token of which..."

V

TEN

Honey-cakes after, if you don't mess up

The night had been glorious, in the end. It was the first thing she remembered, waking at last with Vivi snoring yet beside her: especially after the ceremony, everyone eating everything and milling together, the emperor mobbed by little children gazing at him in snot-nosed wonder, all his immaculate pages getting drunk on Veranthan punch while her friends—she had no memory of having invited her friends, and was sure that Vivi had had no chance either, no time, which meant either that they had heard about it from her people and invited themselves, or else the pages had assumed a licence she wasn't quite sure that they had, to invite on her behalf—her beloved friends got up an impromptu orchestra and played what Veranthan tunes they'd had the chance to learn, so that there was dancing once again in the ballroom, and she was thrilled.

Now, though: now it was the morning, and not glorious. Her head ached and her stomach felt ... unusual; it was possible that she too had drunk a little too much of the punch, despite being born and bred to it, of the pure Veranthan blood. Shouldn't she be immune? Both her pages were at her bedside, her side of the bed, in need of her. Which wasn't fair, because it meant she couldn't even nudge Vivi awake to help with whatever it was, what new crisis had fetched them here.

She made extravagant signs of shushing, and wriggled carefully out of bed, and almost fell except that Ash caught her. He and Alder helped her into the robe that they had ready, and supported her on either side—not that she needed it, once she was moving, she was quite recovered, yes—through to the dressing room, where a bowl of hot water waited and apparently that was all the bath she'd have this morning.

"What is it?" she hissed, once the door was safely shut behind them.

"Lady, another ship has come to port—"

"—what, with more Veranthans? The gods only know where we'll put them, but very well. Let her highness sleep, I'll—"

"Lady, no. Or yes, but no. Clath sent troops to the harbourside, and claimed them as their own."

"Clath did what...?" She was abruptly dizzy, and nothing to do with punch. Ash pushed a stool behind her knees; Alder held her hands, as she subsided onto it.

"They said they were Clathian now, and not Veranthan. They marched them away under escort, to their house."

"Under arrest, you mean."

"Yes, lady, that."

"Clath has no right..." No right to seize her people, and surely no right to make arrests in Feremendas, on the emperor's own streets and quays. Half of her wanted to storm down to Clath's house right this moment, floating on fury, and demand the Veranthans' return then and there.

Happily, her other half was wiser. She remembered how many guards had been on watch, the night of the soirée; there would be more now, after this. She would only imperil herself—and whoever came with her, for she was under no illusion that the pages would let her go alone. And such an

214

exhibition would be futile in any case. At best, Clath would ignore her, bar the gates and let her rant on the wrong side of the wall. The worst ... didn't bear thinking about.

No, she would have to address this the other way, the only way: loudly, and in public. By good fortune, this was a Friday, too.

"Can you two get me in to see the emperor, before court at noon?"

"No, lady," emphatically. "He will be preparing, with his ministers. He sees nobody this morning."

"Well. Who can you get me to? One of those ministers? Anyone who can have the emperor's ear..."

The youngsters consulted, a single flash of eye contact. "Perhaps the chancellor," Alder said. "He goes in to his grace last; he may be willing to see you beforehand."

"Very good. Have the carriage ready by the time I'm dressed, will you?"

"It's waiting at the door, lady."

Oh, she did love them sometimes. "Thank you for that. Now, how many of those Veranthan gowns did her highness actually order for me?"

Ash smiled. "Enough, lady. For both of you. She thought there might be a need."

So: Kinner, the carriage, the pages once again. The Strangers' Gate. No hope of a private interview with the emperor this time, riding around his estate. No Vivi at her side, either. Oh, Vivi would be so *cross* at being left behind! She would scold and scold. But Malance was ambassador, not Vivi; and this had to be done formally, before the court. It couldn't look as though a favourite niece was asking his grace to do her lover a favour. Besides, it was time she stepped properly into her role. Now that she had people to represent, people who depended on her. People she hadn't even met yet, currently detained, those above all: Veranthans in need. In need of someone to speak for them. In need of her.

As usual, the pages were marvellous. They led her briskly through halls and courtyards where she would have been totally lost, and brought her to an anteroom already thronging with petitioners. Of course the chancellor would have dozens of people hoping that he would take up their case, take it directly to the emperor, plead on their behalf.

Malance despaired, almost. But Alder squirmed away through the crowd, to where a harassed secretary sought to protect the chancellor's door. Malance was tall enough to watch her progress—and of course Alder didn't go to the secretary himself. She went to the pages who actually opened the door for those allowed to pass, and closed it behind them, and stood guard with their bodies in between times, to ensure that no one tried to push their way in without consent. The lucky few went in, and never came out; there must be another door beyond.

One of the pages nodded at Alder's request, and slipped through the door himself. Alder wriggled her way back, and just as she arrived, Malance felt a touch on her arm. That same page had come quietly in behind her, and was now beckoning her out the same way they'd come in.

Out into a courtyard, and around by an unobtrusive path to an unobtrusive door. The page knocked lightly, and another of his kind opened it to admit them.

A short passageway brought them to yet one more door. Here they waited, until two frustrated—no, make that furious—women were shown out and directed to the exit. An exchange of page-nods let them in this quiet back way, and here was the chancellor, rising to greet her. "Madam Ambassador. I am sorry about the crush out there; next time, if you send one of your people ahead, you will be brought directly to me, of course."

"Thank you, Chancellor, that's very kind."

"Not at all; it is my duty, rather. How may I have the honour of helping you today?"

Straight to the point; she appreciated that, and was equally blunt—no, even blunter—in response. "Some of my people, newly come to the city, have been detained in the street by Clathian soldiery and taken under guard to the Clath house. That cannot be legal, under Feremendan law."

"Indeed it is not." He had known, of course, already. That too was his duty. "Do you have their names?"

"No, unfortunately; they were straight off their ship when they were seized."

"Mmm. In that case, how can you be sure they are Veran-than, and not Clathians greeted with an honour guard?"

She could find no quick answer for him; it hadn't even occurred to her to question their provenance. Happily, she had pages.

"Lord," Ash murmured, "the captain of the ship confirmed it, and other passengers as well."

"Very well. I will take that provisionally as testament, and send my own people to the harbour to confirm." Malance caught her breath, hoping that the boy hadn't simply made it up; he seemed unconcerned, but that was his palace face, long practised at showing nothing. "In the meantime," the chancellor went on, "I can take some action on my own behalf, but you will want me to take this to his grace, yes?"

"If you please, my lord." He too would know already, that was understood. "It must come before the court today; the situation is intolerable, and my people are under threat. Clath is not known for kindness to its prisoners."

"Clath," he said judiciously, "has no call to be taking or possessing prisoners, under his grace's watch. Thank you for bringing this to my attention, excellency. The matter will be addressed, you have my word."

A swift exchange of compliments, and his brisk pages were ushering her out again, the interview over.

B ack in the courtyard, she was suddenly somewhat at a loss. The energy that had carried her to the palace and through the interview had dissipated, all in a rush. Now she only felt hollow, drained and a little shaky. Oh, and hungry, that too. Another missed breakfast, with hours to wait yet before the noonday court.

"I ... don't want to go back to Verantha," she told her pages. *She will scold and scold*—and then she'd certainly insist on coming with Malance, despite her professed loathing for the whole panoply of court affairs. And that ... would not be the right move. No. Malance was still sure of that. "Can you find me somewhere here, where we can just sit quietly and wait? And perhaps eat something, that too. All of us, I mean." No doubt they'd been up before dawn, to be ready to feed early Veranthan appetites and organise the day's work, but that didn't mean they'd paused to eat on their own account.

"We could go to her highness's apartments, perhaps?" Alder suggested, a little hesitantly.

No, that was wrong. She wasn't sure why, at first—Vivi certainly wouldn't mind—but she was quite certain of it.

Ah. Yes. She shook her head firmly. "It's too far from the reception hall. I can't be late, of course, but I really don't want to be early." She couldn't, she could *not* conceivably stand around for half an hour nibbling snacks and making smalltalk, even with Brion, in the same room as Clath. She would do something premature and foolish, lose all dignity in the process, and very possibly ruin whatever hopes she had of recovering her people safely. The emperor wouldn't like it if two ambassadors fell to brawling in his own reception hall; and she might enjoy his favour, but Clath was the one with influence. He needed to maintain relations with the Clathians; there was nothing at all he needed from Verantha. Which was just as well, she thought wryly, since they had nothing at all to offer.

The pages shared another of those mute and lightning-fast consultations; then Ash said, "Lady, we could take you into our room, in the hall. The pages have a room to gather in, where the food comes up from the kitchens and we take it through and serve it. Nobody would mind if we settled you in a corner there, out of the way. We could find you something to eat downstairs, and you'd be absolutely there when the bell strikes to call the court into the main hall."

Malance tried for a mighty frown, but suspected it looked more like an ineffective scowl. "Ash, this is insubordination by neglect. I said we would all eat together."

"Yes, lady," he said, quite unabashed.

"Good, then. That sounds ideal, if you're sure the current batch of pages won't mind being invaded. You aren't actually one of them—two of them—any more, you know."

They just grinned at her, as if she'd made a joke.

Once a page...

They brought her to the reception hall, though not to the main entrance. Around the side was a quiet, unassuming pair of doors standing open, letting into a small hall. Stairs led down to the kitchens, busy already, noise and steam rising with the scents of spices; a corridor drew them forward, to where one more door stood open.

Her two might wear a different livery now, but that didn't affect their welcome. The kinship was deep and undeniable, despite being largely unspoken. Malance was ushered in with perfect imperial manners, found a chair and a table—and then two more chairs, when she absolutely insisted, when she refused to sit down herself until her pages could join her.

"Lady, we ought to help," Alder murmured. "There's everything to be got ready, and hardly time enough to do it all, even before the guests arrive and the food starts coming up."

Indeed, their host pages were keeping brisk and busy, folding napkins and polishing glasses, opening bottles by the score, running to and from the kitchens with questions and responses about the foods they'd have to serve.

"Later," Malance allowed, "so long as you don't show yourselves in public. I don't want Clath knowing I'm here, and she'll know as soon as she sees either one of you. And don't suggest swapping livery, she's regrettably sharp-eyed, and I won't have you disguising yourself as something you're not in any case—and don't change the subject, either. Scoot down to the kitchens, the pair of you, and come up with three solid platesful of food. I don't care what. Not sea-snail larvae, jellyfish tentacles, or kelp."

They laughed, and promised, and disappeared promptly; and just as promptly returned with loaded plates and glasses. She got wine, she noted, while they had brought water for themselves. She rolled her eyes at them, but was weary of scolding; and they had brought eggs and cheese and pickles for themselves as well as her, and had enlisted a diminutive kitchen boy to follow them up with a pot of coffee and three cups, and a bread-basket over his arm. She slipped him a silver penny, which made his eyes bulge alarmingly before he vanished.

Ash smiled across the table. "He'll be sneaking you up treats all morning now. You own his soul."

"I can be devious too," she confessed, even in such devious company. "And you two won't have time for me," and there were still hours of waiting. Treats sounded like something to look forward to. The day was tolerably devoid of that, else.

The pages were enlisted as promised by their former cohort as soon as they'd finished eating. She waved them away and settled back to watch, nibbling on one more sesame bread roll, finishing the pot of coffee before she even thought about reaching for the wine.

Long familiarity had honed these children into a formidable team. The youngest among them were the napkin-folders and glass-polishers, scrupulously careful at every step. Their elders were already bringing up great wooden trays of cold appetisers, stacking them in purpose-built racks against one wall until they could be redistributed onto the attractive salvers used for service.

Her two helped with that, trooping down to the kitchens and back until the racks were full. Then there was silver-ware to be polished, because not everyone liked to use their fingers; and every single salver had to be inspected and half of those too repolished urgently on discovery of a smear or a scratch. The youngsters put on cotton gloves to avoid any risk of a smudge as they transferred glasses onto salvers that had been passed as perfect. Malance didn't know if it was her presence suppressing chatter, but the pages hardly spoke between themselves. Maybe they no longer needed to; Ash and Alder communicated in glances as often as not, so it was probably a skill that came with the livery. Even if all they were communicating was palace gossip.

She was so fascinated, watching the well-oiled turnings of the imperial backstage machine—and taking mental notes, to try to discover how much of this her pages had already introduced into her own household, and how much further they meant to go—that she was taken by surprise when the little ones started pouring wine oh so carefully into glasses, for others to carry out through another door. She glanced through, and saw a familiar space from an unfamiliar angle; and some familiar faces already gathered. The court was assembling, for their traditional informal meet before the emperor came out at noon.

Now she was nervous again, and now she did reach for her wineglass. Not even the arrival of hot dishes from the kitchens and their rapid distribution onto trays could dis-tract her; not even the aromas those hot dishes brought with them. She felt uncomfortably full suddenly, and uncomfort-ably alone. She still knew she was right, not to have brought Vivi with her—and wondered abruptly whether Vivi might have brought herself regardless, whether she might be out there now mingling with ambassadors and nibbling treats and wondering quite where Malance was hiding—but she missed her company regardless. And found both her pages abruptly at her elbow, and wondered if their telepathy had extended itself to her now, or if her face had given her away, if that was a different thing.

"Lady, you should come with us now."

Yes. If she could see out, others could see in, every time that door opened. She did not want to be spotted, lurking among the pages. So she followed hers out into the corridor and down to another door, which brought her into—

Oh. Another room, another set of pages. She was still lurking, then. These were a pair almost as old as hers, she thought—certainly friends of hers', to judge by glances, smiles—and another pair much younger, who must surely have been twins. A boy and a girl, but much of a height, at least while they waited for an adolescent growth spurt; and their faces had been entirely stamped from the same mould. Along with their matching page-cut hair, they could easily have been mistaken for each other.

Those two were being fussed over by the older pair, brushed and combed into an ideal, the last fleck of dust picked off their liveries. Too young to have acquired the perfect imperial-service neutral face, though they were trying, they looked nervous and excited and solemn and proud all at once, as well as frankly adorable. It was easy to guess what they were about to endure. Finally satisfied, their elders sent them off through a private curtained doorway with words of encouragement and pats on the bottom, "Remember how we greet him, now, and you only call him 'your grace', nothing grander—and try not to look so scared. He's a pet really. Honey-cakes after, if you don't mess up."

The curtain fell behind them, and their two mentors grinned around at Ash and Alder, before greeting her with the same deep nod they gave the emperor. Which was wholly inappropriate, of course, and yet somehow comforting, strengthening, spine-stiffening.

"I don't suppose we can follow the emperor in," Ash murmured, "right on his heels, as though we're all together?"

"No-o—but we can slip you in right immediately ahead of him," the girl offered, "as though you've just come from a private meeting, and he had to hurry after you for fear of being late?"

"Perfect," Alder said. "Thanks, Liss. Lady, are you ready? It'll be any moment now—"

And indeed it was exactly then, the great deep boom of the noon bell seeming to shake the very stones around them; and her pages seized her elbows and positively *hustled* her through yet one more doorway as Liss pulled it open for them, and here they were somehow on the verge of the reception hall itself, again from an unfamiliar angle, a way she'd never come; and there on the other side of the arch was a different door swinging open, held open by one of those adorable twins, so that must be the emperor's private apartments and yes, he was coming out right now, she could see his shadow looming.

Ash and Alder released her now, and dropped respectfully back where they belonged, two measured paces behind. She drew herself up and did her best to measure her own pace to the emperor's behind her, so that they should indeed seem to be together as they entered. And here was the familiar crush of Friday court, and there were all the officials and all the ambassadors and all the other guests making a respectful aisle between them to let him pass, and she could almost have sailed down it herself, all the way to the dais; but she could not afford to be that crude today, so she slipped into place among her colleagues and let him pass, remembering in time not to curtsey here but merely to bow as he came by, barely more of a nod than his pages gave him.

And then she stepped out again immediately behind those little pages, to take shameless advantage of that aisle before it disappeared, before they all thronged together at his back.

Of course others had the same idea, wanting to be first to catch his eye. But she trod hard on his pages' heels, while her own closed up tight at her back; she wasn't even entirely sure they weren't using judicious elbows to keep the importunate at bay. So when the emperor mounted his dais and took his seat with his pages positioning themselves carefully behind him and looking unconscionably relieved at that first duty done, she was right there before him, directly in his eyeline, should he choose to look straight forward and straight down.

Which he did, bless him, because of course he knew everything that was in her mind, everything her tongue needed to tell him; and he said, "Verantha? Are you first today?"

"If it please your grace." She took a moment, took a breath. Registered without caring that Clath was suddenly here too, shoving through to the front. Both her pages moved to stand between them. Good; that was protection enough. That was more than she could conceivably need, here in the emperor's presence; and *they're both carrying knives, and they're faster than a striking snake and more vicious than a cornered rat*, just in case she should need that. If she couldn't have Vivi herself, these two made a fine substitute.

"I learned this morning," she declared, pitching her voice to carry, though the acoustics were so fine in here and the silence so profound that she hardly need trouble; everyone here would know already in any case, and would be breathless to learn her response, Clath's, the emperor's, "that citizens of Verantha, my own people, fled here for sanctuary from the invader, were seized at swordpoint and marched away to Clath's compound, where they are currently held in peril of their very lives. And this in broad daylight, in your grace's capital, on your grace's very streets. I dislike to make demands, before your grace's court; but necessity drives the devil, we are told. Verantha demands, *demands* her people's immediate release, and their restoration to Verantha's territory and protection."

There. That should set the cat amongst the pigeons. There was an undercurrent of whispers at her back, until the emperor raised a hand to still it.

He cocked his head and said, "Clath? Do you have a response to Verantha in this matter?"

"Merely that there is a mistake, your grace. These people are not Veranthan; no one is Veranthan any more, nor can be. These are Clathian citizens now, and so fall under my aegis and our laws. By which laws they are suspected of being rebels, and so I sent a force to fetch them to me, until they can be questioned."

"You feel they fall under your laws, Clath? In my city?"

Oh, he was unhappy about that. She really was the most undiplomatic of diplomats. But experienced, none the less: she pulled herself together rapidly. Once a general serving multiple kings, no doubt you learned to do that. "You are right, your grace, of course. I should have asked you to send your own men to detain them, and deliver them to me. But there was no time. Had I delayed long enough to send messages, long enough for your troops to arrive, they would already have scuttled up to supposed Verantha, where your grace has deemed that I may not follow." And then a stabbing glance at Malance, and a hissed, "Even you. Even you are subject to Clath now, whatever you pretend and whoever offers you their protection. Your day before our justice, that will come."

In honesty, she didn't doubt it. The emperor needed Clath, and not Verantha. He found her useful just now, as an irritant; it couldn't last.

But Clath's day was not yet, so long as she could argue against it with clarity and power. She said, "Your grace, my countryfolk are Veranthan born and raised, in flight from a cruel invader. She cannot claim their persons, any more than she can their allegiance. We are Veranthans yet, for all that strangers occupy our home and threaten us even here, under your grace's eye."

"Your grace." Clath again, scanning the assembled, fascinated throng. "I see people here, your own people, from Albertin and Morrow, from Scand and Hark and Leverine. All territories claimed by your own illustrious forebears, claimed at point of sword when they would not submit peacefully. Are they any the less Feremendan? I myself was born in Merandia, and remain proud to claim that heritage; nevertheless, I am Clathian first and foremost. The minute we annexed those lands that had been called Verantha before, all their peoples became ours. Even this one, yet," with a scornful sideways nod of her head towards Malance. "We have no use for her, but she is ours nevertheless. Your grace may not deny it."

"Oh, may I not?" She was making mistake after mistake, and a heartsunk Malance thought that she would win in any case. Her argument was strong. "You were born Clathian, excellency, for all that your forebears were born free." Ouch; that was telling in itself. From the emperor, it was striking. She felt Clath flinch, but refused to look at her. "My own people, from lands my ancestors seized in conquest, yes: they were born within the bounds of Feremendas, under the peace of Feremendas as it has been for centuries. We no longer invade foreign peoples, nor will we begin again. Nor, advisedly, should you." That, surely, was an answer to her oblique approach at the soirée: that he would not ever agree to a division of the lands that lay between them, and that he would respond if Clath tried to seize them anyway. It wasn't a rescue for Verantha, too late for that, but it might save all her neighbours, if his voice could carry sufficient conviction back to the Council of Kings.

"Your grace—"

"No. I have no patience with strangers' squabbles being fought out in Feremendan streets. You will return your prisoners to Veranthan custody, where they belong."

And there it was, what she had so much needed to hear; but she barely managed one breath of relief before Clath's harsh voice was back, undiminished.

"Your grace, we hold them as Clathian citizens on Clath territory. Your grace's edict does not run that far."

"No, perhaps not; but in this instance Clath territory sits amid mine. I will not cross your borders, Clath, without your invitation, as I will not cross Verantha's,"—oh, did that mean Clath still did not know about his visit the other night? She wasn't certain, but she could certainly hope—"but I might station my troops all around your compound, to ensure that no more similar excursions were perpetrated by your guards."

"Your grace, my embassy's people here enjoy the same protections as myself, under your grace's kindness."

"Do they so? I do not believe those protections extend to going about in armed packs, arresting newcomers to my city who have committed no offence here, people who might also and quite reasonably expect to benefit from my protection. That I will not tolerate again, excellency. And, of course— should I feel obliged to invest your compound so, should I not achieve your word that such an encroachment will not occur again—you might well find my own people reluctant to cross my soldiers' lines, to bring the food and drink and other supplies that you and your people depend on."

There, now: there was a threat of another kind.

And Clath was reckless now, goaded beyond wisdom. "If you were to impose such a barricade, your grace, it might be that our detainees under investigation would be the first to experience deprivation. Rebels have no great claim on our resources."

And now the emperor rose to his feet, and strode to the edge of the dais, and after one frozen instant his little pages startled forward to stand either side of him, supremely focused on the aggressor here, hands on hidden knives, ready to hurl themselves down and protect him with their lives should that prove necessary. *Your grace, you owe those two a present,* she thought, ridiculously, even while she noted a number of lithe liveried figures passing rapidly through the press, to be on hand if needed. The emperor paused a moment longer, merely breathing, surveying the hall; and then he thundered, in a voice she hadn't known he owned, "Clath, if I learn—and I will learn, depend upon it—that you have starved or tortured or otherwise maltreated Veranthan citizens, or Clathian citizens, or citizens of any polity at all, here within the bounds of my city or anywhere else within my borders, then you may depend upon this too, that your embassy will be immediately revoked and my protections withdrawn. You will leave all your many citizens here and elsewhere without a voice within my lands; you yourself may not find a way to leave my lands at all, if I lay hands upon you. I do not harbour torturers, under the guise of diplomats or any other. Am I exactly clear?"

Now Malance did look, out of interest. Clath was more pale than ever, and she visibly swallowed before she could speak. "You are, your grace."

"Very well. I require—and this is not a request—that you immediately release your captives to the possession of my own troops, whom you will already find before your gates on your return, I think, Chancellor?"

He knew exactly where to look, in the crowd. Malance followed his gaze, just in time to see the chancellor's nod.

"Good. *Immediately*, excellency. That means now."

From pale, Clath went to vividly flushed; but she turned and blundered her way almost blindly through the massed court, no aisle opening for her, while Malance's heart rejoiced. And then she found her hand unexpectedly claimed and squeezed, rather remarkably hard; and she looked down—she knew that would be the right direction—to find Vivi there after all, ferocious, hissing, "You and I, we are going to have a *conversation*, as soon as neither your pests nor mine can overhear us; but right now, I think we should

beg his grace's permission to depart, don't you? We have
new people to accommodate, and absolutely nowhere to put
them yet."

Malance wanted to hug her, and to apologise, and—a little
bit—to run away from that promised conversation. What
she did instead was offer a bow to the emperor in gratitude,
which he acknowledged with a nod; and then turn her lover
and herself in a single swift movement, hissing back, "Verantha does not *beg*, Vivi, nor ask permission, even of the
emperor. When we choose to go, we go. Hurriedly, in this
case," with Vivi's pages to break a path ahead and her own to
guard them from behind, as all the court sought to congratulate her and make their own separate marks with the emper-
or's new apparent favourite, when she had been no more
than his apparent pet before.

Vivi kept her word all the way home, saying nothing that
all four pages crammed up behind could not help but
overhear; which meant in fact that she said nothing at all.
Malance bit back a smile, and played with Vivi's hand that
she had not yet snatched back nor Malance relinquished; and
when they drew to a halt in Verantha, before Verantha's front
door—and how strange was that, that a country could have a
door? and yet here they were, on their country's very doorstep—she briskly dismissed all four of their followers. "You
know what's coming, children; we have more Veranthans on
their way, as soon as the emperor's troops can escort them
here. And the way things are going, it seems probable that
we should expect more after these. At least a trickle, maybe
a flood. Do what you can to prepare for them, here and now,
and start thinking about the future. You know we depend on
you, so shoo."

Vivi's youngsters grinned, at being shooed; her own
two scowled at being sent away, knowing they'd be missing something climactic. Nevertheless, they all went on the

instant, making rapid plans between themselves, who should do what.

Left alone, there in her doorway, Malance faced Vivi and said, "You're going to yell at me, aren't you?"

Vivi was somehow holding both her hands now, in that same fierce, nearly painful grip. "I was," she allowed. "I was going to yell at you so hard. How *dare* you leave me out of a fight? Especially a fight like that, before the court, where I have so many friends?"

"That was the point, though—"

"Oh, I know. I always knew, even as I chased you down— and you might have thought to send the carriage back for me, so I could chase you down in comfort, by the way—and that doesn't stop me being furious with you. Nor does the fact that you were brilliant, and Uncle played along exactly as you must have wanted, and Clath will never live down the shame, which is glorious. Just don't you ever, *ever* leave me out of something so lovely ever again, do you hear?"

It hadn't been lovely in the least, not to her; but Malance would rather like her fingers back unbroken, and there was only one way to achieve that, so she said, "Yes, Vivi, of course, I promise, never again," and bent down to kiss her beloved in token of her oath.

Which turned inevitably into a wholly other kind of kiss altogether, and Malance was infuriated when she heard that kind of cough behind her which meant *your pardon, lady, but I really need to speak to you right now.*

It wasn't one of the pages, though, which she would absolutely not have taken kindly; they had their instructions, and no need to be bothering her. This was Felid, looking sweetly anxious at the interruption, but driven none the less; and he said, "Forgive me, lady, highness, but Farl swears he will leave your service if one more demand is laid upon him, and Alder says there are still more Veranthans on their way and possibly imperial troops who might want feeding also, and *please* can you come and tell him he mustn't go?"

There was something more than worry in the poor boy's voice, and Malance realised that she'd been neglecting her own and closest people, with all that had happened these last weeks. If Farl and Felid were bonding so tightly—or more, binding together—she'd had little idea of it; and of course Farl could leave her in a tantrum or on a whim, and of course Felid could not, unless she sold him or gave him away. She wanted neither of those occasions to occur, so she said, "I'm sorry, Vivi, but I really do need to deal with this. We can't lose Farl now," *and if he goes I'd have to give him Felid, apparently, and I love the boy too much to lose him willingly,* "so will you let me—?"

"I will not," said Vivi determinedly, still keeping hold of her hand, albeit more loosely now. "We will go together, and address this crisis as one voice in two delightful bodies. Felid, my love, come with us. If Farl sees that we're keeping you come what may, then you and I at least know that he isn't going anywhere, whatever he may say."

V

ELEVEN

They knew her intimately,
and they were always right

It wasn't only Clath's released prisoners, and it wasn't only Farl. More Veranthans came, it seemed, with every ship that docked. The house was too small already; if they turned the entire gardens into a camp, pavilions cheek by jowl, there would still barely be room for them all. The kitchen couldn't feed them, the laundry couldn't keep them clean, there wasn't enough water in the well.

Malance organised daily wagons back and forth—or no, Malance gave the orders and her pages did the work, as they should. Her people were fed and decently clothed, they had water to wash with, all at great expense to the emperor. It wasn't enough. The house was chaos, overcrowded, loud; the gardens were worse. Even peace-loving Veranthans could grow fractious and quarrelsome, Malance learned, packed too close together for too long with too little to do.

"It can't go on," she said, walking through the park to Brion's house with Vivi, supposedly to consult the older man, probably to beg him to take in some of the refugees himself—she hadn't quite decided yet—and mostly just to escape the turmoil for an hour. To make no decisions—maybe not even that one—and settle no arguments, hear no reports on what more they were short of and how the pages proposed to address that, comfort no distressed children and find no distracting tasks for mettlesome adults. Even, she was astonished to discover within herself, to speak nothing but Feremendan. Not to act as interpreter between two misunderstanding peoples, just for a while. There were others in her house now who could translate, but it felt as though everyone still came to her.

"Of course not," Vivi agreed. "And yet it will. People will keep coming, you know that. It's a good thing."

"It is." The more of her people who escaped Clath, the more who came here to build a new community, Verantha-in-exile, the better their future would be. And yet. "They can't all come to us, though. They simply can't."

"No."

"And if I let them scatter all over the city, then they'll lose touch with each other and with us, they'll lose that sense of being all Veranthans together, one cohesive whole. The children won't have anyone to speak Veranthan with outside their families, they'll lose the language and forget the culture," and she would have failed entirely.

"Which," Vivi said, "is exactly why we're going to talk to Outlands."

"It is?" This had been Vivi's idea, and she did seem even more pleased with herself than usual, but Malance hadn't realised she had any particular scheme up her sleeve.

"It is." A firm nod, and Vivi would say no more, other than "Wait and see," which was exactly as annoying as she clearly wanted it to be. One of Vivi's pages giggled softly at their backs. So those children were in on it too, were they? Whatever it was? Very well. Bodyguards and conspirators, apparently. She would be dignity personified, Madam Ambassador to the core; she would indeed wait and see. And reserve some terrible revenge for some other occasion, because oh, all three of them were going to suffer for this.

Ever predictable, Brion greeted them with a table of small plates to sample. Malance sighed internally; he would discuss no business, she knew, until they had tasted and discussed everything: how rare the ingredients, how exacting the preparation, what would go well with which other dishes. He was perfectly capable of sending orders down to his kitchen that those other dishes be instantly prepared, to prove his point or otherwise.

Very well. She would be complaisance personified, his personal friend; she would taste and try, debate and argue for as long as it should please him; and Vivi would suffer for this too, at some later date. Her pages were suffering already, at that age when they were permanently hungry, standing quietly against the wall watching, smelling everything, tasting nothing. If they'd been her own, Malance would likely have softened and sent them down to the kitchens by now, to beg what they could and amuse themselves till it was time to leave. Vivi was less merciful. Good.

It seemed to take an age of the world before Brion was satisfied. He had his servants clear away the debris, served one last bright fresh wine as a palate-cleanser, then leant contentedly back in his chair and said, "So. How may I help you today? This wasn't just a pleasure-jaunt, I know."

Well, at least he wasn't in on it as well. *He* hadn't been toying with her, making her wait all this time. She smiled beneficently on him and said, "Apparently not—but *I* don't know what Vivi has in mind," *or in store,* "only that there's something, and she needed to bring it to you."

"There is, and I do. Have you a chart of the city, and its waters? This will be easier if I can point."

Of course he had a chart. So did Malance, so surely did every embassy. Two minutes later Vivi was sprawling across a detailed plan that covered half the table, and Malance was still bewildered.

"There." One fine finger, stabbing down. "That's Outlands' harbourside allotment, isn't it? Where your ships berth, where you warehouse what they bring in before taking it to market?"

"It is. I may have mentioned to the emperor more than once that it is too small and too inconveniently far from the centre to be ideal, that we could do more trade if we had more space, but he's never seen fit to accommodate me, alas."

"Good. Sell it to me."

"*Sell* it...? My dear girl, that's been Outlands' base in this city for a century and more. Without it, we would have nowhere at all."

"Yes, you would. Here." Another stab of that determined finger. Malance was growing interested now, though she still didn't quite see the point. "Where the emperor's building all that new wharfage. It's perfect for you."

"It would be, yes. I understand that it's intended to benefit Clath."

"It was, I know. His grace is quite unhappy with Clath at this time. *Quite* unhappy. He is probably not inclined to be generous. I believe I can persuade him to look kindly on Outlands instead."

"Ah. You haven't discussed this with him yet, then?"

"I have not." Now she smiled up at Malance, her eyes alight. "I thought I ought to present it to those who stood to gain, before seeing if it could actually be managed. Three voices are louder than one."

"Vivi—I'm sorry, but what is this all about?" Malance was merely bewildered. "My people don't need wharfage and warehouses."

"Not yet, but they will do. Look, Mal, see this area behind?" A broad gesture, sweeping across the chart. "My family owns all this land, from here to here. It's beyond the city limits, but only just. A grant from a previous emperor, for services rendered. We've done nothing with it, in honesty: sheep and goats to keep it from getting overgrown, but no more than that. Without the waterfront, it's never seemed that useful. *With* the waterfront," and here she beamed from one to the other, "it's ideal. Don't you see, Mal? It's what your people need: land, access to the river, a good road into the city but still a place to be apart, a place to be themselves. Little Verantha. And plenty of room, however many eventually make it this far. Room to grow, room to build, room to work. Kiss me, I'm brilliant. And then we'll work out how to convince his grace that Outlands really does deserve an opportunity to expand their trade with the city and the empire."

"Will, will your people really let you give all that land away, though?"

"Sweetling, I'm not *giving* it to you. Not yet. My parents still have an interest at least in appearing to be in charge of the family's affairs. It's nonsense, of course, they never come to the city, but even so. Which is why I will lease you the land, and he doesn't know it yet but the emperor will pay for it until your people have established themselves and found ways to be independent of his help, and my family will be delighted with their clever daughter for finding a use for the land and making them a handsome profit, even if most of that profit goes back into new buildings and roads and a marketplace and workshops and all sorts; and when I'm finally actually in charge I *will* give it to you, to us, to we Veranthans, and that'll be that. Kiss me again, I deserve it."

Of course it could never be that easy. Clath was predictably livid at the proposed loss of the new wharfage, and raised voices of opposition at court and among the city's powerful merchant guilds. What did Outlands have to trade, after all, compared with Clath? Wool and dried fish? It was risible. Worse, it was insulting. Did the emperor truly care so deeply to offend the other power of the world, and his greatest trading partner?

Clath had more friends, many more friends than Verantha. Outlands had always been welcome at court, a minor voice, an amusement, little more; Brion was personally popular, but that held small sway in matters of business or affairs of state. Some weeks—some Fridays, in the main—Malance despaired, while the emperor listened to arguments from all sides and kept his own counsel and promised a decision in due time.

In the meantime, though, even without the waterfront, there was no reason why the Veranthans shouldn't start work on the land itself. That lay entirely in Vivi's gift, at least until she had to ask the emperor to start paying for it. Not yet: so far she hadn't even let her family know she'd found a use for it.

At this season, Brion's warehouses stood empty. That was one of the arguments used most heavily against his notional tenure of the new wharfage; Outlands ships could only make the voyage through eight months of the year, thanks to winter storms and ice at home. Brion was addressing that with notions of their fleet staying here in the south those bitter months, trading locally back and forth until the thaw could see them sailing north again. For the moment, though, he had no goods to store; which meant he could offer spacious, weathertight accommodation for as many Veranthans as chose to leave the embassy. There was protection, too, behind his dockyard walls and watchmen. Vivi's original suggestion had been to move those pavilions out of the gardens and set them up on her family's land, but Malance had vetoed that. She didn't trust Clath not to send her guards down to attack a vulnerable camp.

For the same reason, she insisted on keeping the children at the embassy: *for their schooling* was what she said, but *for their safety* was what she meant. Her house was still busy, then, with kids and their parents, and those few too old to work the land, some others who chose to stay; and with constant comings and goings between house and land, supplies to manage, problems to solve; but it was an ordered kind of busyness at last. Racket was mostly confined to the pavilions, where the children studied with her friends and played together—again, often with her friends—through the day. Malance found time to organise her own thoughts at last, time to consider her options, time even to rest occasionally. Vivi was often at the palace or elsewhere, pursuing Veranthan interests with all the fervour of an adoptee or a convert; but when she was home she would rub Malance's feet for her, and tell stories of her family and her childhood, growing up alternately in the palace here and on their country estate, a far way away and a far, far cry from royal luxury.

When Vivi wasn't home, Malance had her pages do the foot-rubbing, while they passed on court gossip and tales of palace wickedness, almost all of it perpetrated by pages, none of whom were somehow ever themselves.

They were insinuating little beasts, finding some back way into her heart; perhaps she might keep them after all. Also they gave very good foot-rubs.

Also, the more they and Vivi told her about the training of pages, separately or together, the more they gave her cause to think. Clath was growing genuinely dangerous again, she believed, angry even with the emperor now, and blaming everything of course on Verantha, her people, Malance personally. The ambassador could barely constrain herself, seemingly, making untimely threats even in public, even at Friday court, even in the hearing of the emperor. She hadn't again tried to interfere directly with the Veranthans, but that was surely coming, one way or another. Sooner or later, it must come; such fury could not be bottled up for ever. There would be a trigger, and then there would be an explosion, and Malance anticipated violence. Clath had the troops for it, after all; she kept almost a private army behind her embassy walls, and the emperor did nothing.

Very well, then. Malance would do anything to protect her people. Anything.

She had the Veranthans cut down a row of trees in the park, to give clear line of sight from her house to Clath.

"Mal, you did *what*? You had no right! No right at all! The emperor will be furious, when he hears. If he hasn't heard already, and I expect that he has. All the parklands are his, and every tree is precious to him."

"I know he'll be angry—and I also know that he'll understand. I couldn't have asked permission, he never would have granted it; but I expect his forgiveness. Eventually."

And indeed, she had to endure a bitter interview with his grace, which sent her home in tears, with Vivi saying "I told you so" all the way back. But it meant that she could station sharp-eyed children to keep watch on the road, and run to warn her if ever they saw a party coming out of Clath in this direction.

At night she had the embassy gates closed and locked, and set volunteers to watch them and to patrol the walls. Veranthans were not a warlike people, but they hunted game in their mountains with enthusiasm. They were no strangers to moving quietly, and they did know how to kill.

She had done, she felt, what she could. Now there was only waiting.

It wasn't soon, but soon enough: a boy careering through the house, calling for her, sprinting to her elbow: "They're coming! I saw them, we all did!"

"How many?"

"Six men, and a woman."

"All on foot?"

"Yes, lady." All the children had borrowed that mode of address from the household servants, and used it delightedly.

"Very good. Thank you, Merl. You know what to do now?"

"Tell my father," he recited, counting the list off on his fingers. "Tell Garrel's mother. Make sure everybody leaves the pavilions and comes into the house. Take care of the little ones, so they're not frightened." He was all of eight, and so no longer counted as a little one. "Don't go near the windows, and don't come out until we're told."

"Good. Off you go, now."

She looked around, but her pages had vanished already. That was a load off her mind. Vivi wasn't home yet; that was another.

She took a breath, walked through the hallway and out of the front door. Heard it locked and bolted at her back. Good.

Alone and empty-handed, she walked halfway down the drive, to where that handy bench awaited her by the dry pool. She sat: quite still, quite calm.

Was it really so far, from the Clathian embassy to Verantha? She didn't think of Clath as a slow walker under any circumstances, but she seemed to be taking an age to arrive.

Finally there she was, a shadow at the open gate, six men in silhouette, in line abreast, behind her. A wall of weaponry.

She didn't hesitate to pass the gateway and advance up the drive. Neither did her men.

Malance rose from the bench, stepped into the middle of the roadway. Waited.

Clath came within half a dozen paces, then stopped.

"This is Veranthan territory," Malance said, surprised to find her voice so forceful. "Clath is not welcome here."

"There is no Veranthan territory. There is no Verantha. You are all my people now."

"The emperor says otherwise."

"He does; which is why you still live free and make mock of our rights and entitlements. No matter. This is his city; I abide by his rules. As must you."

"Indeed. What do you want?"

"You have given shelter to a man of mine, a Clathian."

"No."

"I say yes. His name is Breck, and he fled my house in shame. I will see him returned. It is the emperor's decree, that no embassy may knowingly give sanctuary to the citizen of another power. Breck has hidden here long enough. He is

mine to hold and mine to punish, and you will give him to
me."

Her men bulked themselves up behind her, touched hand
to sword-hilt, hand to dagger. Malance sighed.

"Brion talked, I suppose? That man never did know when
to keep silent. In this matter, though, he is misinformed.
There are no Clathians here. I have a man named Breck in
my household, yes, and he is as Veranthan as I am."

Clath snorted. "Which is not at all, as I keep telling the
emperor. He will not listen—yet—but he will listen to me
on this. You shall not pass him off as yours, in some peasant
charade. I have his papers; I know his place of birth, his age,
his family. We are record-keepers, we of Clath; we know all
our people."

"I congratulate you. That must be so useful, when you
want to threaten them. Good papers keep good order, I am
told. Nevertheless: there is one paper of his that you do not
have. Breck has renounced Clath, and is now a citizen of
Verantha. Please leave."

Clath snarled. "Ridiculous! He has no such right, and you
have no such powers. The emperor will not—"

"His grace was kind enough to stand witness to the deed,
and chose to hold the paperwork himself. I know he will be
pleased to show you how absolutely we have followed Feremendan law in this."

In this, and in two dozen other cases too: all her people,
all Vivi's. All Veranthans now. Even the pages, even Vivi.
Apparently Feremendans could hold two citizenships at
once without having to renounce either. She didn't really
understand how that could work, but it was the law and she
had embraced it gladly. Even her boys had gone through the
ceremony. She'd been fairly sure that they counted as Veranthan already, since they belonged to her, but it was better
to be safe. Besides, they had loved the idea of having papers
of their very own, and those in the possession of his grace
the very emperor himself. Who had come to their house,

and *spoken* with them! "Malance's famous boys," he'd called them. She'd never seen them so ridiculous, or so ridiculously happy.

Clath pinched her lips together and took a slow, tight breath through flaring nostrils. She looked more dangerous than Malance had ever seen her: a hawk, mantling to eat.

She gestured rapidly to her men, left and right. "Find him. Leave this one to me." And then she drew a dagger from her belt.

And then, again, Malance felt the sudden appalling power of a passing bolt, a sound laid physically against her skin, so near it was; and a darkness bloomed in Clath's eye, and she fell dreadfully backwards.

Malance stood quite still. Clath's men yelled, startled, stumbled backwards; and recovered themselves, gasping, and reached for their weapons with their killing eyes fixed on Malance.

She gestured, and a dozen men and women stepped out of the pavilions to left and right. The crossbow is the hunting weapon of choice, in the Veranthan mountains; these were experts all, and each man of Clath saw two points aimed right at him.

Expecting no resistance—the ambassador was a general before, but there had been no strategy in her today, only rage—the Clathians carried no bows, only blades.

Malance said, "Lay down your weapons, take up your mistress, and return to Clath. Wait there. The emperor will send." When they hesitated, glancing from one to another, she added, "There is nothing but death for you here, if you delay. I am not of a generous mind today."

One by one, sword-belts clattered to the gravel. The men came forward, hoisted Clath's slack body awkwardly onto their shoulders and stumbled away down the drive. If it had seemed a long walk here, it would be a longer one back.

Stock-still, she watched them out of the gate. Then she beckoned, without looking back. Her two pages stepped up, one on either side, each with a cocked and loaded crossbow in their hands.

She said, "Ash—no, Alder, you're the swifter. Run to the palace, see the emperor. You'll know how. Tell him this. Tell him that Clath has once again invaded Verantha, in arms, and threatened her citizens. Tell him that we have driven them off, but I fear their return, in numbers. Ask him to send help for my people, whom he has helped so much already. Oh, and tell him this too, that he should send to Clath for a new ambassador. Go."

Alder handed her crossbow to Ash, and ran lightly for the gate. And nearly collided with the carriage, turning in; and ducked around it and ran on and out of sight, while Kinner cursed and settled his startled horses and brought them slowly up to where she stood waiting.

Vivi leapt from her seat behind—no nonsense about waiting for her pages, they were transfixed by what awaited them, so she simply vaulted the low door without troubling the latch—and came forward, her eyes darting from side to side but always returning to Malance.

"My gods, Mal. You made them into an army."

"Of course I did. Clath had one; we needed one."

"Clath came? I saw a party on the road ahead, making towards Clath, but I couldn't be certain."

"Oh, Clath came. Unfortunately for Clath, as you see, I had the means to meet her." And two pages up on the roof, and she was not ever going to ask them which had loosed that immaculate shot, so close to her, so deadly.

"You, what, you scared her off? My hero!"

"We killed her."

Apparently even Vivi could be shocked into absolute silence. That was good to learn.

"She drew a weapon on our lady," Ash said, soft and certain.

"Hush," said Malance sharply. "Mind your manners, page boy. Don't interrupt your betters." She would have preferred to leave Vivi with the impression that one of the adult Veranthans had shot Clath. Too late now. Probably it had always been too late; Vivi would have had the truth from one of them, if she hadn't guessed it already. There was probably honour among pages, in that regard. Or terror, faced with a determined Vivi.

"Yes, lady." He did not sound noticeably chastened; nor did he sound particularly shaken. Only cool, competent, in control of himself and ready at her orders. Alder had been much the same, quite collected in her manner and not at all uncertain on her legs. One of them had killed this day, this hour; whichever it was, neither one of them seemed overmuch affected.

Vivi had stepped forward, and was standing directly in front of Malance now, holding both her hands, gazing up, assessing. What she saw seemed to satisfy her; she said only, "What do we do?"

"Close and lock the gates. Guards at every wall, but particularly watching Clath. Eyes on the roof, too. Not the children now. Everyone on alert, in case Clath comes back before the emperor sends troops." The emperor would most certainly send troops. Whether they came to defend her or arrest her, time would tell.

In the meanwhile, she had Vivi's hands in hers, Vivi's eyes on her, all of Vivi's attention: Vivi's readiness at her command, as though she were a page again, another gift of the emperor's. Well, except that Malance didn't tend to hold her pages' hands, nor hold their eyes this deeply in her gaze.

"Someone thump on the door," she said, "until they open it. I forgot, we should have had a secret knock or something, to say that it was safe now."

For the moment. Good enough.

"Excellency," he said, "you have used me. And his excellency the Outlands ambassador, and doubtless more besides, and I shall hear from them all in due course, no doubt; but mostly, I believe, you have used me."

"Your grace, I have. And I think you knew you were being used, from the very beginning; and if you had minded, you would have put an end to it then and there. Meanwhile you have also used me, and used my friend appallingly, *appallingly*, and I knew nothing of it."

"Ah." He smiled somewhat, and gestured to a page—one of those pretty little twins again; that pleased her, obscurely—to serve them wine. He waited until she sipped, then sipped himself, and closed his eyes in pleasure. "Carallen grapes, from the south. A rare pleasure."

Her fingers were trembling; she had to set the glass down, and take a breath. "Marmon," she said, and apparently that had taken her whole breath, just his name, so that she had to breathe again, "Marmon was from the south, your grace, and a rare pleasure in himself."

"Yes." His eyes were open again, and regretful. "I was sorry to lose him. I liked the lad. His work, at least, and his reputation. A cat among the courtly pigeons; I enjoy that."

"And yet."

"And yet," he agreed.

That wasn't enough. "And yet you killed him." Her voice was strangely flat to her own ears, as though all her passion were spent already, all her fury, all her grief. That couldn't be possible, surely. Not yet.

"I needed a death, and his was the one that offered in the moment."

At least he was prepared to be candid, at least about what she already knew. "Because he died that night," she said slowly, spelling everything out to be certain, to be clear, "and because either Vivi or I might have been the one intended to die, therefore she stayed that night, because the house was guarded—but she'd been meaning to stay anyway, so..."

"Yes. She would have stayed, and left in the morning, and come back when the fancy took her, and I would have waited another six months or a year for you two to make up your minds. You were being an unconscionable time about it," he said, frowning at her, scolding.

Did he expect her to laugh at him? Her hands were fists, nails cutting into her palms. She said, "That wasn't it, though. It wasn't just to hurry us up, to find commitment in duress."

"No, of course not. My niece had dithered half a dozen times before; she could dither a dozen times more, she could dither lifelong if she chose, for all that I liked you so much and hoped you'd be her choice. But I needed a tool against Clath, more than the needle that you already were. I needed a weapon, which was Vivi, in your hands. Unless it was the other way around. You took your own action in the end."

"I did; but you had given me the weapon, and it wasn't Vivi. I found her for myself."

"Mmm." He looked a little smug, as though his hand had steered that from the beginning. Perhaps it had. That was an idea that ... she didn't actually want to interrogate at all, thanks. Let it go.

"So," she said, "Marmon died because Clath had to be provoked, and there was no better way to do that than a princess of the blood imperial allying herself with Verantha, under the emperor's own favour?"

"Something like that, yes. The Council of Kings will hold now within its established borders, and not threaten any more of our neighbours for a while yet. An ambassador going rogue in Feremendas herself, taking armed men into another embassy while it was under my personal protection? That is too much for them to bluster away. And she is dead, and her body on its way home, with a strong protest in my own hand. They will assume that I was responsible for that death, and take note, and take care. I expect a more amenable representative to be sent this time, and we may have peace for a generation. These are the games we play, Malance. Verantha."

"Yes, your grace. I do understand, I think." Although she hated it, and almost him, and almost herself for being so understanding. "Thank you for your time, and your honesty."

"Both are yours to command at any time, Verantha. Malance. I look forward to the next occasion."

She wondered if she could come to court on Friday next, if she could bear it. If she could look at him ever again without seeing Marmon in her mind's eye, her friend, cut down for strategy. A rose blooming in his throat.

The carriage took her home, the pages jumped lightly down, Ash opened her door for her while Alder trotted ahead to be certain that all was how she'd want it within. Her house, her people, Vivi. Everything. They knew her intimately, and they were always right.

She knew them too, and she knew exactly how it had gone. One last service for the emperor, before they came to her. The boat had been a decoy, of course, sailed no doubt by another pair of pages. Hers had run from the watchtower to where they'd left horses waiting. A swift ride along that same path that Partin would run in their wake to carry the news to the emperor; except that it was no news to him, and they would have handed their horses off to another waiting pair of pages somewhere near her house, and changed into clean livery no doubt, and arrived at her door at his grace's order, in plenty of time to take charge while she was slowly tiding it home.

And she loved them yet, she found, and she wanted to keep them for ever; and no, she would never ever ask which one had loosed the shot. Perhaps they took turns.

ABOUT THE AUTHOR

Chaz Brenchley spent his childhood in Oxford, generally with his nose in a book. At the age of twelve he met J R R Tolkien in a theatre dressing room, and his fate was sealed.

He sold his first stories at the age of eighteen, and has been a professional writer ever since. His work ranges from science fiction to epic and urban fantasy, from mysteries and thrillers to romance and horror. He's published upwards of fifty books, and many hundreds of short stories.

A decade ago he moved from bachelordom to marriage, from Newcastle to California, along with 120 boxes (115 of which were books), two squabbling cats—now gone, alas— and a famous teddy bear.

http://www.chazbrenchley.co.uk/
https://www.facebook.com/chaz.brenchley/
@chazbrenchley on Blue Sky
@ChazBrenchley@wandering.shop on Mastodon

ALSO BY CHAZ BRENCHLEY

The Crater School Series

Mars, the Red Planet, farthest-flung outpost of the British Empire. Under the benevolent reign of the Empress Eternal, commerce and culture are flourishing along the banks of the great canals, and around the shores of the crater lakes. But this brave new world is not as safe as it might seem. The Russians, unhappy that Venus has proved far less hospitable, covet Britain's colony. And the Martian creatures, while not as intelligent and malevolent as HG Wells had predicted, are certainly dangerous to the unwary.

What, then, of the young girls of the Martian colony? Their brothers might be sent to Earth for education at Eton and Oxbridge, but girls are made of sterner stuff. Be it unreasonable parents, Russian spies, or the deadly Martian wildlife, no challenge is beyond the resourceful girls of the Crater School.

1. Three Twins at the Crater School
2. Dust Up at the Crater School
3. Mary Ellen, Craterean!
4. Radhika Rages at the Crater School

The Outremer Series

Outremer—a harsh and barren kingdom born of blood and at war with the world around it.

For forty years, the Order of the Knights Ransomers has been the sword-arm and conscience of the kingdom. Their stronghold, the Roq de Rançon, is the key to Outremer's defence. But nomadic tribes on the kingdom's borders threaten to reclaim this land that was once theirs.

Marron, a young man training to be a Ransomer, and Julianne, a noble-born girl betrothed to a man she's never met, are journeying to the Roq. There each of them will be put to the test, as they become inextricably bound up in the coming upheaval that will decide the fate of Outremer.

CHAZ BRENCHLEY

www.ingramcontent.com/pod-product-compliance
Lightning Source LLC
Chambersburg PA
CBHW020358030726
47496CB00007B/2206